WHISPER OF TREASURE
AND LIES

ALSO AVAILABLE BY TRISH ESDEN

SCANDAL MOUNTAIN ANTIQUES MYSTERIES

The Art of the Decoy

A Wealth of Deception

WRITTEN AS PAT ESDEN

NORTHERN CIRCLE COVEN TRILOGY

His Dark Magic

Things She's Seen

Entangled Secrets

DARK HEART TRILOGY

A Hold on Me

Beyond Your Touch

Reach for You

WHISPER OF TREASURE
AND LIES
A SCANDAL MOUNTAIN ANTIQUES MYSTERY

TRISH ESDEN

Whisper of Treasure and Lies

Scandal Mountain Antiques Mysteries Series

Book 3

Edited by Katherine Quimby
Proofreader ~ Lydia Johnson
Cover Design by Book Covers by Melody ~ Melody Simmons
Interior formatting by Painted Wings Publishing Services

Library of Congress Catalog-in-Publication data available upon request.
ISBN (hardcover): 979-8-9926975-1-3
ISBN (paperback):979-8-9926975-0-6
ISBN (eBook): 979-8-9926975-2-0

For all my golden girls,
Haley, Gypsy, Ellie Mae, Lucy, & Seven,
Gone but never forgotten.

Secrets. Everybody has them, large and small, the white lies and the deep, dark soul crushing ones. Some are revealed with the slightest prompting, often for money or love. Others are buried with their keepers.

Antique dealers and collectors, like me, are notoriously adept when it comes to holding our secrets close. Just try and discover where we acquired a prized piece or how much we paid for it. Perhaps we'll brag about the procurement, more likely we'll dance away from the subject as lightly as an auctioneer moving on to the next bid. Even if we offer up the information, can you be certain you've learned the truth?

Maybe. Maybe not.

Some say all secrets eventually come to light, even if it takes decades or the passing of the older generation. I'm not so sure about that. Some secrets lie in graves so thick with damp moss, ferns, and brambles that they resist the light, only to become more deeply buried with the passing years.

On second thought, I'm probably wrong. I know better than to make sweeping assumptions. Plus, I've crawled under those brambles and dug in that dank earth. I've excavated bottles and bits of china, silver coins and gold rings...a million small treasures from cellar holes and abandoned privies, remnants of lives long gone, pieces capable of revealing the most closeted truth—even those left unsaid until it was too late.

—Edie Brown

CHAPTER ONE

"You okay?"

My uncle Tuck rested a hand against the small of my back, a comforting gesture as we joined the crowd flooding toward the old feedstore building, currently home to Fisher's Auction House.

"I'm fine," I said. In truth, sadness pinched at the back of my throat instead of the jittering excitement I usually felt when attending an auction. I loved antiques and art. I lived for auctions. I craved the adrenaline rush of bidding.

Tuck hushed his voice even further. "Seriously, Edie. I don't mind if we skip this."

I managed a smile. "I want to stay. It just feels..."

"Like the end of an era?"

I nodded. Today, Bucky Sander's estate was going on the auction block. Bucky had been a renowned Vermont antique dealer and one of my grandparents' closest friends. I'd learned most of what I knew about antique bottles from him—historical flasks, medicines, poisons, mineral spring bottles...the rare and the common. It'd been over ten years now since we'd lost my grandparents. Bucky had passed five years after that. His collec-

1

tions, mountains of antique inventory, as well as the accumulated contents of the farmhouse he shared with his wife had sat untouched until recently when she put their home on the market and moved into a smaller place.

Tuck's hand left my back. He chuckled. "Bucky was quite the character."

"That's for sure." Smiling wistfully, I glanced ahead to the auction house's front stoop. I could picture Bucky standing there with his buddies: faded overalls, his beard stained with tobacco juice, looking like a total hick. But he was no average hick. He was one of the shrewdest, most brilliant antique dealers I'd ever known, aside from my grandparents.

Tuck lengthened his stride, hurrying up onto the auction house stoop ahead of me and a pair of middle-aged women. He opened the front door and held it for us. Tuck, always a gentle bear of a man in action and looks, especially this time of year, when autumn-brown corduroy and tweed were in season, and he let his graying beard grow fuller.

As the women moved on, I stepped into the warmth and rumble of the auction gallery. The sight of aisles and tables piled with all manner of antiques made my skin tingle. Primitive cupboards, blanket boxes, blue decorated stoneware, Vermont country store and farm relics. Paintings. Folk art carvings. Decoys. Handmade baskets. Boxes full of tins and old bottles.

I breathed in the aroma of coffee mingled with old wood and leather, the vanilla scent of early books, and even a trace of gasoline from things stored in a barn...an untouched estate fragrance as enticing to me as the scent of apple pie hot from the oven.

If I'd had a million dollars—better make that five million—I would've bought everything in the place without a second thought. Unfortunately, though our antique shop's bank accounts were more liquid than they'd been a few months ago when I'd returned home and took over running the business, I still wasn't in a position to bid without caution—ten thousand dollars at the most, less than five made more sense.

I scanned the gallery again, this time taking in the competition. Martina Fortuni, a dealer who had a shop in a neighboring town and was a general thorn in my side, was scrutinizing a silver teapot with her jeweler's loupe. It was doubtful that she'd be bidding on much today, not enough jewelry and glittery things for her taste.

Only a few yards from her, Marissa Lavelle—a forty-something bigwig dealer from New Hampshire, overdressed as usual in white slacks and a swing coat that Cruella de Ville would've been proud to wear—was chatting up the much beefier and a whole lot less pretentious Sparky Collins. An electrician by trade, Sparky was also a dedicated Vermont bottle digger and collector. Rumor had it, he'd recently discovered a stash of early bitters bottles inside a wall while rewiring an old house. He'd sweet talked the homeowner into letting him have the entire lot in exchange for a hundred dollars off the wiring bill, a stingy offer considering one bottle could easily bring a hundred bucks or a whole lot more.

Joie Bascom, the director of Scandal Mountain Museum, was deeper into the stacks of antiques, flipping through an old postcard album. Plump and dressed in orange leggings and a marigold-yellow sports jacket, she resembled a Turk's turban squash. She glanced up, smiled and posed as Francois-Baptiste, the eldest living member of the infamous Lefebvre family and co-owner of the *Scandal Mountain Gazetteer* panned his video camara her way. I hadn't seen Francois, or Frenchie as everyone called him, in several years. His hair was now nothing more than a crescent of white frizz, but he was as lanky and buzzing with energy as I remembered.

The more I looked, the more people I recognized from both the in-town and out-of-town antique dealing communities. Sure, anyone could bid by phone or online. The online preview of the items being auctioned had been available since mid-August. But I suspected I wasn't the only one who wanted to honor Bucky by participating in this auction the old fashion way—namely, in person.

Tuck touched my wrist. "I'm going to register and get a bidding paddle."

"Great," I said. "I'll save us some seats."

I headed for the rows of folding chairs that spanned the center of the gallery. Lots of the seats had boxes on them or coats draped over their backs, marking them as reserved. I peeled off my sweater and laid it across two chairs in the rear row.

"Hey there." The familiar voice came from behind me. I turned to see Pinky Woods with her rooster-comb of blond hair strutting toward me. She worked at Fisher's Auction House as well as bartending part-time at the Jumping Café's pub. We hadn't hung with the same crowd in high school, but we'd gotten along then and become even closer since I'd returned home.

"Quite the crowd," I said.

She rested the box of vintage records she was holding on one hip. "Frickin' madhouse if you ask me."

I smiled. "Bucky would have loved it." I quieted my voice. "I haven't seen Jules and Rosetta Ramone. What's up with that?" Jules and Rosetta were dealers who disliked my mom and had recently extended that feeling to include me.

Pinky rolled her eyes. "They're vacationing in Paree." She pronounced Paris with the same affected accent as Jules would have used.

I laughed. "I bet he wishes he'd put that trip off for another time."

"They probably left bids online." She leaned closer. "Did Kala ask you about the puppy?"

A twinge of tension pinched at the base of my skull. Kala lived with Tuck and me and worked for our antique business. In fact, she was watching the shop today. She and Pinky were also currently an item, and the golden retriever puppies were Pinky's most recent fundraising scheme. The portion of the puppies' cost that didn't go toward expenses was being donated to the Scandal Mountain Humane Society. I toughened my voice. "A puppy isn't a good idea right now. I already told Kala that."

"You should at least take a look at them. They're adorable."

I crossed my arms. "I imagine they are."

"You have the perfect place to raise a puppy—" She abruptly stopped her sales pitch and glanced toward the front of the auction house. Alfred Fisher, the head auctioneer as well as the owner of the place, was at the podium tinkering with the mic. Pinky shifted the box of records off her hip, once again holding it squarely in both hands. "I better get going before Alfred bursts a blood vessel. We can talk more later."

"Sure," I said. *But not about puppies*, I added silently. Tuck, Kala, and I had enough to do without the complication of a pet.

I gave Pinky a head start, then followed the same route she'd taken, down the center aisle between the chairs to the front of the room. But instead of heading for the podium and Alfred, I veered toward a glass showcase. The showcase as a rule contained the auction's most valuable smaller pieces. Today that meant one thing: the Glass Widow.

The Glass Widow was a legendary mineral springs bottle, the only recovered example of a case of thirty-six bottles made for the grand opening of the Mountain House Resort, a vast Victorian-era hydropathic spa built high up on Scandal Mountain near the ever-flowing Maiden Spring. The resort was intended to become a destination spot, but on the eve of its grand opening a fire flashed through the massive structure, killing guests and the resort's newly married owner. However, that wasn't the worst of the tragedy. The following investigation revealed the fire was arson, ignited to cover up the owner's murder.

I moved up behind two women who were looking into the showcase.

"I can't believe that old bottle's estimated to sell for between forty and fifty thousand dollars," one woman said.

"My brother had a brown one like it," the other woman said.

I clenched my teeth, resisting the urge to speak up. As far as I was concerned, the estimate was low for such a rare mineral springs bottle. Sure, the other thirty-five so-called Glass Widows were rumored to be somewhere in the vicinity of the resort ruins, an elusive treasure waiting to be found. Still, this bottle was beyond rare. And the amber-brown ones like the woman's brother had? Manufacturing records showed twenty-four cases with forty-eight amber bottles in each had been delivered to the resort, destined to be filled with healing water and sold after the grand opening. Those bottles were excavated by scavengers soon after the fire and carried off as souvenirs of the tragedy. One of them recently sold at auction for five thousand dollars.

Finally, the women relinquished their spot in front of the showcase. I slipped forward. As I bent close, nose all but pressed against the case's glass, the clamor of the room around me seemed to fade. The bottle was blueish emerald in color, quart-size with a squatty body and a long neck. The likeness of a plump Victorian bride was embossed into the glass along with the words: *Maiden Springs. Healing Water. Scandal Mountain, Vermont.*

I'd only seen the bottle once before, back when I was sixteen. That summer, I'd spent every spare minute digging bottles in an old dump near our house and selling them at the Jumping Café flea market. Bucky Sanders had often stopped by to see what I'd found. That day, he'd reached into his barn coat and taken out the Glass Widow as reverently as if it were a crown jewel.

"Is that what I think it is?" I'd asked, stunned. The town museum had a display devoted to the Mountain House resort tragedy. It included a tattered pamphlet advertising the resort's grand opening. On the pamphlet's cover was a depiction of the Glass Widow bottle. I'd dreamed of seeing one for real, but I'd never thought it would happen.

Bucky handed the Widow to me. "Amazing, isn't she?"

The bottle's glass glimmered in the hot sunshine like cool water in a mountain lake. I willed my hands to remain steady as I studied it with awe. Fine whirls of bubbles created during its manufacturing were trapped within the glass, frozen motionless for all eternity. There were no chips or dings. No scratches. The bottle was perfect, except for a few flecks of cork and red crud that clung to the inside of its lip.

"Someday, Edie," Bucky said, "it might not be me or your grandfather that finds the rest of the Widows. Might be you. You've got enough love of the hunt and the smarts to do it."

Heat flushed across my cheeks. It was one thing to have my grandparents say flattering things, and quite another to have an unrelated and esteemed dealer like Bucky do it.

I looked up. With all my heart, I longed to ask where he'd found the bottle, but I respected him too much to pose such an impertinent question. It was his secret to keep or reveal.

Still, something puzzled me. I'd always assumed the thirty-six Glass Widow bottles would be found together somewhere around the resort ruins or perhaps in the attic of a local home, if they'd been carried off by a scavenger like their less valuable amber cousins.

I turned the bottle over in my hands, feeling its coolness and shape. I asked, "Do you think the rest of them are out there?"

"I know they are," Bucky said.

I blinked at him, surprised by the confidence in his voice. Even my grandparents, who'd had a running bet with Bucky as to which of them would locate the cache of bottles first, had admitted they might well have been destroyed in the resort fire, though not as much as a single broken shard of one had ever been unearthed.

He pressed his hand over his heart. "I feel it right here."

Trust your instincts, my grandpa had told me a million times. In that moment, I became certain Bucky was right. The other thirty-five Glass Widows were out there somewhere, waiting to be found.

"Ahem." The sound of a man clearing his throat yanked me from my thoughts. "If you're done window shopping, maybe you could let someone else preview."

A bitter taste crept up my throat. I knew that voice. Felix Graham.

Pasting on a smile, I turned to face him. No way was I going to let him see that his snide comment had ticked me off. Graham was a jerk—a condescending, conceited, womanizing jackass in the first degree—and I didn't feel that way just because I suspected he was involved with my mom going to prison for art forgery. He had also refused to let the world in general forget that I'd slipped up and bought stolen property by mistake a few years back.

I widened my smile and met his eyes. "I assume you're planning on bidding on the Glass Widow."

"None of your business," he snapped.

"Well, good luck if you do," I said. I could see how a certain type of woman would be drawn to his custom suits and salt-and-pepper hair good looks, but it was beyond me how anyone could be blind to his snake oil personality.

I turned my back to him and stepped to the left, moving on from looking at the Glass Widow to where a Bible box with a slanted lid sat atop the far end of the same showcase. It was a beautiful, rustic piece, about the size of a large portable type-writer case. Dark finish. Heavily carved with vines and flowers.

As I pulled the Bible box closer and began to examine its exterior, I half-listened to Graham call an auction house employee over and asked them to take the Glass Widow out from the show-case so he could examine it. In reality, Graham was right, whether he was going to bid on the bottle or not wasn't any of my business. And, as much as I hated to admit it, he was also right to think I was just ogling it. No way could I afford to spend the kind of money the Widow was going to bring.

I opened the Bible box's lid. The preview on Fisher's website had stated that it was full of Vermont ephemera, but it had failed to list the items individually.

The lid's interior was decorated with a folksy painting of a farmhouse and sheep, a nice, unexpected addition, but not particularly notable.

I turned my attention to the contents. Victorian-era brochures and advertisements—all from Scandal Mountain and nearby towns. Plus, photographs from the same time period: tiny cartes-de-visite images that often were used as calling cards as well as so-called cabinet cards, a larger type of photo mounted on thick cardstock that were produced from the 1860s until the mid-1920s. Old letters, invitations.... I'd seen similar items at the town museum—like the pamphlet advertising the resort's grand opening. I'd also seen them in the book Frenchie Lefebvre had written in the 1980s for the centennial anniversary of the resort tragedy: *A Mystery in the Mountains.* All in all, the Bible box contained exactly the sort of ephemera that was highly sought after by local history buffs.

My eyes zeroed in on a larger booklet:

~Mountain House Resort~
The Secret to Health and Happiness
Maiden Mineral Springs and Spa

Okay, this was even more interesting. Local history, a piece I'd never come across before. Very sellable.

I reached deeper into the box and pulled out a stack of three identical notebooks—medium-size with black and white speckled cardboard covers. Modern composition notebooks. What were they doing in with Victorian-era items?

Curious, I opened the top one. Every page was filled with dates, weather, and handwritten notations.

June 21. Miserably hot. Tunbridge. Purchased contents of Floyd Renfrew shed chamber. Lunch with Ruby Rice.

August 6. Rainy. Bennington. Stopped by museum to research flint glass creamer...

Bucky Sanders's personal journals? The Bible box was from his estate, so it only made sense for the notebooks to be his as well.

My pulse picked up. My throat went dry. What if the journals contained clues to where he'd found the Glass Widow, perhaps even information that could lead to the rest of the cache?

I forced my face into a mask of indifference and studied the next journal entry: *August 10th*. For the most part, it was indecipherable, smudged and written in some sort of shorthand or perhaps drunken hen scratches. Bucky did like his drink, though in the end it was a massive stroke, not liver disease, which took his life.

Worried that the time I was spending looking at the notebooks would give away my high level of interest in them, I slid them back under the other pieces of ephemera. As I did, I spotted a sealed, business-size envelope, modern in appearance. It hadn't been stamped or mailed, but was addressed to Bucky in cursive handwriting, large looping letters with an unmissable right-slant. The tail on the 'y' arced like a fishing hook—

My grandpa's handwriting.

My mouth fell open, and I whipped the sealed envelope from the box. Judging by its weight and thickness, it contained something, though perhaps only a single piece of cardstock or a folded note. Small dots of yellowish-brown stained the envelops exterior. It looked to me as if color from something inside had bled through the envelope.

I sniffed the envelope. A whiff of mildew and an oily-chemical smell infiltrated my nose. Perhaps the odor of what lay inside.

More likely a scent absorbed from all the old photographs and papers that had laid on top of it for who knows how long.

My breath quickened as I turned the envelope over. One corner of the seal was slightly peeled up...Bucky and my grandfather had been rivals and friends for decades, trading and haggling over antiques and art, betting about who'd find the resort mineral springs bottles or acquire other prized pieces first.

I drew a fingernail lightly across the seal, stopping just short of the peeled up corner. Why had Bucky never opened or thrown the envelope out, even after my grandparents had died? What did it contain?

The hairs on the back of my neck prickled. My fingers trembled. With all my heart I longed to shove the envelope into my pocket, dash to the ladies' room at the rear of the auction house and rip it open in the privacy of a stall. But I wasn't a thief, even if I had been accused of it on several occasions. Asking Albert Fisher to open it only minutes before the sale began wasn't an option either. He'd undoubtedly turn me down since it wouldn't give other potential buyers time to preview the contents. There was only one solution.

I glanced around, looking for Tuck. He stood a few yards away, examining a book. Probably the volume of *Meehan's Native Flowers and Ferns of the United States* that he'd planned to bid on.

As if he felt my stare, Tuck looked my way. That was one thing I loved about him, the way we always seemed to be on the same wavelength.

He set the book down and hurried over. "What is it?"

I made sure Graham's attention was focused on the Glass Widow and not us, then I discreetly showed Tuck the envelope, including the sealed flap and the handwritten address on the front.

His eyes widened, telling me he recognized my grandpa's—his father's—writing. He whispered, "Where did you find that?"

I answered by placing the envelope back in the Bible box and closing the lid. After that, I took Tuck by the elbow and propelled him toward our reserved seats, safely away from Graham and any other potential competition.

Moving in close to him, I whispered, "I'm going to bid on the box."

Tuck gave me a sidelong glance. "The envelope could be nothing. There could be a Christmas card inside or a sales receipt from your grandfather. Bucky bought lots of things from him over the years."

The cords in my neck tightened. "The box itself is wonderful. There are a lot of sellable Victorian photos and booklets in it, and some of Bucky's personal journals."

Tuck chuckled. "So, what you really have on your mind isn't just the envelope. It's using Bucky's journals and the ephemera to go treasure hunting for the other Glass Widows."

I cuffed his arm playfully. "Alright, I admit it. But even if I keep the journals, that doesn't mean we can't make a profit. I'll make copies of the ephemera, then sell the originals and the box. There's a nice folky painting on the inside of its lid."

"You realize the chance of you being the only person who noticed Bucky's journals is slim to none?"

"That doesn't mean it's impossible."

He laughed. "You sound like your grandfather."

Smiling, I settled into my chair. Tuck was right. 'That doesn't mean it's impossible' was something my grandpa had said quite often, a motto I preferred over giving up.

A motto that had also gotten me in trouble more than once.

* * *

Ten minutes later, promptly at nine o'clock, the auction began. To get everyone in their seats and quiet, Albert Fisher started by briskly auctioning off the first half-dozen items. They were lower value, but they did the trick. With the crowd settled, he moved on, mixing more desirable pieces in with ones of moderate value. The lead pieces didn't begin to come up until a good two hours into the sale. At noontime, the crowd hushed as the Glass Widow went up on the auction block.

The bidding started with online buyers and those on the phone butting heads in rapid fire. Within seconds the Widow surpassed the low pre-sale estimate of forty thousand.

After it hit fifty-five thousand, the people in the audience took over. Joie Bascom from the town museum jumped to her feet, her unbuttoned marigold-yellow jacket flaring out and blocking my view as she bid fifty-six. Someone else bid fifty-seven. Joie bid sixty thousand. The other person bid sixty-five. She bid seventy...

"Will anyone give seventy-five thousand for the Glass Widow?" Albert Fisher chanted from the podium, "Do I hear seventy-five thousand?"

Bucky Sander's wife, Doris—a dowdy, gray-haired woman with a dry personality—sat in the front row of chairs, tightly gripping a silver-haired gentleman's hand. As a rule, Doris had rarely gone antiquing with Bucky, so I'd never gotten to know her very well. Still, I couldn't help but wonder who the gentleman was—a family friend or perhaps even the reason she'd decided to move on with her life at this point? Whatever her reason, this auction would go a long way toward making her future comfortable, especially with the Glass Widow doing so well.

"Last call," Albert Fisher chanted more slowly, drawing out the words. "Anyone seventy-five thousand? Anyone...seventy-five... Going once. Twice..." He raised the hammer to end the bidding.

"Seventy-five," Felix Graham's voice boomed from the back of the room.

A ripple of awe rushed through the audience.

"I've got seventy-five!" Albert Fisher shouted gleefully.

Joie Bascom was on her feet. She wheeled to glare at Graham.

Tuck leaned close to me and whispered, "I didn't think Graham was that into bottles."

"He could be bidding for a collector who wants to remain anonymous," I suggested.

An auction house employee waved a hand in the air. "I've got eighty thousand on the phone."

"Ninety," Graham said.

If a ripple of awe had gone through the room before, this time it was a roar of excitement.

Albert Fisher glanced at the employee who'd called out the phone bid. "I have ninety thousand for the Glass Widow, do I hear a hundred?"

"One hundred," someone said from the left side of the room. The voice was loud and clear. A woman. Everyone in the room shifted to look in her direction. All I could see was the back of those people's heads and stacks of furniture waiting to be sold, not an inch of the woman bidding.

"A hundred and ten." Graham's voice again.

"We have a hundred and ten thousand on the floor," Albert Fisher said. "A hundred and twenty anyone? Hundred and twenty...?" He paused, a long silence stretching out for a good sixty seconds. "Fair warning, the bid on the Glass Widow mineral springs bottle is at one hundred and ten thousand dollars. Going once. Twice—" He hesitated again, then brought the hammer down. "Sold!"

As applause rose, I craned around, watching as a runner carried the Glass Widow back to where Graham stood against the wall. He was as puffed up as a rooster in a hen house, chin raised in triumph.

"Next item up for bid is lot number 158," Albert Fisher's voice once more filled the gallery, "a late nineteenth century Bible box filled with local ephemera. I trust everyone had a chance to view the contents."

My attention snapped back to the front of the room. My mouth dried. I gripped my bidding paddle hard, readying to make my move.

Albert Fisher took a breath. "Let's start the bidding at—"

"Three thousand!" Graham shouted.

Tuck's hand landed on my wrist, holding it down before I could raise the paddle. "That's way too much. Let it go."

I scowled and shouted, "Four thousand." We'd caught up on the overdue bills and major home repairs. We had an upcoming decoy auction that would bring in a tidy sum, though that wasn't until the end of November, a full two and a half months from now.

"Five thousand!" Sparky Collin's voice sang out.

"Seven," Graham countered.

"We have seven thousand," Alfred Fisher jumped in, taking back control of the auction.

Tuck gave me a warning glance. "Edie. No."

My face heated. I gritted my teeth. *Damn it.* He was right. Three thousand dollars wasn't smart. Seven thousand on a simple Bible box and a bunch of ephemera was foolish, though if the contents could lead me to the legendary cache of Glass Widow bottles it would be worth it, and then some. Plus, there was the mysterious envelope.

"Going once! Twice..."

I scrunched down in my chair, pressed my hands over my ears. I didn't want to hear any more, especially not the word 'sold' or the explosion of applause for Graham as he scored not only the Glass Widow but the Bible box and its contents as well.

No two ways about it, I couldn't stand Graham. Not in the least.

CHAPTER TWO

While the auction crowd was still in an uproar over the prices the Glass Widow and Bible box had realized, the copy of *Meehan's Native Flowers and Ferns of the United States* that Tuck hoped to buy came up for sale. He bid fast without waiting for Alfred Fisher to drop the opening bid to a lower level, and Tuck ended up taking the book for that single bid. Unlike the overpriced Widow or Bible box, the cost was reasonable, and the book was just the sort of item we needed to add to our inventory.

A runner scurried down the aisle to bring the book to Tuck. As they handed it to him, a dried leaf escaped from between its pages, drifting to the floor and landing at my feet.

"Sorry about that," the runner said, voice hushed.

Tuck waved off the apology. "Don't worry. It's nothing."

I bent over, picked up the leaf. It was a piece of pressed maidenhair fern, crispy with faded green on one side and specks of brown spores on the other. Like Bucky Sanders, my grandpa had also pressed examples of plants in his field guides as a way to keep track of which varieties he'd located in the wild. And, yes, I'd spent a lot of time fern hunting with my grandpa as well as bird-watching with Grandma. Why live surrounded by nature if you didn't take time to get to know it?

Tuck let the book fall open to the page where the leaf had been stashed. As I put it back in place, I noticed stains on the paper from the spores. They devalued the book, but that thought was quickly replaced with the memory of the yellowish-brown dots on the Bible box envelope.

I caught Tuck's eyes, nodded at the stains. "Does that remind you of anything?"

Wrinkles spanned his forehead as he thought for a second. His eyes brightened with understanding. "The stained envelope."

"Interesting, huh?" I said.

I swiveled in my chair, looking to see if Graham was still standing at the back of the room. He was walking away from the nearby payment window, Bible box in hand as he headed out the auction house's front door.

Perhaps the idea of a pressed fern being the source of the stains on the envelope should've killed my enthusiasm. A dead leaf had zero monetary value to anyone, including me. Still, it piqued my curiosity. For one thing, maidenhair ferns grew around Maiden Spring—the source of the mineral water that had inspired the building of the ill-fated Mountain House Resort, the healing water which the Glass Widow bottles were intended to contain. I'd seen the ferns when I'd hiked up to the resort's ruins both with my grandparents and alone. *If* I was right about the stains on the envelope being from fern spores, then the question was: why had Grandpa given Bucky a piece of fern? Was it a clue to where he suspected the cache of Glass Widows were hidden? If so, why hadn't Grandpa or Bucky retrieved them?

Albert Fisher's booming voice broke through my thoughts. "Next item up for bid is a barrister bookcase."

I looked toward the front of the auction gallery. The item up after the bookcase was a folky Vermont oil painting, followed by a plastic milk crate full of bottles wrapped in newspaper, both items I'd intended to bid on.

But Graham was leaving. And, after winning the best pieces in the auction, he was undoubtedly in a good mood. Maybe, just maybe, I could weasel the envelope out of his clutches, despite his dislike for me.

I tapped Tuck's shoulder. "I'll be right back."

He gave me a puzzled look. "What about the oil painting?"

"You bid on it and the crate of bottles."

Moving quickly, I left my seat, dashed up the aisle and out the front door. The sounds of the auction muffled as it glided closed behind me. A medium-size box truck was parked to my left. Beyond it were a dozen vans and cars, and Graham's unmissable Mercedes SUV with the Golden Stag Antiques & Gallery logo on its side. He was just opening the driver's door.

I stepped off the stoop, intending to shortcut around the box truck to get to him faster, when I spotted Joie Bascom storming toward him. She shook a fist in the air and screeched, "Why in god's name did you do that?"

He set the Bible box on the SUV's front seat—I could only guess he'd rearranged the ephemera so he could fit the Glass Widow inside for safekeeping. He wheeled and snarled something at Joie. I couldn't make out the words, but the hostility in his tone was unmissable.

I crouched down, hiding in the shadow of the box truck. I was dying to watch the fight, but I didn't need to get caught in the act.

Joie jabbed a finger at Graham's chest. "The Widow belongs in the town museum. I told you I was going to bid on it."

"You did," Graham said. "I also heard you solicit several other potential bidders the same way. I'd call that an attempt at bid rigging." He looked down his nose at her, his expression nothing but disgust. "Bid rigging's illegal. I'd never be involved in something as lowlife as that."

I crouched a bit lower. That was laughable. In my experience, there wasn't much Graham wouldn't do to get what he wanted.

Joie's voice rose, ear-piercing sharp. "I wasn't bid-rigging, and you know it. I'd raised fifty thousand. I was going to put in twenty of my own money. If you'd stayed out of it—"

He laughed. "Don't get all worked up. If you're nice, I might loan the pieces to the museum for special occasions."

"You're a jackass, Felix Graham. Someday you're going to get what you deserve."

As she swung away from him and stomped back toward the front door, I crept around the box truck, staying out of her line of sight.

I glanced toward Graham. After that confrontation, he probably wasn't in a receptive mood anymore. Still, if I wanted the envelope, I needed to talk to him. But how could I do that without looking like I'd been spying?

I was about to step out from my hiding spot, when another woman's voice echoed across the parking lot. "Hello-oo, Felix Gra-ham!"

Graham glanced toward the voice. A youngish woman dressed in a little plaid skirt and modest cardigan was jogging in his direction. She was my age, late twenties. Average height. Average weight. Bland brown hair.

"I've been trying to catch up with you," she said. "I didn't know if you'd gotten my messages. I don't mean to be pushy..."

As she chattered, Graham pinched the bridge of his nose as if her rambling was giving him a headache. I could relate to that kind of stressed feeling. I almost felt sorry for him, almost.

She gulped a breath, then started again. "My grandmother said you were looking for help. I sent you a resume last week. I can stop by anytime for an interview. I—"

Graham raised a hand to stop her. "All right. I'll give you an interview. Tomorrow. Nine o'clock sharp. Before the store gets busy."

The woman bounced on her tiptoes. "I'll be there. I will. You can count on me."

"If you waste my time by being late, you can forget the job."

"I'll be on time. I promise."

In one quick movement, Graham turned back to the SUV's open door, shifted the Bible box onto the passenger seat, and jumped in. Leaving the woman barely enough time to skitter out of the way, he slammed the door shut, then peeled out of the parking space.

A heavy feeling weighed in my stomach as I watched the SUV speed toward the parking lot exit. But it wasn't the car's taillights or the shine of its rear window that I saw. The only thing in my mind was the envelope with the mysterious contents and my grandfather's unmistakable cursive writing on the front.

An envelope I desperately wanted to get my hands on—and that wouldn't be easy.

CHAPTER THREE

O ur house was on the outskirts of Scandal Mountain village, just off the main road, past the airstrip where my grandparents died in a single-engine plane crash, and up a steep driveway lined with trees. Every time I saw the Federal style brick house I grew up in my heart burst with joy. It was especially beautiful this time of year when autumn tinted the maples orange and scarlet, and the gardens transformed into a riot of gold and lavender. They were part of why I'd moved back home to help Tuck rebuild the antique business after Mom went to prison for art forgery back in May. Even the thought of the business my grandparents founded going bankrupt and the forced sale of the property that would follow was unbearable to me.

I tapped the brake pedal and slowed to pull up in front of the carriage barn that housed our antique shop. Kala rushed from the store to meet us. She looked as bright as the autumn maples in a burnt-orange smock dress that matched the recently-dyed tips of her lion's mane afro.

Her hands went to her hips. "So, what did you buy?"

"Just a plant identification book and some mediocre bottles," I said, getting out. I opened the car's back door, retrieved the crate full of antique bottles that Tuck had bought while I was eaves-dropping on Graham. Some of the bottles were wrapped in yellowed pages of the *Scandal Mountain Gazetteer*, others were partially uncovered, a few were totally visible. Not outstanding bottles, but very sellable to beginning collectors.

Kala groaned dramatically. "You two had all the fun. This girl's been bored to tears."

"No customers?" Tuck asked, as we went inside the shop.

"It wasn't totally dead. I sold that charcoal drawing that was up in the loft and a couple of early Nancy Drew books and some other stuff. Nothing exciting." She snagged a wrapped bottle from the crate and began to undo it. "You didn't get that mineral springs bottle you were all excited about?"

"Graham ended up with the Glass Widow," I said.

"That stinks."

"He had to pay up to get it. A hundred and ten thousand dollars to be exact. Plus, a twenty percent buyer's premium."

"Wow! Maybe we should go hunt for the rest of them," she said.

"Maybe..."

I set the crate of bottles on the shop's front counter. While we started removing the newspaper from the fully wrapped bottles, I told Kala about Graham buying the Bible box too and about its contents, including the envelope addressed in my grandfather's handwriting, and about Joie Bascom arguing with him in the parking lot. I even mentioned the younger woman cornering him about the job.

Tuck chuckled. "I bet Graham was ready for a stiff drink after that."

I smiled. "Not Graham. If he stopped somewhere for a drink, it was so he could buy a round for all his cronies and gloat over his new acquisitions."

Kala finished unwrapping a dark brown bottle and held it out for me to see. "Is this one worth anything?" She didn't know much about early antiques and bottles, though she was brilliant when it came to mid-century collectables, stuff I'd tended to dismiss until I'd discovered how much we could get for them online. Not to mention her other areas of expertise, including dubious lock-picking and serious computer *skills*.

I took the bottle from her. It was from a pharmacy, pint-size with a wide mouth and matching ground glass stopper. Machine made. First quarter of the twentieth century, perhaps a few decades earlier. No chips or cracks. The remains of a paper label wrapped its middle.

I wiped a finger across the label, cleaning it off enough to read. "Potassium ferricyanide."

Kala's eyes went wide. "Cyanide? That's not good."

"Luckily, it's empty," I said. Over the years, I'd come across antique bottles containing all sorts of dangerous substances, including strychnine and arsenic. Poisons were something antique dealers and bottle lovers in general learned to be careful about. I gave the bottle another onceover. "It's not worth that much. But it'll sell if we keep the price low."

Tuck took the bottle from me and set it on the further end of the counter. "I didn't expect to find anything fantastic in the crate. Fishers wouldn't have auctioned them off without unwrapping them all, unless they had reason to suspect there wasn't anything special in the lot."

I raised my eyebrows. "Unless Fisher's ran out of time to do it."

We all dove in, quickly unwrapping bottles, uncovering one average but nice condition one after another: more brown ones, a clear bottle embossed with the name of an early Scandal Mountain pharmacy, a similar one from Burlington, basic hair tonic bottles, a nice bitters...

As I fell into the rhythm of removing newspaper and examining the bottles, the smell of the musty paper combined with chemical and oil scents was reminiscent of the smell I'd detected on the envelope with my grandpa's handwriting on it. "Maybe not from fern spores," I mused aloud.

Kala stopped unwrapping. "What did you say?"

Tuck waggled a finger at me. "She's thinking about the sealed envelope again."

Kala laughed. "Not another obsession."

"Exactly," Tuck said.

I shot a glare at both of them. "I'm just curious about it. If that's alright with you two?"

"If Graham's got it, you might as well forget it." Kala echoed the advice Tuck had given me on the way home from the auction.

I sighed heavily. "You're right."

As I reached back into the crate to snag another wrapped bottle, my fingers bumped against something wedged against one side of the crate. A piece of cardboard?

I pulled it out. It was a manilla envelope about the size of a birthday card. The word 'Original' was written on it in pencil.

"Another envelope," Tuck said. "Is it from your grandfather?"

"Unfortunately, not." I showed them the unfamiliar handwriting. "But it feels like there's something inside."

I unfastened the envelope's brass clasp, slid the contents out. It was an antique photo mounted on thick cardstock, about four inches high and six across, a cabinet card showing a formally dressed Victorian-era woman sitting on an ornate wicker settee. A paunchy, bewhiskered middle-aged man stood beside her. Behind them, velvet curtains and an enormous urn of what appeared to be white roses, apple blossoms, and bells of Ireland formed a backdrop. Unfortunately, unlike the nice cabinet card-type photos I'd noticed in Bucky's Bible box, this photo was in horrendous condition, faded and mouse chewed.

"Pretty much garbage." I turned it over. As was customary, the back was elaborately decorated and stamped with the photographer's information:

Louis Beaumont Photography ~ New York Studio. 961 Broadway.

"It really is in bad shape. I wonder why Bucky didn't throw it out?" Tuck said.

"Maybe he bought the crate of bottles just before he died and never had time to sort through it." The best of the best had passed through Bucky's hands over the years. But he wasn't purely an upper-end dealer. He enjoyed buying boxes of odds and ends and rusty barn junk as much as high-end items. Basically, he loved anything old, especially things with local history or lore attached to them, hence the massive auction when his wife, Doris, decided to put their home on the market.

Along the bottom of the cabinet card's backside something faint was scrawled in pencil. I picked up the jeweler's loupe we kept by the register and used it to magnify the writing.

Kala leaned forward. "What are you looking at?"

"I'm guessing it's the names of the people in the photos." I held the loupe closer to my eye, struggling to make out the faded handwriting. *"The Betrothal.* George...Maybe Fielding. Her name is Sophie—" My voice cracked from shock as I realized what I was reading. "It's freaking Sophie Stebbins and George Fielding."

"You're kidding?" Tuck said.

"See for yourself." I passed the loupe and the cabinet card to him. "I think we know now why Bucky kept it."

Kala puffed out a frustrated breath. "You want to fill this girl in? I have no idea who you're talking about."

"Sophie Stebbins *is* the Glass Widow," I said.

She gawked. "The woman the bottle was named after?"

"The one and only." Apparently, I'd made a couple of narrow-minded assumptions. First, that Kala had listened closely to my rambling monologues about the bottle's history during the weeks leading up to the auction—aka about Sophie Stebbins, George Fielding, and the Mountain Resort tragedy. Then again, I wasn't certain how much of the story I'd actually told her, and it wasn't something anyone was likely to know unless they were local history buffs, bottle collectors, or fans of infamous true-crime stories.

Tuck handed Kala the photo and loupe. "It's quite the story, lust, out-of-wedlock pregnancy, an arranged marriage with a most unusual dowry—and murder."

"So, this is like a pre-murder engagement photo," she said.

Tuck chuckled. "Exactly."

As Kala studied the card, I told her the story, filling in as many details as I could remember. My grandfather or Bucky would've done a much better job. At any rate, I explained how Sophie Stebbins had been in her thirties, a sour-faced spinster whose father owned a large bottle manufacturing company in Upstate New York. The company specialized in custom bottles, including ones for the mineral springs resorts that were popular in the era. George Fielding had bought up most of the land on Scandal Mountain and begun to build the Mountain House Resort in the early 1880s. The autumn before the resort was scheduled to open, Sophie and her father came to visit George in hopes of getting a large bottle order.

Kala wrinkled her nose in distaste. "Let me guess, the visit also included Sophie's father arranging a marriage between her and George?"

"Pretty much. George Fielding was supposedly running out of money to finish the resort. Sophie's father offered him a financial partnership. Plus—if he married Sophie the Virginal Spinster—he'd receive a dowry consisting of twenty-four cases of basic amber mineral springs bottles, and an additional thirty-six custom bottles for the resort's grand opening with Sophie's likeness on them."

Kala tossed the photo on the counter. "I never liked that whole 'spinster' thing. Sophie was probably gay and didn't want anything to do with marrying a guy."

I shook my head. "Not in this case. It's accepted fact that she arrived a week before the wedding with the dowry of bottles and a bun in the oven, as they used to say."

"Okay, so not gay—but maybe she was bi...."

"Who knows." I continued the story, telling her about George's murder and the fire that gutted the resort only hours after his and Sophie's marriage, on the night before the resort's grand opening when the Glass Widow bottles were to be distributed to the guests as gifts.

She interrupted. "But Sophie wasn't killed?"

Tuck jumped in. "She was seen just before the fire, furtively slipping into a house owned by the local pharmacist, Jeb Warner. He was accused of killing George Fielding, his secret lover's husband, and starting the resort fire to cover up the murder."

"Wow. That is awful," Kala said.

As she looked down at the cabinet card again, Tuck went into more detail. "Apparently, Sophie and Jeb Warner formed a friendship on her first visit to town. At some point, after Sophie's marriage to George was arranged, Jeb Warner went to the Stebbins's company in Upstate New York to purchase bottles for his pharmacy... Let's just say they must've consummated their relationship at that point." Tuck tapped a finger on the counter. "There's a new exhibit about the Mountain House Resort tragedy at the town museum. I hear it's fabulous. We should go see it."

My thoughts went to Joie Bascom yelling at Graham in the auction parking lot. Her reaction may've been excessive. Still, she had a point. The Glass Widow really did belong in the town museum. It was an important part of Scandal Mountain's history.

CHAPTER FOUR

I went to bed a little before eleven. I was relaxed and sleepy. In fact, I'd had a hard time keeping my eyes open while watching TV with Tuck and Kala. But as soon as my head hit the pillow, my brain switched back on; the story of the resort fire, the cache of missing bottles, Graham's attitude at the auction, the envelope with my grandfather's slanted writing all replayed over and over on an endless loop.

Around midnight, I gave up tossing and turning, snagged my phone from the bedside stand, and texted my boyfriend, Shane.

Wish I was there with you. We could go for a midnight skinny-dip.

I spent most Saturday nights at his cabin, but this week we'd put date night on hold because he was a state police detective and had an early morning training session.

I hit send. Then I closed my eyes, visualizing him surfacing from the warm water of his pool into the cool autumn air, his sandy curls wet from a swim, looking like he belonged on the cover of *Fitness* magazine. Man, how had I gotten so lucky? Shane wasn't just great looking either. He was kind and smart, and patient. Alright, so his devotion to law enforcement sometimes caused friction in our relationship, but no more so than the things I tended to get myself into as an antique and art dealer.

My phone pinged. *Shane.*

I'll stop by tomorrow if I can get away. Need to get sleep now.

I scrubbed a hand over my face. I was such an idiot. It wasn't like we hadn't video chatted about the auction earlier.

I scrunched under the covers and answered. *Sorry. I was bored. Couldn't sleep.*

That's okay. I just got home. XO. Goodnight.

My fingers cramped as I forced myself to not draw out my apology with another message. Instead, I tossed the phone onto my bedside stand, safely beyond reach. Then I rolled onto my back and stared at the shadows and moonlight shifting on the ceiling.

* * *

I crawled out of bed not long after sunrise. Bleary-eyed, I scuffed downstairs and made a pot of coffee. A single mug of joe wasn't going to do today, so I put the entire pot on a tray along with the jug of creamer, and a handful of snickerdoodle cookies. Yawning, I carried the tray out onto the front porch and plopped down on the wicker settee.

The air had a crisp bite to it. Overhead, migrating geese honked, then moved on into the distance. A picture-perfect autumn morning. Except for my mood.

I fixed my coffee and was about to take a sip, when the house door creaked open, and Kala straggled onto the porch. Her hair was poufy on one side and bedhead-flat on the other. She had on yoga pants and an oversized '*Jaws*' T-shirt with a frayed neckline. She thrust out her mug. "You do know hogging the coffee pot is against house rules."

I cringed. "I didn't think anyone else would be up for a while."

29

"I figured you'd head to Graham's shop first thing. Thought I'd go with for moral support. You are going, right?"

"Am I that predictable?" I asked, pouring her coffee.

"Yup, totally." Kala added creamer to her mug, took a sip. "Yum. Hazelnut. My favorite."

My hours of sleepless ceiling-staring had led me to a single conclusion. As much as I despised the thought of groveling to Graham, asking to buy or at least see the contents of the envelope was the only way out of my funk. I also knew for certain he'd be in his shop first thing in the morning. After all, I'd overheard him make an interview appointment for nine with the pushy, younger woman in the parking lot.

I cradled my mug in two hands, took a sip, then said as much to myself as to Kala, "I get why Graham paid so much for the Glass Widow—bragging rights, potential resale in the future—but his overpaying for the Bible box doesn't make sense. Even if he thinks it contains clues to the cache of Widows, I don't see him as the treasure hunting type."

"I'm with you there," she said. "I can't imagine Graham digging around in a cellar hole or abandoned dump for old bottles." She thought for a second. "Someone could have paid him a commission to buy the box for them. They could be the treasure hunter."

"I suppose." That was a good way for someone to remain anonymous, even to the auctioneer.

A wily smile played at the corners of Kala's mouth. "Not to change the subject, but have you given more thought to the puppy? Pinky says people are putting dibs on them really fast."

I closed my eyes, barely resisting the urge to groan. Not this again. I was starting to feel like the mean parent. "You can't really think getting a dog right now is a good idea."

"Our customers would love it."

I clenched my teeth. "Just what we need in the shop. Puppies pee on rugs. They chew things, like antique furniture and books."

"They're really cute."

"They're furry trouble-machines," I said. To get my point across, I added, "In other words: it's not happening."

* * *

Just after nine Kala and I climbed into my car. Technically, the classic Volvo wagon belonged to my mom, but I used it full time and cherished it since it had been my grandpa's baby.

I drove toward Graham's shop. Golden Stag Antiques & Gallery was in Burlington, about an hour from our house. I was relieved Kala had dropped the puppy subject, at least for the time being. I was also relieved to find the parking lot of Graham's shop empty of cars. He and his employees parked around back of the building so the lack of vehicles didn't mean the shop wasn't open. It simply meant there weren't customers around to interfere with my talking to him about the envelope.

"Here goes nothing," I said.

Kala quieted her voice. "Just stay cool. Don't let Graham get under your skin."

"Easy for you to say." I took a deep breath, got out of the car. I never liked talking to Graham and this was going to be even worse than usual since I had to be on my best behavior.

As always, the air inside the Golden Stag smelled like clove-studded oranges. Light from sparkling chandeliers and Tiffany-style lamps illuminated the glossy hardwood floors and a myriad of showcases. A farm table surrounded by rabbit-ear chairs occupied the space closest to the shop's front counter. Two large oil paintings of harvest scenes hung on the wall behind it. My entire body tingled from the nearness of so many wonderful pieces. Whether Felix Graham was a womanizing ass or not, he did have good taste and an amazing shop.

Janet, one of Graham's long-time employees, breezed out from a nearby storage room to greet us. With her upswept gray hair, lace-collared blouse, and knit cardigan, she never failed to remind me of Agatha Christie's Miss Marple.

She smiled warmly. "Edie and Kala. What a nice surprise."

"Glad to see you as well," I said. I liked Janet. She'd helped us on more than one occasion, feeding us information that Graham probably would have preferred she keep to herself. That said, she'd also told him things I'd have rather he didn't know. Still, she was a good-hearted person.

A familiar younger woman peeked out from the storage room, then tentatively crept into full view. I recognized her from the Fisher Auction House parking lot.

Janet's powder-pink lips pressed into a proud smile as she motioned at the woman. "This is my granddaughter, Alison. We're hoping she's going to be working here soon."

Whoa, I thought. I hadn't noticed the resemblance before, but it was unmissable now. Gray-blue eyes, pale complexion, conservative sweater and skirt, the woman was pretty much a clone of Janet—definitely not your average look for someone my age.

I offered a smile. "I hope you get the job," I said. Miraculously, I managed to keep any hint of sarcasm out of my voice. In truth, I was taken aback. I understood how someone who didn't know Graham might want to work at the Golden Stag, but it seemed like Janet would've warned her own granddaughter off. He was the slippery, self-centered sort of boss I wouldn't wish on anyone, except perhaps a masochist.

Alison sighed. "Doesn't look like it's going to happen, anyway."

"Why not?" Kala stepped up beside me.

Janet lowered her voice, her concern plain to hear. "Graham was supposed to be here before opening—at nine o'clock sharp—to interview her. He hasn't shown up yet."

"I didn't see his Mercedes out front," I said. "I assumed he'd parked out back. He's really not here?"

"No." Janet's voice quavered, "And he's never *this* late for appointments."

"Did you try texting him?" Kala asked.

"Yes. And we phoned."

"Maybe you should try again," I suggested. "He could've been taking a shower or something."

Janet picked up the shop landline from the counter, punched in a number. As she waited with the phone to her ear, she continued, talking faster, "Alison was going to drive to Graham's house to make sure everything's okay. We really are very worried. Except, if Graham arrived here while she was gone, he'd assume she was late for her interview. Even if I told him the truth, he'd think I was making excuses for her."

After the conversation I overheard outside the auction house, I suspected Janet was right. Graham probably would've gleefully used any excuse to avoid hiring Alison. Then again, there was an equally likely and self-motivated reason for his tardiness. It would've been just like Graham to top off last night's celebration of his auction wins in his hot tub with Dom Perignon and a married woman-friend. Janet herself had told me about walking in on Graham in exactly that sort of compromising situation. Perhaps avoiding a repeat of that awkward event was the real reason Janet didn't want her granddaughter going to Graham's house to check on him.

Kala frowned. "Doesn't Graham have voicemail?"

"He does." Janet's voice pitched higher. "But it's not on—and usually it is. Something's wrong, I know it."

I rubbed the back of my neck to ease a pinch of tension. This wasn't how I'd expected our visit to go. But Janet really did sound worried. Plus, I had to talk to Graham if I wanted the envelope. "How about if Kala and I check on him. He lives near the country club, right?"

"Stonecrest Way. His house is on the cul-de-sac. It's easy to find. Near the Vermont National Country Club..."

As she chattered on, giving more detailed directions than was necessary, Alison caught my eye and softly added, "I'd really appreciate you doing this. I was counting on getting the job."

"No problem." My stomach tightened with worry. I wasn't sure checking on Graham was going to do any good for either of us, but I was equally certain standing around here wasn't going to get anyone anywhere.

* * *

It only took ten minutes to drive to Stonecrest Way, a short street with a half-dozen posh colonial-style homes on large, private lots. There were views of Mount Mansfield to the east and the golf course to the north, interrupted by manicured lawns and forested windbreaks.

Like Janet had said, Graham's home was on the cul-de-sac and up a short driveway. His Mercedes SUV with its ostentatious Golden Stag logo sat in front of the four-car garage, a sign that he was most likely still home. To the right of the garage, a walkway led to the front door. To the left, a lattice topped stockade fence hid the view of the backyard, including, I suspected, his infamous hot tub and party oasis.

"If Graham answers the door," I said, pulling up next to the SUV, "I'm not going to mention the missed interview thing."

Kala shot a look my way. "You're not going to tell him we talked to Janet?"

"I'd rather keep it simple. I'll tell him we stopped by the store. Since he wasn't there, we decided to check here."

"Whatever—" Kala abruptly stopped talking. Eyes wide, she gestured through the windshield toward the stockade fence. "What—what's that?"

A gate in the fence stood open. Something the shape of a large duffel bag lay in the middle of the walkway. It looked like... "Is that a person?"

I leapt out of the car. Kala's footfalls pounded behind me as I raced across the driveway toward it. It was, in fact, a person. A man. In a navy-blue bathrobe. He lay face down with his naked legs exposed. He wasn't moving.

"Oh, my God," I gasped. "It's Graham."

CHAPTER FIVE

I dropped down next to Graham's body.

"Is he dead?" Kala asked, hovering over me.

I touched his shoulder. It felt warm. But he was totally still. Maybe dead. Maybe not breathing. I gave him a shake. "Graham. Are you alright?"

He didn't respond.

Kala let out a squeak. "He really is dead."

Heart attack. Massive stroke. I pressed my fingers against his neck. There was a slight throb. "He's got a pulse." I gave him another shake. "Graham. Can you hear me?"

He slurred, "Leavvve me alone. Let me sleeeep."

"Are you okay?" I asked.

He turned his head, staring blankly at me. His face was as white as a frog's belly. It was slick with sweat. Blood crusted his nostrils. Drool bubbled from one corner of his mouth. "Why-s you in my bedroom?"

Kala snickered. "He's drunk—or really high."

He crawled onto his hands and knees. "Where's bed. Needs to go…"

If he got up, he might stumble and hurt himself worse. I

glanced over my shoulder, through the open gateway to where a chaise lounge sat beside the infamous hot tub. It wasn't a bed, but it would do for now. I looked at Kala. "Help me get him over there."

He staggered to his feet. "Don't need—s help."

"Yes, you do." I grabbed him by one armpit before he could collapse. Kala took hold of the opposite arm. It was like hauling an anesthetized elephant to its feet, but we got him up. With his arms over our shoulders, we dragged him toward the chaise lounge.

Kala grumbled. "He's as heavy as a corpse."

I could only nod. She wasn't kidding, it was like lugging a mattress. As we neared the chaise, my gaze went past it and the rest of the patio furniture to a set of atrium doors that led into his house. They were wide open. "Let's get him inside."

Graham swayed, and all his weight landed on me. I braced my legs to stay upright and shifted my arm to around his waist. He reeked of vomit, blood, and sweat. I should have been repulsed, instead all I felt was worried. The blood might've come from him hurting himself when he fell. But he wasn't into drugs that I knew of. I'd never seen him sloppy drunk. Something was wrong. Very wrong.

My shoulder muscles cramped as I all but carried him through the open doorway and inside the house. To the left was a living room. Huge fieldstone fireplace. Oil paintings. Country antiques. A massive sofa upholstered in brown leather. Classy. Expensive. Exactly the sort of surroundings I'd envisioned Graham living in.

I edged past a coffee table, then lowered him onto the sofa. Kala grabbed pillows off a recliner and slid them behind his head. He closed his eyes, and once again went motionless.

"We need to call an ambulance," I said. "Something's seriously wrong."

Kala took out her phone. "One time, there was this girl in my dorm who acted exactly like this. Somebody had roofied her."

"I don't think that's the case here," I said. I rethought.

Drugged? It wasn't just women who got roofied. And it wasn't always about date rape. Graham was rich. What if someone had been after—

My stomach lurched from a jolt of fear. The Glass Widow. The Bible box. Robbery.

Frantic, I scanned the room. A mahogany desk sat against one wall. Papers were haphazardly strewn across its writing surface. The desk lamp lay broken on the floor.

"No." The word slipped from my mouth as brittle and heavy as leaded glass. The Widow. The Bible box. I couldn't see them anywhere, though Graham could've left them in another room or at the shop, I supposed.

I studied the rest of the room. One oil painting was likely an Emile Gruppe. Another appeared to be Maxfield Parrish's *Hilltop*. If I recalled right, the Parrish painting had last sold for somewhere in the millions... A Tiffany favrile glass vase sat on a side table along with a bronze nude. Lots of incredibly valuable things hadn't been taken.

The glass doors to a display cabinet were wide open. Miniature carved songbirds were displayed on the top and bottom shelves. The middle shelf contained a pair of early glass flasks on one side, and a decanter and two brandy snifters on the other. The center section of that shelf was conspicuously empty, as if the crown jewel of the display had been removed. Had that crown jewel been the Glass Widow?

Graham mumbled, "Was sleeping. Heard somethin'..."

I knelt by the sofa, gave him a shake. "Were you robbed?"

"Tried—to stop them," he slurred.

I swiveled to Kala. "We need an ambulance and the police."

Graham shifted as if attempting to sit up. "No. Don't call."

"You need help," I said, voice firm.

"Call my doctor. He's closer."

Kala poised a finger over her phone. "What's his number?"

Spittle slid from Graham's mouth. "802—802-8..."

"Call Janet," I told Kala. "She'll know the number." Maybe Graham had an ongoing medical issue. Maybe he was on medication and drank on top of that. He could've knocked over the desk lamp and left the display cabinet doors open in his confusion.

"Is that you, Janet?" Kala said into the phone. "Graham is— acting weird. I need the number for his doctor." She was silent for a second, then recited back a phone number. I listened closely, memorizing it in case she didn't.

Graham lifted his head. "Dr. Gabriel Stanhope. Lives next door."

While Kala made the call to Dr. Stanhope, I rushed to the front door, unlocked, and opened it in preparation for his arrival. Next door was good. Someone other than us to make decisions about the situation was even better.

Before I could even turn away from the door, a man dashed from the house across the street with a medical bag in his hand. Gabriel Stanhope, I assumed. He was a squat, muscular man with thinning blond hair and a deep tan. He loped across the cul-de-sac. When he reached the front walk, I waved him inside. "Graham's in the living room."

He pushed past me, golf shoes squeaking against the polished floor as he sprinted down the short hallway. "How long ago did you find him?" he asked over his shoulder.

"A few minutes. He's acting drunk or high, but maybe it's something else."

Stanhope rushed into the living room, dropped his medical bag on the floor between the coffee table and sofa. He crouched, checked Graham's eyes and pulse. He took his blood pressure, then asked Graham what had happened.

"Felt dizzy," Graham said. "Laid down." He raised his head, glanced toward the coffee table. "The box was there. Saw someone leaving. They took it."

"Who?" Stanhope asked.

"Don't know. Tried to follow… Too dizzy. Maybe should call cops."

Stanhope took out his phone, put it to his ear. "This is Dr. Gabriel Stanhope. I need the police and an ambulance at 26 Stonecrest Way. Possible drug overdose and burglary." Still on the phone, he rose from his crouch, then walked out of the living room and into the hallway. His voice hushed until it was impossible to hear what he was saying.

Kala nudged me with her elbow. "What do you think he's talking about?"

I shook my head. I didn't dare say anything with Graham only feet away. Maybe Graham had a medical condition the doctor didn't want us to know about.

Stanhope strode back into the room. He eyed me and Kala. "You two need to stay put until the police arrive. They want to ask you a few questions."

I nodded, but the accusatorial tone of his voice took me aback. I said, "We don't know anything."

Kala folded her arms across her chest. "Like less than nothing."

"You are the ones who found him."

"Yeah, but we don't know any more than you do," I said.

He picked his medical bag up from the floor. As he started to set it on the coffee table, I spotted smudges on the tabletop, including a ring-shaped one, perhaps from the bottom of a glass. I rushed forward, thrusting out a hand to stop him. "We shouldn't put anything on there. There might be evidence on its surface. Graham said it's where the box was. I'm pretty sure he was referring to an expensive Bible box he bought yesterday."

Stanhope set the bag back on the floor, narrowed his eyes. "For someone who knows nothing, you seem to know a lot about what Graham owns."

"I was at the auction yesterday when he bought it. That's the only reason—"

Graham interrupted, "Water. Thirsty."

40

Stanhope glanced at Kala. "Get a glass for him from the kitchen, and a roll of paper towels while you're at it." Without missing a beat, he swiveled to me. "Go upstairs and find a blanket. We need to keep him warm until the ambulance arrives."

My face heated. Stanhope was as much of a domineering jerk as Graham. Still, the need for blankets and water made sense.

I hesitated. Then again, maybe it was a ploy to get Kala and me out of the room and give him time to talk to Graham in private.

CHAPTER SIX

No sooner had I returned from upstairs with the blanket and Kala from the kitchen with the water and towels than the wail of sirens sounded and rapidly moved closer.

"I'll show them in," I said, heading for the front door. My offer wasn't just about being helpful. Getting some fresh air and away from Stanhope was more than a little appealing. Kala hurried to follow me, undoubtedly feeling the same way.

As we reached the door, an ambulance sped into the driveway and stopped behind Graham's SUV. A police cruiser winged in beside it. Two officers emerged, a young woman and an older man, sprinting toward us a step behind the EMTs with their stretcher.

I flagged them inside. "Graham and his doctor are in the living room."

"Thank you," the woman officer said as the group passed by. After they had all disappeared through the doorway, I realized the older cop—a gruff looking man with an oddly bulbous forehead— was still in the driveway, shining a flashlight in through the back window of the Volvo. What the heck?

I strode toward him. "Hi, I'm Edie Brown. That's my car."

"Would you mind if I took a look inside?" he asked.

Confused, I frowned. "Why?"

"Just a formality."

Even if I didn't watch a lot of crime shows on TV, his curiosity would have pinged a warning bell. My mind went to Stanhope walking into the hallway and out of earshot when he called 911. What had he told the operator? That he thought we were involved with the robbery and Graham's condition? Why else would the officer want to look inside my car?

I gestured at Kala, said to the officer, "This is Kala Acosta. She works for me. We're the ones who found Graham. He was laying just over there." I pointed at the gateway. "We brought him inside through the atrium doors that are at the back of the house. He was acting out of it."

The officer walked to the driver's door, then once again shone the flashlight's beam inside the vehicle. "You knew the atrium doors were unlocked?"

I clenched my teeth. I'd been questioned by police enough that the way he phrased the question stood out to me. "The doors were wide open. We had no idea if they were unlocked or not before then."

The officer—Sergeant Nelson according to his nametag—looked at Kala. "Is that right?"

She nodded. "We're antique dealers. We were at Graham's store. Janet—she works for him—was worried because he was late for work. We came over to check on him. You know, like a welfare check." Her eyes narrowed to slits. "And before you ask, we didn't wander around inside his house looking for valuables. We helped him onto the couch and called the doctor. That was it."

Without missing a beat, his attention swung back to me. "Is this your vehicle?"

"Yes, I already told you—" I stopped talking as I realized he might have checked the license plate number, and that I might have unintentionally lied. "It's registered in my mother's name.

Vicki Tuckerman. I have permission to use it." No way was I going to mention her current address—federal prison—though chances were, he discovered that already. I swallowed drily, closed the distance between us, then opened the driver's door for him as a show of cooperation. "Go, on. Look if you want."

"Thank you." The officer leaned in. He fanned the flashlight beam across the floor.

I felt the touch of Kala's hand on my arm. She whispered, "You don't have anything suspicious in there, do you?"

A sick feeling crawled up my throat as the beam of the officer's flashlight went under the driver's seat and I remembered my stash. I cleared my throat. "Um… Officer?"

He looked over his shoulder at me. "Yes?"

"I picked up some sterling silver flatware at a yard sale the other day. I believe it's still under the seat. There might be a sugar bowl and some hunting knives under there too."

He reached under the seat, fished out a box. Thankfully the yard sale price was still taped to the flatware—*$5 for all*—a super deal for so much sterling. He put the box back, then moved on, searching the rear of the car more quickly, most likely because there was nothing to be seen other than aging granola bars, stray travel mugs, and haphazardly folded shopping bags.

I was on the verge of telling him that my boyfriend was a state police detective when he backed out of the car and closed the door. He smiled. "Thank you for letting me look. If you don't mind, I have a few more questions."

"Sure," I said. What else could I do? Put myself back on his suspect list by objecting?

He asked for our contact information. As he moved on to reviewing what had happened in more detail than before, the EMTs wheeled Graham out on the stretcher, loaded him into the ambulance, then took off, red lights strobing.

The officer chatted with us for a few more minutes. Finally, he let us go.

* * *

Once we were out on the main road, heading away from Graham's house, Kala rolled her eyes and said sarcastically, "Now that was a lot of fun, wasn't it?"

"I couldn't believe it when he wanted to search the car," I said.

Kala lowered her window, letting the breeze blow on her sweat-shiny face. "I don't know about you, but I could use a treat. Something cold, like an ice-cream sundae—salty and sweet—nuts, caramel sauce, marshmallows..."

I laughed. "With a shot of Bailey's Irish Cream on top."

"Definitely."

I tapped the brakes, slowing as the car ahead of us put on its turn signal before veering into the golf course's driveway. "How about we pick up ingredients for sundaes and take them home. Tuck's going to need a little something special too, at least once we tell him what happened." I hesitated. "Before we do that, we should stop at Graham's store and tell Janet and Alison everything."

"I agree." Kala softened her voice. "I hope whoever stole the stuff from Graham doesn't just toss or burn that envelope from your grandfather."

My thoughts staggered. With everything that had been going on, the envelope had slipped my mind. But now it came back in a rush, leaving me feeling hollow. If the chance of finding out what was inside it had been low before, now it seemed impossibly slim.

CHAPTER SEVEN

I was glad Kala was in a talkative mood. When we reached the Golden Stag, she was happy to tell Janet and Alison everything that had happened at Graham's, while I quietly hung back. All I wanted was to get the visit done and get home where I could escape to the solitude of my bedroom to think.

Thankfully, we were back on the road in less than a half-hour, speeding out of Burlington toward Scandal Mountain. The tension pinching in the back of my neck subsided. My shoulders relaxed. We were almost to the village and Quickie's Quick stop where I planned on buying the sundae supplies when Kala's phone pinged.

She looked at the message, texted back, then swiveled in her seat to face me. "Do you mind stopping at Pinky's apartment before we go to Quickie's? She's got a shirt she wants to give me."

I longed to say no, but Kala had been a lifeline, and her day hadn't been any easier than mine. "Is that what you were texting about?"

"Yeah." She grimaced. "We probably should tell her about Graham. You know she'll find out."

"That's for sure." Pinky didn't miss much. In fact, she may have

already heard about Graham's robbery thanks to her cousin Edgar
and his scanner. Our names wouldn't have been mentioned, but—
My thoughts hit their mental brakes as something occurred to me.
"You're sure the something Pinky wants to give you is clothes and
not a puppy?"

Kala grinned, a sly tilt of her lips. "I told her you hate puppies."

"I don't hate puppies. They're just a huge commitment, that's
all."

Still smiling, Kala flopped back against the seat. "No puppies, I
promise."

I steered off the main road and down the side street that led to
Fisher's Auction House. Pinky's apartment was directly behind it
in the granary building; an old, dilapidated structure that
zigzagged upward three-plus stories to a ventilated top.

"While we're here"— I pulled the car in by the concrete steps
that went up to Pinky's front door—"we should ask if she knows
who the underbidders on the Widow and the Bible box were. One
of them might be involved in the theft."

"Sounds likely to me," Kala said, as we got out.

I raised a hand to stop her from thinking I had anything else in
mind. "I'm not suggesting we deep dive into this robbery thing."

She laughed. "I've heard that before."

"I'm serious this time."

Kala knocked once on Pinky's front door, then opened it and
stuck her head inside. "It's us. Are you home?"

A chorus of dog barks and puppy yips answered, as loud as a
pack of excited coyotes. Pinky's distant voice shouted. "Back
here!"

We walked into her entry and living room. Well, it was actually
more of a bohemian open-plan living space. Vintage stuff and
used furniture were stacked and strewn everywhere. A flight of
repurposed fire escape stairs went up to a loft, partly hidden from
view by a mishmash of drapes. Life-size statues of St. Francis and
the Virgin Mary stationed on either side of the bathroom door

were new additions since my last visit. An odd mix of ham soup and wet dog smell hung in the air as thick as incense smoke in a Buddhist temple.

A few yards away from St. Francis, Pinky sat cross-legged in the middle of a puppy playpen. Balls of golden fluff crawled over her lap and wiggled under her arms, vying for attention while their mom watched attentively from outside the pen. I counted ten before Pinky untangled her legs, freed herself from the puppies, and lumbered to her feet.

She smiled at Kala, eyes lingering for a beat. "You're going to love the shirt I found for you."

"It has to be better than this." Wrinkling her nose, Kala flicked the sleeve of her sweater. "I would've taken it off, but I honestly didn't realize how gross it was until now."

Pinky frowned. "What are you talkin' about?"

"It's got body fluids on it—Felix Graham's to be exact."

I glanced at her sweater sleeve. I'd noticed a damp spot on mine earlier and avoided thinking too much about it: Graham's drool, most likely. On the other hand, Kala's sleeve was spattered with nastiness, including blood-colored globs.

Pinky leapt out of the pen. "Oh my God. What happened? Are you okay?"

As Kala explained how body fluids ended up on her sweater sleeve, I slumped down on an empty spot at the end of the couch. The rest of it was piled with enough old blankets and pillows to overfill a castoff bin at Goodwill. Except Goodwill would've never allowed them on their shelves. They stank of dirty dog.

"The police even searched Edie's car," Kala said.

Pinky's gaze shot to me. "They did?'

I shrugged. "It ticked me off at first, but they were only being thorough," I said, though I still suspected Stanhope had said something incriminating to the 911 operator.

Pfffft. The sound followed by a rotting cabbage stink came from the other end of the couch, then a graying dog snout emerged from underneath the stinky blanket pile, only far enough that it could sniff my pant leg.

Ignoring the stench, I patted the dog's nose and mumbled, "You really should learn some manners if you're going to be around guests."

Pinky rolled her eyes. "That's Sandra. She's...antisocial."

I jerked my hand back, not wanting to get nipped, and shifted away from the dog. "Ummm...should I get up slowly and sit someplace else?"

Pinky laughed. "Not antisocial as in vicious. She's hiding from the *terrifying* puppies." She swiveled back to Kala and returned to the previous topic without a pause. "You said Graham was acting like he was on something."

"We think the robbers drugged him," she said.

Pinky grinned, a devious Kala-like smile that set off warning bells at the back of my skull. "I could find out for sure, if you want."

"Like how?" I asked.

"Kala's sweater. All we'd have to do is give it to my little brother. He's got 24/7 access to the state forensic lab. He could run some tests on the blood, saliva...whatever else is on it."

We'd called Pinky's little brother Butthead Bill all the way through grade school and even after he left for college. He was odd as a kid—an outsider with chubby chipmunk cheeks, a love for plaid pants, and creepy hobbies like stuffing and mounting things he collected along the roadside: skunks, frogs, crows. However, his pastimes had paid off bigtime when he scored a job working for the state as a forensic scientist right out of college.

I squinted at Pinky. "Can't Bill lose his job for doing something like that?"

"Trust me, no one will ever know."

"Ah—I'm not sure." I nibbled my bottom lip. "Kala and I were going to ask you who the underbidders were at the auction, but testing the sweater might be a step too far..."

Before I could fully gather my thoughts, Kala yanked off the sweater, revealing *The Exorcist* T-shirt she wore underneath. She tossed the sweater to Pinky. "I vote we go for it."

Pinky caught the sweater. "I'm bartending at the Café later today. Bill is supposed to stop by. I'll give it to him then."

I opened my mouth to object, but clearly I was too late and outnumbered, and I couldn't deny I was more than a little curious. Still, there was another issue. Pinky loved doing favors like this for people. However, they never came without a price, and I imagined her brother's walk on the illegal side of forensics wasn't going to be a pro bono job.

I eyed Pinky. "What's this going to cost us?"

"Don't worry about that," she said.

I narrowed my gaze. *Yeah, right. Famous last words.*

Her grin grew broader as she set Kala's dirty sweater on the back of a chair, then picked up a paper bag off its seat. She handed the bag to Kala. "This is the shirt I texted you about. I saw it at the church thrift shop, and I couldn't resist buying."

Kala reached into the bag. Her eyes brightened as she took out a charcoal gray hoodie bedazzled with an image of the three wise monkeys.

I laughed. It was perfect. Kala had a major crush on the trio, especially See No Evil.

"I love it." Kala beamed. "It's—it's sparkly and just my size!"

"It really is perfect," I said.

Pinky caught my gaze. "Before, you said something about wanting to know who the underbidders were. I assume you mean on the Glass Widow."

"That and the Bible box." If we were going to go out on a limb by having Bill test the fluids on Kala's sweater, there was no sense dialing back on what I'd originally contemplated asking. "I know Joie Bascom was bidding, but she wasn't the only one."

"After the auction," Pinky said, "Albert Fisher was talking

about how high Joie bid. The museum doesn't have that kind of money to spare."

"I know for a fact Joie raised fifty thousand," I said, "And she was ready to kick in another twenty of her own." I didn't expand to explain how I'd overheard this in the parking lot. Pinky had her own secrets, and I could keep some of mine as well.

She stroked her chin, thinking for a moment. "There were loads of phone and online bids. I don't know who placed those or everyone who was bidding on the floor." She gave the pen full of puppies a meaningful side-eye glance. "I could find out, if you want."

I pressed my lips together. Okay, now I knew where this was going. Kala wanted a puppy. I was the only thing standing in the way.

Pinky grinned. "You asked before how much Bill would charge for testing the gunk on the sweater for drugs. I know you hate puppies."

"I don't hate puppies," I snapped.

Without missing a beat, she continued, "As I was saying. I know you don't like puppies—" She glanced toward the pile of blankets beside me, once more wiggling as antisocial Sandra's head poked into view: a sugar-faced golden retriever with soulful brown eyes— "and neither does somebody else."

"Oh," I said as I caught her drift. She wasn't talking puppy. She was talking grumpy, old, stinky dog.

She went on, "Sandra belongs to Bill. I've been watching her as a favor while he's hunting for a new apartment. She hates it here. You wouldn't even have to buy food. I have a huge bag of kibble. Bill thinks she's going senile, so he insists she eats special brain-enhancing stuff. She likes people food better, French fries, cheese-burgers... It wouldn't be a forever situation, only until Bill gets settled in."

I looked at the dog. She stared back at me, big eyes opening wider as if pleading to be freed from her current situation. The main reason I didn't want a puppy wasn't just the peeing and chewing. If Kala moved out and left the puppy behind, then said puppy would become my problem. And I wasn't certain if I'd even continue to live at home after my mom got out of prison and returned—which was only five months away, if not less. What would happen to the puppy then? It wasn't fair to assume Tuck would want it.

Pinky continued her sales pitch. "Sandra won't be any trouble. She mostly sleeps. She loves being outdoors. She doesn't really smell that bad."

I closed my eyes. Dear Lord, Tuck wasn't going to be thrilled about this—and even less so when he learned the reason we owned Bill a favor. But how could I say no with both Sandra and Kala's eyes pleading for me to say yes.

CHAPTER EIGHT

Kala and I decided to skip the ice-cream sundae idea. It seemed wiser to not leave Sandra the Cranky alone in an unfamiliar car, for her sake and the car's upholstery. We also rode the rest of the way home with the windows down. Pinky was wrong about Sandra not smelling that bad.

"I think she rolled on a dead fish," I said, as I turned into our driveway and started up the hill.

Kala snickered. "Maybe Bill took her on a walk at the state body farm."

"Don't even suggest that." Somewhere in Vermont there was a plot of wilderness where human bodies were left to naturally decay, so they could be studied by law enforcement and forensic scientists like Bill. I might've loved digging in old dumps for bottles, but the idea of messing around in pits full of rotting bodies was nothing short of disgusting.

As the shop came into view, I spotted Shane's Land Rover parked in front of it.

"Were you expecting your boyfriend?" Kala asked.

"Not this early. It's barely three o'clock." I pulled in next to the Rover.

"You don't want to mention Bill and the blood test thing to him, right?"

I cringed. "He'd probably prefer to not know."

Kala laughed. "See no evil, know no evil."

"Partly that," I said. "At this point, we aren't even sure Bill will agree to do the test. We just have Pinky's word for it. Besides, maybe he'll do the testing at home on his own time. That wouldn't be illegal, maybe."

She laughed again. "I can see it now—Bill in his apartment-size mad scientist laboratory, testing body fluids and doing who knows what else."

"That might explain his hunt for a new place to live." I parked, got out of the car, and opened the back door for Sandra. "Welcome to your new temporary home."

Sandra plunged out of the car, tail going a million miles-per-hour as she made for Shane's Rover, sniffing its tires before she changed direction and galumphed toward where Tuck was emerging from the shop.

Lengthening my strides, I zinged in front of Sandra, blocking the way before she could slip past Tuck and into the store. I glared at her and hardened my voice. "No. You're not going inside."

Tuck chuckled. "That tail does look like it could clear a shelf of pottery with one swing."

"She also stinks like roadkill," Kala said.

Tuck gave Sandra another look and raised a bushy eyebrow. "Exactly what is the furry, little skink-ball doing here?"

"Ummm...We're sort of babysitting her as a favor to Pinky," I said.

"Short term?"

"Supposedly." Instead of going into more detail, I glanced past him and through the open shop door. "Where's Shane?"

Tuck nodded toward the house. "He went inside to get beers and sandwiches for us."

"Isn't it a little late for lunch?"

"The shop was busy earlier, and I lost track of time. Now my stomach's growling like a bear."

He led Kala and I over to where a cast iron table and chairs sat close to the shop's front door. I was surprised no one had bought the set before now. It was fabulous and reasonably priced.

Once we'd all sat down—except for Sandra who wandered off to give Shane's tires another sniff—Kala perched on the edge of her chair and said, "Do you want to tell him what happened or should I?"

Tuck's gaze winged to the Volvo as if expecting to see a dented fender.

"Not that kind of problem," I said. "More like Graham's in the hospital and the Glass Widow and the Bible box were stolen."

His mouth dropped open. "You're kidding?"

"I'm afraid not." I took a second to peel off my sweater—it wasn't that gross, but it sure felt good to be out of it. After that, I gave a *Cliffs-Note* version about finding Graham. When Shane returned with the beers and sandwiches, I shared everything again in detail—or almost everything.

"Do you remember the name of the officers who responded?" Shane asked.

"They were city police, South Burlington," I said.

Kala jumped in. "The old white dude's nametag said Sergeant Nelson. Squinty eyes. Big forehead. Suspicious of everything."

Shane nodded. "I know who he is."

Something butted my thigh. I looked down. Sandra was staring up at me with watery eyes. She snorted like an exasperated old woman.

"Why the sad look?" I asked. "Didn't anyone give you a bite of their sandwich?"

"She got plenty of mine," Tuck said. He made a face. "What she really needs is a five-gallon drum of doggie shampoo and a trip to the pond."

Shane looked at me. "If you want to do that, I could use the walk."

At the mention of the word walk, Sandra started barking and wiggling like someone had offered her a plate of steak and gravy.

"How about *swim?*" I emphasized the word to see her reaction. Her barks turned to whines and her tail jumped to supersonic level. "Okay, but this is about getting clean as well as fun."

We didn't have doggie shampoo hanging around, but in the shop's storage room there was a dusty box of Nature's Beauty pine tar soap—48 desiccated bars to be precise. Buying a case of the so-called 'old timey soap' and its corresponding bath bomb balls had been one of my mom's hairbrained business schemes. She'd insisted it would bring in customers and sell like crazy. I suspected the purchase had more to do with her attraction to the Nature's Beauty salesman than the idea that the overpriced items would make us money, which unfortunately and unsurprisingly they hadn't.

Soap in hand, I went with Shane and Sandra across the driveway, through the gardens and down to the furthest edge of the lawn where an apple tree I'd given to Mom as a child hung low over the grass. Mom hadn't acted impressed the day I gave it to her, but every spring she cut branches of blooms off the tree and used them to decorate her art studio, which was attached to the shop. According to her—and Victorian floriography—apple blooms symbolically meant 'I have a preference for you', though Mom always warned that thorn apple blooms referred to someone having 'deceitful charm'.

Lost in thought, I slowed my steps. Mom was such a temperamental mix of ups and downs...

"Don't eat that!" Shane's shout snapped me back to the here and now.

Sandra was under the apple tree snagging half-rotted apples off the ground and downing them as quick as a vacuum cleaner, a colon-cleaning snack I suspected we might regret later.

We chased her away from the tree to where a short path led to my family's tiny pond. It was fed by a spring that burbled down from high up on Scandal Mountain. It was similar to Maiden Spring in that way, though nowhere near as impressive at any point. At the pond's inlet there was a patch of deep green watercress, and a shade garden where my grandfather had planted ferns he collected, including maidenhairs.

When we reached the edge of the water, Shane picked up a stick and tossed it into the pond. "Go get it, girl!"

Sandra flew into the water like a Dockdog on a mission. In a second she had the stick and was back, dropping it at Shane's feet. He tossed it again, and once more she was off at light speed.

"That certainly brought the old girl to life," Shane said. "How old is she anyway?"

"I have no idea. All Pinky said was that she didn't like puppies."

"She seems to like it here."

This time when Sandra returned, I managed to get a hold of her and scrub her with soap. I ended up getting as soaked as she was, but it was warm for an autumn afternoon, and I was for anything that would eliminate the stench.

I tossed a stick, sending her back into the water to rinse off, then turned to Shane. "You haven't said how your day went. How was the training session?"

His eyes brightened. "I expected it to be boring. It was a HAZWOPER refresher class, emergency response and hazardous waste. Usually, those things are 'Death by PowerPoint' dull, but the instructor was great."

He moved in close to me, brushed a lock of damp hair out of my eyes. "You had quite the adventure."

I blew out a breath. "That's for sure. Disappointing, too."

"You're talking about not getting the envelope?"

I nodded. "I know it sounds self-centered...What happened to Graham was serious. I do feel bad for him."

His voice became grave. "Whoever did it is dangerous. They

risked a lot by committing a robbery while someone was home, not to mention picking someone like Graham."

He was right about both, especially the last. I not only suspected Graham was involved with my mom being set up for the art forgery charge, but I also knew for a fact Graham was complicit in the theft of a decoy collection, though the police had failed to find anything other than hearsay evidence against him. In other words, Graham was connected on both sides of the law.

"This isn't going to be an easy case to solve," Shane said.

"That's for sure. Pinky said there were tons of people interested in the pieces." I thought back to the auction, shook my head. "It couldn't have been someone bidding online. They wouldn't have known who had the winning bid in time to go after Graham so fast."

"What's to say it was only one person or that they were bidders? Anyone in the audience would've seen who ended up with the pieces." He rested his hand on my arm. "Do me a favor, stay out of this. Let the South Burlington police handle it, okay?"

I playfully shoved his hand away. "Just because I'm curious about a stupid envelope, doesn't mean I'm crazy enough to get tangled up in Graham's—"

The *brrring* of my phone interrupted.

Fishing it out of my pocket, I answered, "Hello."

Tuck's voice came from the other end. "You won't believe who just called the shop."

"Ahhh—who?"

"Graham."

My mind went blank. Graham? "Shane and I were just talking about him. What did he want?"

"They're releasing him from the hospital. He wants you to come to his house tonight to talk," Tuck said.

"About what?" I asked, dumbfounded.

"He said his memory of last night and this morning is foggy."

"But Kala and I don't know anything."

Tuck was quiet for a moment, then said, "Graham didn't mention Kala. He just wants to speak with you." His voice deepened. "I have a bad feeling about this."

"Well, yeah. Graham's not exactly our family's biggest supporter."

He hesitated. "We can talk more when you get back up to the house."

"Alright." I hung up.

As I slipped the phone back into my pocket, Shane folded his arms across his chest. "What was that about?"

"You jinxed me. That was Tuck. Graham wants to talk to me in person—tonight."

Shane rubbed a finger over his lip, then said, "I think you should do it."

I gawked. "You just told me to stay away from him."

He shrugged. "Maybe I was wrong. It would be handy to know Graham's version of what happened, or at least the version he chooses to tell you."

"The great Detective Shane Payton is admitting he's curious?" I teased.

His expression once more went serious. "Just don't let Graham pull you into anything, like agreeing to backing up a bogus story for him."

I laughed. "You mean, like an insurance scam?"

"I wouldn't leave it past him."

"Neither would I."

CHAPTER NINE

Tuck and I arrived at Graham's a little after seven. Kala had been more than happy to stay behind and babysit the new and improved, less stinky version of Sandra. Shane had gone home. As much time as he spent with me and at work, I suspected his day-to-day home chores had gotten ahead of him.

We went up Graham's front walk and rang his bell. A moment later, Dr. Stanhope opened the door. He nodded curtly at the hallway behind him. "Graham's waiting in the living room."

"How's he feeling?" I asked.

"Better than before." With that said, Stanhope breezed right past us, his stout legs carrying him swiftly in the direction of his house.

"Guess he's anxious to get home," I whispered to Tuck.

"Seems as though."

We headed down the hallway to the living room. Graham sat in a wing chair with his feet up on a hassock and a throw blanket pulled over his legs. His face was pale and unshaven. He wore a gray sweatshirt with a stretched-out collar, not at all his normal richer-than-thou look, made even more intense by a scabbed-over abrasion that striped the end of his nose.

He took a sip from the glass he was holding—ice water by the looks of it—then he set the glass on a stand beside his chair. There was a thin book on the stand. My heart sped up, thumping hard. The book was the size and shape of Bucky's journals. Had the journals somehow escaped the hands of the thieves? If Graham still had them, did he have other things as well, like the envelope?

"Hope you don't mind I tagged along," Tuck said.

Graham dismissed Tuck's comment with a flick of his fingers. He nodded at the sofa. "Make yourselves comfortable."

"Glad to hear you're feeling better," Tuck said as he settled down on the end of the sofa closest to Graham.

I remained standing in hopes of catching a better look at the book or journal. "You were in pretty bad shape this morning," I said.

"I only vaguely remember most of it," he admitted.

I craned my neck. The book was dark brown with bright patches of gold lettering. Not one of the journals. *Damn it.*

"Edie mentioned you might've been drugged," Tuck said.

Graham scowled. "I don't generally make a habit of passing out on my front lawn."

I resisted the urge to smile. Tuck's choice of comment had been perfect. Graham hadn't denied the possibility of drugs, a fact we'd soon have confirmed or ruled out thanks to Pinky's little brother.

I lowered myself, sitting on the edge of the coffee table, up close to Tuck. "You were robbed though, right?"

"Bastards took the Widow and the Bible box."

Tuck gentled his voice. "Is anything else missing?"

Graham picked up the water glass again. He took a sip. Cleared his throat. "I haven't had a chance to go through everything, but it doesn't appear so."

I gave the room a quick scan. The lamp was back on the desk next to a short pile of neatly stacked papers. Nearby, the display cabinet's doors were shut. Through their glass, I could see everything was exactly as it had been earlier, except the decanter and snifters were now gone. "Did the police find any evidence? Fingerprints? Traces of the drug? Did they take anything?"

He set the water glass down. "After I left, they supposedly came back and went over the entire place. Upstairs, the garage, the yard...They took the decanter and snifters with them, but I can't see as they did much else. Certainly not a thorough job." His eyes locked on mine. "That's why I asked you here."

I frowned. "What are you talking about?"

"I want to hire you to find out who did it."

I froze in shock. It was good I was seated, or I might have toppled over. "You can't be serious."

Tuck rose from the sofa. "It's been nice talking to you, Graham. But you're barking up the wrong tree. We're antique dealers, not private investigators." He touched my shoulder. "C'mon, Edie. Let's get out of here."

Graham's gaze remained on mine. "You two, and that employee of yours, can fly under the radar. Cops can't. It could be years before they get to the bottom of this, if they even try that hard." His voice lowered and pinched. "You have connections."

My entire body went hot, sweat stuck my shirt to my back. Logic screamed for me to scramble to my feet and make for the door like Tuck suggested. Curiosity glued me in place. I scowled at Graham. "What about your connections? You have millions more than we do—and don't try to tell me you don't, Tuck and I know better."

"That might be true. However, in this instance, I'm not inclined to trust them."

"You think one of them did this?" I asked.

"It wouldn't be the first time someone was backstabbed by a business associate."

Tuck squeezed my shoulder. "Definitely time to leave."

I rested a hand over his. "In a minute." Something Graham had said to me a few months earlier pushed into my head: *I heard about your trouble—arrested for selling stolen property. Your mother's in prison for forgery. I don't need or want to be connected to people like you.* I looked at Graham steadily. "I thought you were too high and mighty to stoop to associating with people like us?"

"I didn't say I want us to become best friends. This is purely business, and I expect you to keep our arrangement under wraps." A smile flicked at the corners of his mouth. "You're good at this sort of thing. On top of that, no one will suspect you're working for me." He was silent for a beat. "Name your price. Cash under the table. I know you can use it."

Careful to keep my face expressionless, I stalled as if mulling over the proposition. Shane had said it would be handy for me to hear Graham's side of the story, a version that perhaps would differ from what he'd told the police. "First, I want to know everything you remember from the moment you left the auction gallery until now—blow by blow. Did you go straight home?"

"I went to the Jumping Café first, had a drink, and talked to a few people."

"People from the auction?" I asked.

"Sparky Collins was there. I spoke with him."

I paused for a beat. I was surprised to learn Sparky hadn't stayed until the end of the auction. There were tons more Vermont bottles going up on the block that he would've normally bid on.

Graham continued, "I had dinner with Rene."

I resisted the urge to gag. Rene St. Marie lived across the street from us. He and Graham were both on the state Chamber of Commerce board of directors. Like Graham, Rene was on my list of least favorite people, mostly because it was no secret that he'd love for us to be forced to sell our property so he could snap it up and develop the land. Still, his friendship with Graham was long-standing and Rene had little interest in antiques. The chances of him being involved with the theft were nil.

As Graham went on, his voice grew quiet as if he were

recounting the events as much for his own benefit as ours. "I ordered Chicken Florentine. I couldn't eat it all, so I had the rest put in a to-go box. I don't usually bring home leftovers, but it tasted particularly good. I left the Cafe about seven, stopped at the shop and picked up the money bag, then went home. By that time, it was eight-thirty."

"Did you set your alarm system when you got home?" Tuck asked.

He shook his head. "I always do that just before bed. Quite often I have *friends* stop by."

I ignored the meaningful way he jutted an eyebrow when he stressed the word *friends*. Yeah, I got it. He meant women. I asked, "But you remember locking all the doors?"

He tilted his head, thinking. "I secured the front door. I'm certain of that."

That coincided with what he'd previously told us. "How about the atrium doors?"

This time his pause was longer. "I'm...not sure. Before I locked the front door, I brought the Bible box and the to-go container in from the car. The Glass Widow was inside the box." He nodded at the coffee table. "I put the Bible box and the food right there, went upstairs and showered. When I came down, I finished the rest of my dinner while I went through the box's contents."

"But when you were at the Jumping Cafe, you left the Bible box and the bottle in your SUV, right?" Tuck asked.

"No. I brought them inside, sat down at a booth, and never left them unattended."

"Did you sell some of the ephemera while you were at the café?" I needed to eliminate the possibility of him claiming all of the contents were stolen when in fact that wasn't the full truth.

"Certainly not. I didn't even go through any of it until I got home. Then I skimmed one of the journals and some of the papers before I put them in my safe. I planned on looking at the rest later in the evening."

"So, everything wasn't stolen," I said. This was great news. "Did you tell the police that?"

He looked at me as if I were crazy. "Of course. I just wish I'd put everything away. If I had, we wouldn't be sitting here now." His tone shifted, barely noticeable but it was there—a note of fear, trepidation as he went on, "I took a snifter and my decanter out and had a nightcap around midnight." He glanced toward the display cabinet. "I could swear I left them on the coffee table and I'm certain the decanter was half-full. But when the police came the decanter was empty and everything was back in the cabinet, at least I think it was. I wasn't exactly at my best. I only vaguely remember Stanhope and the rescue squad, you, and that black girl."

I bristled at the way he referred to Kala. "You mean, Kala, the woman who works for me?"

"Whatever, yes."

I clenched my teeth, pushing back my dislike for him. Still, I wasn't totally devoid of sympathy. Not remembering a long space of time had to be unsettling. "I saw the decanter and snifters in the cabinet at that point," I said to reassure him. However, I didn't mention the ring of smudge I'd noticed on the coffee table. I'd assumed it was from a glass, now I was certain—and not just any glass, a snifter.

Tuck spoke up, "Edie, told me there was an empty space in the middle of that cabinet shelf."

Graham closed his eyes. "The last thing I clearly recall is putting the Glass Widow in the cabinet. I stepped back to admire it. The room began to spin... I woke up on the sofa. Someone was standing in the living room, holding the Bible box. I got up, tried to chase after them... two people, maybe three, maybe one. Everything was hazy. The atrium door was open. I remember that and the cool air. I tripped over something. Might have been my own feet."

"Do you remember us finding you?" I asked.

Graham opened his eyes. "Stanhope said I told you to call him." It was a statement ripe with finality, and it didn't answer my question. His voice hardened. "We have a deal, then? You'll take the job. You'll find out who did this to me."

I laughed. I couldn't help it. Graham's arrogance was nothing short of astounding. I rose to my feet, scoffed. "I don't think—"

He cut me off. "Name your price. You can have the Bible box and the Widow for all I care. All I want to know is who had the balls to do this to me."

My chest squeezed and the urge to say 'yes' buzzed in the back of my brain like a giant poisonous insect. Graham had just paid close to a hundred and twenty thousand for the two pieces. Receiving them as payment would be one heck of a score—if we succeeded. But he was a manipulator in the first degree. Nothing Graham did or said could be taken at face value. Not when, above all else, I was convinced he was somehow involved in my mom going to prison for art forgery.

Still, Shane had said it would be handy to know Graham's version of the robbery, or at least the version he chose to tell me— and I'd achieved that goal. A warm, deliriously happy feeling uncoiled in my chest, a sense of satisfaction and power.

I lightly folded my arms in front of me, drawing out the moment, savoring it, then I said to Graham, "Tuck's right. You're barking up the wrong tree. Thanks for the offer, but no thanks."

CHAPTER TEN

O n the way home Tuck drove, and I phoned Shane and filled him in. I was taken aback when Shane admitted to wishing we'd covertly videoed the conversation so he could see it. I couldn't help wondering if it was also so he could pass the recording on to the South Burlington police, though I couldn't think of anything we'd learned that Graham wouldn't have told them already.

When we got home, Kala had two pizzas from the Jumping Cafe waiting in the living room, still in their boxes, nice and hot. "A reward for bravery," she said. Her voice grew excited. "So, what happened?"

Between bites, I told her the story. When I reached the fun part about turning Graham down, she scowled. "Are you saying I sacrificed a sweater to forensic science for nothing?"

I set my slice on the coffee table. "All it means is that we're not doing anything on Graham's payroll. Personally, I think knowing more is a good idea."

Tuck nodded. "I haven't said anything to either of you, but I am still concerned about the police searching the Volvo, and what Dr. Stanhope might have said to them."

"They didn't find anything in the car," Kala said.

Tuck's voice remained firm. "Did you stop to consider where you went while you were inside Graham's house? You went into the kitchen to get water. Edie told me Dr. Stanhope sent her upstairs for a blanket. What if your fingerprints are the only foreign prints in the house? What if—"

I held out my hands to stop him from going on. "I like to think the police are smart enough to not jump to conclusions. But you're right, that could be an issue."

Out of the corner of my eye, I spotted Sandra spring like a cobra toward where my pizza slice sat on the coffee table.

"No!" My shout came too late. She snagged the slice, rocketed for the hallway, and galloped upstairs, leaving a trail of pizza-dribble behind.

Kala laughed. "I think the white on that dog's muzzle is powdered sugar, not a sign of age."

"She sure can move like a puppy when she wants to," I said.

Tuck got to his feet. "If everyone's done eating for now. I'll hide what's left in the fridge—out of sight, out of mind."

"I wouldn't be so sure about that," Kala said. "Sandra'll probably wait until we're asleep, then open the fridge and filch the rest."

* * *

Sandra's antics had driven off the gloom, and for the rest of the evening our discussion of the robbery was less ominous. But later, when I went to bed, a delicious dream of making out with Shane in his swimming pool turned menacing as soon as I noticed the pool's floor was covered with rotting maidenhair fern fronds and yellowed envelops.

The dream's meaning wasn't hard to interpret. Beneath my conviction to not work for Graham, a small part of me wondered if I'd made the right choice. What if my grandfather's envelope was one of the items that had made it into Graham's safe? Now that I'd refused to work for him, Graham would never show it to me. No question about it, getting tangled up with a slippery jerk like him was the definition of foolhardiness. Still, Tuck didn't have a monopoly on wondering what if…

What if the envelope wasn't among the stolen items? And what if grandpa had put something important inside it?

* * *

The next morning, Tuck and Kala were out in the shop, and I was in the upstairs hallway vacuuming Sandra's trail of pizza residue when the landline rang—my mom, right on time for her scheduled call from prison. The house rule was that Tuck would answer and talk to her first. After a few minutes, I'd chime in and say hello. It was the best way to keep peace between me and her.

As I waited for Tuck to answer on the shop extension, I turned the vacuum cleaner off. The phone rang. It rang again, and again…

Finally, I rushed to where a phone sat on the hall table and answered, "Hey, Mom. Sorry it took me so long. How are things going?"

I squeezed my eyes shut waiting for the inevitable poor-mes to commence. I shouldn't have led with that question, not with my mom on the other end.

"Just fabulous," she twittered.

Shocked by her answer, I stared at the phone in disbelief. "What happened?"

"The powers that be are letting me teach an art class."

"That's great news." For months, she'd been plaguing the warden and anyone else who'd listen with endless requests to do that very thing.

"The volunteer who was supposed to teach the class was

69

caught by a security camara slipping pills to one of the inmates. It was wonderful. They took her away in handcuffs."

"Lucky you," I said. *Stupid volunteer*, I thought.

"They'd already bought the art supplies. I'm much more qualified than she was..."

As my mom went on about her teaching qualifications, I spotted Sandra partway down the hall, slinking towards the front of the house. She dashed into Mom's bedroom. What was she up to this time?

Still listening, I headed down the hall toward the bedroom. It was strange that Sandra had managed to get inside since the door was always kept shut.

Mom took a breath, then continued, "Yesterday, I talked to the class about signatures on art and the importance of marking replicas."

"That's nice," I said, still walking toward the bedroom. I suspected the inmates had gotten an earful about how Mom had been arrested while attempting to cross into Canada with a Maxfield Parrish that she'd painted but forgotten to mark as a replica on the back or even on the sale slip. Plus, the painting had mysteriously acquired a flawless, forged Parrish signature.

Mom claimed she hadn't signed the piece. The sticking point for me was that I'd seen her practicing Parrish's signature only a short time before. The day I'd caught her, she'd asserted emulating the signature was a way for her to step into Parrish's persona before painting. I hadn't been convinced then and for some time later. But recently, I'd started to wonder if she was telling the truth. Using a signature to get in the zone was the sort of Zen-like thing she might have done.

Thump!

The sound came from inside Mom's bedroom followed by little digging noises. I hurried my steps and rushed inside. Sandra had jumped onto Mom's four-poster bed, undoubtedly the source of the thump sound. She was now circling in the center of Mom's antique quilt as if preparing a nest. I rushed over, yanked on her collar to put an end to the circling.

"Just lay down, already," I said to Sandra. Dog toenails and antique quilts weren't a good combination.

"Did you say something?" Mom asked.

"No, nothing. Everything's fine." I scratched Sandra's belly with my free hand. Thankfully, she responded by collapsing onto her side and kicking one leg up, exposing a wider expanse of belly.

Mom's voice hesitated. "I hear Graham was robbed."

I stopped scratching. "Who told you that?" Was the inmate grapevine that fast?

"Vincent told me."

I let out a breath. Vincent was her lawyer. "Do you remember the Glass Widow bottle? They took that and some local ephemera Graham had just bought at Fisher's."

She hissed. "I never liked those bottles. They're cursed. Look at what happened way back when, all those people killed in that horrible resort fire...I swear your grandparents would be alive today if your grandfather hadn't gone looking for them."

My throat tightened as the plane crash that killed my grandparents pushed into my mind. Their plane descending toward our airstrip. Me waiting on the ground to greet them. The crash. The explosion. The flames...Two fires. The resort. My grandparents' plane. So many tragic deaths. But there was over a century and a half between the disasters. Even if Mom wanted to see a cursed connection between them, it didn't exist—except for the unrelenting pain of the truth. Murder in one case and a horrific accident in the other.

I squeezed my eyes shut to banish the thoughts, then pushed a nonchalant tone into my voice. "Bucky owned the bottle for years and it never affected him."

"Believe what you want." Her voice lowered, becoming hushed. "He still thinks I owe him a thousand dollars."

Opening my eyes, I frowned, confused. "Who are you talking about? Bucky? It's a little late to repay a debt to him. He's been gone for five years now."

"Not him. Felix Graham. But don't you pay him a red cent."

"You owe Graham money?" It would have been nice to know this before, like long before now. "For what?"

"The person I made *the* painting for was one of his customers. He thinks I owe him money because of that. But I don't."

The way she stressed the word "the" told me she was referring to the replica Parrish that sent her to prison. Tuck had told me word-for-word everything that she'd revealed to the police from the time of the arrest until she took the plea agreement months later. This specific connection to Graham was not among them. "Does Vincent know about—" I bit my tongue. I wasn't sure where she was going with this, but I also suspected the prison phone line was monitored. "Next time you see Vincent you might want to mention this."

"I didn't mention it before because I know you and Tuck don't like Graham."

"Don't *like?* We don't trust him," I said before I could stop myself.

"Graham was always generous when I needed to pay bills— buying pieces from the shop and paying cash on the spot to help out."

"I imagine he was very helpful." I couldn't keep the sarcasm from my voice. For someone who grew up in the antique and art trade, it was surprising how naïve Mom could be. Graham no doubt paid fast, quick dollars to purchase items for under their wholesale value. The best of the best pieces too, no doubt. Graham was a lot of things, but he wasn't a fool.

"A few years ago," she said. "I was running late with the town property taxes. When I told Graham about it, he purchased one of my replica Parrish paintings. Granted, the buyers he sends my way pay significantly more than he did, but those are custom paintings. The replica he bought—*Hilltop*— was a practice piece I'd created."

My mind flashed to the Parrish painting I'd noticed in Graham's living room. *Hilltop.* The original was worth millions. I should have considered it might have been one of Mom's replicas. And, yes, what she was saying about Graham helping her out made sense. Normally, people who owned fine art hired her to create flawless facsimiles, so the original pieces could be safely stored in secure climate-controlled vaults. Over the years, Graham had sent lots of clients her way—for a kickback, of course.

As a suspicion began to tumble at the back of my brain, I sat down on the bed next to Sandra. "So, this thousand dollars Graham thinks you owe him, what exactly was it for?" Ears listening in or not, this was something I needed to know.

"Well, ah…the people I painted *the* Parrish for are customers of his. But they approached me on their own about doing the replica. Technically, he didn't refer them to me…"

As she went on about an argument she'd had with Graham over creating the painting for his customer and not giving him a kickback, a twinge of sympathy gave way to a devious thought. Perhaps it was brought on by the ghost of her familiar perfume, lingering on the quilt beneath me, maybe it was her yearbooks and artist journals whispering in the drawers of the nearby secretary desk, or the soft sweaters and smocks embroidered with folksy wildflowers murmuring behind her closet door. Whatever it was, as her voice rose to a hysterical pitch, my conviction to avoid becoming entangled with Graham did an about-face, and I came to a dangerous decision.

I hated Graham. I didn't trust him. But when he'd asked me to name my price, he'd opened up an opportunity I'd failed to consider. Not cash. Not my help in trade for the Glass Widow and Bible box. Something far more important.

Granted, becoming involved with Graham in any sort of deal

was risky, very much so. But I wasn't naïve like my mom. I had Tuck and Kala on my side. And if I succeeded in unmasking the thieves for him, the reward I could now envision would be more than worth the risk. Plus, not only would it be agonizing for Graham, but I'd be able to prove to Mom and the entire art and antique community that I was capable of righting her mistakes, and of breathing new life into the business my grandparents had worked so hard to create.

Mom's voice broke through my thoughts. "...They put me on a new medication."

"What did you say?" I asked. *Medication?* I hadn't even known she was on any.

"It's for—It's not important." She paused. "I need to get off the phone now."

"Mom," I said insistently. "What medication?" Typical Mom. Open up a subject then avoid it like I was still a child she thought was too young for the truth.

"Love you, baby."

"Same here." As she hung up, I glanced at the clock on the nightstand. Normally, she'd have talked for five more minutes, and she hadn't even asked to speak with Tuck.

CHAPTER ELEVEN

"I want two things." I said to Graham.

Tuck, Kala, and I had closed the store at three o'clock, then driven to Graham's house. Sandra'd insisted on coming and was currently biding her time in the Volvo, snout out a partially lowered window as she scoured the landscape for squirrels. The rest of us stood in Graham's living room. Without any extraneous gestures of civility from Graham, we'd gone straight to the point of our visit.

Graham looked down his nose at me. "And exactly what would those two things be?"

I eyed him, watching his body language for signs that he was lying or withholding something. He was back to his smug self, standing so close to me that I couldn't escape the musk of his aftershave. His hair was slicked back, his blue striped dress shirt unbuttoned enough to reveal a swath of chest hair.

I raised my chin, met his gaze. "First," I said. "Yesterday, you mentioned putting some of the items from the Bible box in your safe before the thieves arrived. I want those things. Plus, I need a promise that you'll give us any other information you have or find out while we're working on this. No holding back."

Tuck folded his arms. "Can we safely assume the police didn't take the items you put in the safe?"

"They went through them, but no," Graham said. "I'd be glad to provide you with photocopies of those pieces, but I can't see how they'll do you any good. I've—"

I cut him off. "You can make copies for your own use. I want the originals. We don't know the motive for the robbery. They could've wanted the ephemera for its face-value or for a reason that's less easy to ascertain without closely examining what's left." I hardened my voice. "Of course, the reason for the robbery could be more straightforward. You've made enemies over the years."

He shrugged. "Success has its repercussions."

Kala snickered. "So does sleeping your way through half the county."

Graham glared at her.

I swallowed hard. On another occasion, I'd have laughed at Kala's comment. But her role right now was to avoid attracting attention. We hadn't told Shane we'd changed our minds about doing the investigation for Graham yet. However, we'd been inspired by his regret—which was another way of saying Kala was secretly video recording this meeting on her phone. And, even from where I stood, I could see the lens peeking out from her shirt pocket.

I cleared my throat. "For all we know the thieves could be bottle diggers, looking for a clue to the location of the rest of the Widows." His attention swung back to me, and I bit back the urge to smile. Thank goodness. Disaster averted.

He scoffed. "The chance of the thieves returning sounds like a good reason to keep what's left in my safe."

"We have several safes," I said, "and full security. Plus, we recently adopted a retired police K9. But you didn't know that—did you?"

I didn't dare look at Tuck or Kala. They'd burst into laughter for sure. The idea of Sandra the Weirdo being a retired police K9 was pretty absurd. Sometimes an impromptu lie falls a bit too short of reality.

"All right. You can have the originals." Graham flicked his fingers dismissively. "For all the good it'll do you. Now, what's your other requirement?"

My stomach quivered as if I were standing in front of a judge about to declare my sentence. But I forced my body to remain still, arms relaxed at my sides, eyes trained on Graham's face. I took a deep breath. "In exchange for finding out who took your items, I want you to tell me everything you know about my mother's forgery charge—how she was set up, where, when, and by who.... Everything. Including your own involvement."

His lips went stiff as if he were containing his emotions, just like me.

I hardened my voice. "If you don't tell us the truth or if you try to set us up to take the fall for the theft, if you do anything unwarranted, I will personally make your life a living hell. I won't back down. You won't be able to go anywhere or do anything without me dogging your steps."

At that, he laughed, an open and honest sound that gave me a glimpse of what appeared to be an amicable person beneath the man I loathed. Not that I believed what I saw. I wasn't that gullible.

He nodded crisply. "Don't worry. As soon as you give me the name of the thieves, I'll tell you what I know, though I can't guarantee it'll be the answer you want or hope to hear."

CHAPTER TWELVE

"Is it possible someone tailed you home from the café?" I said to Graham. Now that we'd come to an agreement, it was time to dig in and the theory he'd been followed from the time he left the auction made sense.

Graham harumphed. "No way—and before you suggest I might not have noticed, the police talked to Dr. Stanhope and his wife. They didn't see or hear any vehicles drive past their house that night, other than mine. Their security camaras confirmed that, and also that no one walked down the street or entered my house by way of the front door or garage."

"How about *your* security camaras?" Kala asked.

His voice lowered, slightly submissive. "Unfortunately, mine were off at the time of the robbery. Like I said, I hadn't locked up for the night—"

"Yeah, we know, in case one of your *friends* stopped by," Kala said.

As Graham shot a look at her, I jumped in before he could say a word. "So, the police didn't take anything other than the decanter and snifters?"

He shook his head. "They looked for the to-go container from the café, but didn't find it. Not even in the rubbish."

"That's strange," I said. Very interesting, actually.

* * *

Not long after that, Kala and I went out to Graham's backyard to scout for possible routes the thieves might've taken that were beyond the reach of Stanhope's security camaras. Tuck stayed behind with Graham to finish going over details of the police visit and to help him photocopy the ephemera that had been in the safe.

With Kala beside me, I walked past Graham's hot tub and party gazebo, down a set of flagstone steps to where the stockade fence that enclosed Graham's backyard ran along the rear of his property. A bed of freshly planted mums and asters spanned its length and continued down both sides of the stockade.

Kala took out her phone, brought up a Google Earth satellite view of the area. "On the other side of the fence, there's a field and another development. Someone could have parked there." She looked up at the stockade's lattice top, a good eight feet above us. "They'd have to be in good shape to shimmy up that, unless they brought a ladder."

I studied the flowerbed. "Kind of hard to imagine them landing on this side without smashing a plant or two."

Kala glanced toward the gateway where we'd found Graham. "How about if I search in this direction for breakage while you go the other way?"

"Sounds good."

We headed in opposite directions, walking along the fence and flowerbed. It went without saying that the police had probably followed the same logic. They'd most likely left footprints themselves, but they would've been careful not to cause additional damage to the garden.

Along with the flowers, I scanned the top of the fence, looking for any indication that someone had recently scaled it—threads from a torn shirttail, dirt smears, grass stains, blood... The Glass Widow would have been easy to get over the fence, but the Bible box not so much. It was too bulky to fit in a backpack and would've required two free hands to carry.

"See anything?" I called to Kala.

"There's an enclosure for garbage and recycling. It's padlocked."

Rubbing my neck as usual to relax a knot of tension, I moved on, studying the flowerbed once more. Not a single broken mum branch. The bark mulch was perfectly in place. Nothing disturbed, which was a bit disturbing to me.

As I neared the corner where the fence turned toward the north side of the house, I noticed another gateway a few yards ahead. Unlike its counterpart on the other side of the yard where we'd found Graham lying, this gate was closed. But the hasp intended to lock the gate's latch shut wasn't secured and—judging by the grunge that coated it—hadn't been used in years, if ever. I could only guess that Graham's ego was so supersized that he saw no need to keep it locked. After all, who'd dare trespass on *his* property, I thought sarcastically. I mean, he was pretty nonchalant about locking the house and his security camaras as well.

I tried the latch. It wasn't rusty, though the hinges resisted as I tugged the gate open. I walked through the opening and into an unprotected side yard. The north wall of Graham's house was now to my right. To my left, the lawn sloped downward, ending after a few yards in a thicket of cedar and honeysuckle bushes tall enough to hide a person. I glanced in the direction of the Stanhope's property. It wasn't visible from this angle.

"Kala!" I shouted. "Over here."

She appeared a second later, not jogging through the gateway behind me as I'd expected but dashing around by way of the front yard. She looked over her shoulder toward Stanhope's, then back at me. She grinned. "Looks like you found their security camara's blind spot."

"Sure does." I went back to scanning the edge of the lawn. There was a barely discernable break in the thicket of bushes. It was narrow and overhung with branches, likely an entrance to a game trail used by rabbits or deer to come out at night and feed on the grassy lawn. I nodded at it. "Unless you found a more likely spot, I'm guessing that's the route the thieves used. We should check it out."

Kala wrinkled her nose. "You want to go in there? Clearly, you've never seen the movie *Skeeter*—or *Ticks*. Gigantic mosquitos and insects. That place has to be crawling with them..."

As she chattered on, giving a summary of every bug-related horror movie she'd ever seen, I led the way down to the game trail and into the thicket. I wasn't about to tell her my least favorite horror flick was *Swarmed*, with its mega-aggressive yellowjacket wasps. If I told her, she'd say, "What doesn't kill you, makes you stronger", and she'd force me watch that awful movie again.

Shoving my hands under my armpits, I turned sideways to protect my exposed skin from clawing branches as I made my way along the trail, deeper into the tall brush. A mosquito buzzed my ear. My scalp itched from thoughts of yellowjackets, and all their creepy-crawly relatives.

"We need to buy a drone," she said. "It would be better than doing this bushwhacking crap." She fell silent, then asked, "Speaking of crap, is that poop?"

I turned back to see what she was looking at. A clump of raisin-like nuggets was scattered on the ground at her feet. "Those are deer droppings," I said with authority. As revenge for her horror movie comments, I added, "or giant man-eating bug vomit."

"Wasn't there something in the news about a bear hanging around one of Burlington's golf courses?"

"That's deer, not bear poop. Besides, if there was a bear, it would run away before you ever saw it." I turned back around, then went up on my tiptoes, attempting to see overtop the brush. "I think there's an opening up ahead."

"It's probably the golf course."

"I don't think Graham's house is that close to it."

"According to the arial view, it should be."

I groaned. "Why didn't you mention that before—"

Crash! Crunch!

My heart leapt into my throat as the sound of breaking branches came from behind us.

Crash, crash. CRASH! The sound became louder as something hurtled from up on Graham's lawn, down the game trail toward us.

"Bear!" Kala screeched.

Adrenaline rocketed into my veins. I started to take off, but Kala shoved past me on the narrow trail. A branch snagged her afro.

*Crunch-crash, crunch-crash...*Side by side, we froze, looking back up the trail—

Sandra barreled into view, tongue lolling, eyes glistening. Not a bear. A lame-brain dog.

Letting out a relieved breath, I crouched. Sandra wriggled in close, licking my face as if she hadn't seen me in weeks. I glanced at Kala. "You didn't let her out of the car, did you?"

Kala yanked her hair free from the branch. "Of course not." She rested her hands on her hips. "I'm done with this adventure. Let's find the end of this stupid trail before the real bear shows up."

"Fine by me." I gave Sandra a hard look. "No running off." I couldn't imagine how she'd gotten out of the car. We'd only left the windows partly open.

After only a few more minutes of walking, the game trail ended, and we did, in fact, come out onto the golf course. The view was amazing, sweeping greens, interspersed with teardrops of sand and islands of birch trees. In the distance, the windows of the clubhouse glinted. It reminded me of Luigi Lucioni's painting *Ninth hole at Manchester's Ekwanok Golf Course*, right down to the hint of early autumn gold.

"I can see why people like playing golf here. It's beautiful," Kala said.

"It's also the perfect way for thieves to access Graham's house. Except, the golf course must have security. Plus, assuming the thieves didn't know it was Graham they were going to rob until after he won the bottle and box at the auction, then how did they know the game trail even existed?"

Kala grinned. "I don't think they took the trail." She pointed to a nearby strip of mowed grass that led away from the course. Even from where we stood, I could see it led to the cul-de-sac at the end of Graham's Street. Apparently, Graham's neighborhood came with golf course access.

She grimaced apologetically. "Sorry. I didn't notice that when I Googled."

"That would've been helpful," I said, with more than a little sarcasm.

We started hiking up the mowed strip toward the cul-de-sac. It took maybe two minutes to walk to Graham's house that way. Also, if someone had stuck to the far edge of the grass, especially after dark, it was likely they'd be hidden from Stanhope's security camaras.

As we neared Graham's front yard, I hurried my steps and grabbed Sandra by the collar. "No more free-range dog for you, young lady." I turned to tug her toward the car but stopped. The car's rear passenger door was wide open.

Kala raised her hands. "I swear, I nothing to do with that."

"Dogs don't open doors by themselves," I said.

She rolled her eyes. "Of course, they can. Service dogs do all kinds of stuff—open refrigerators, turn on lights, call 911...It depends on if they're smart enough."

"That rules Sandra out," I said. I wasn't about to believe that Stinky Sandra was some kind of super-trained service dog that had somehow ended up in the care of a less than aboveboard forensic scientist. If she had opened the car door, it was a fluke. I let go of Sandra's collar and pointed at the car. "Back inside. Now."

She lowered her head as if she was sorry she hadn't stayed in the car, then looked up at me and grinned—like she really grinned, teeth showing and everything. She didn't feel sorry. She was proud of herself for escaping.

Where had she come from before Bill adopted her?

CHAPTER THIRTEEN

My thoughts of Sandra's mysterious past faded as we went back inside Graham's house. He and Tuck had finished photocopying the ephemera and were starting to transfer the originals into a cardboard document box to keep them safe on our way home.

Tuck glanced our way. "Kala, do you mind helping Graham finish with this? My back is killing me from hunching over."

"Sure, no problem," she said.

Graham scowled slightly at the new arrangement but surprisingly went back to situating the ephemera in its new home without a word. I suspected he was as eager to be rid of us as we were to finish and go home.

Massaging the small of his back, Tuck walked over to me. I was pretty sure he was up to something. He'd never complained about his back before.

He shook his head as if to apologize, then lowered his voice to a whisper. "*The* envelope—the one with your grandpa's writing on it? It wasn't in the safe with the other items." He rested a hand on my arm. "I'm really sorry. It must be with the other stuff in the Bible box."

It was as if my heart dropped into my stomach. Sure, taking Graham up on his offer was about obtaining information that might free my mom. But getting to see the contents of the mysterious envelope was a bonus I'd counted on.

I shot a look toward Graham. Why couldn't he have put the envelope in the safe with the other ephemera? *Because it didn't pique his interest*, I told myself. Still, it sucked something awful.

* * *

A few minutes later, Graham and Kala finished packing the document box. After that, all four of us moved on to searching the house for clues the police might've missed. There were several closets in the hallway—jackets, tennis rackets, a golf bag and clubs, boots, a rain slicker, and umbrellas... The basement consisted of three rooms: a laundry room, a workout area, and a climate-controlled wine cellar under the stairs. There was no sign that someone had broken in through the cellar hatchway. No specks of tracked-in dirt or grass on the floor or stairs, nothing to indicate that the thieves had been down there.

We returned to the first floor, where the kitchen was incredibly neat. No clutter, no dirty dishes or dishes drying in a rack, no stack of bills waiting on a table like at our house. No water spots on the coffee pot. I even peeked in the fridge. It was as empty as Fisher's auction gallery after a cleanup sale: nothing other than a few beverages, lemons, and jars of condiments.

We gave the living room another look, plus the room off of it that served as Graham's home office. The safe the thieves hadn't opened was in there.

Next, we went upstairs. The morning after the attack, I'd been on that floor only long enough to grab a blanket, but this time I poked around. The only hint of activity was in Graham's personal bathroom. A pair of slacks and belt hung on a hook. Damp bath towels, underclothes, and the raspberry-pink dress shirt I recalled him wearing at the auction were piled in a laundry hamper. Every window upstairs was locked, and none of them appeared to have been jimmied.

Satisfied we'd looked everywhere, we once more went over the terms of our agreement with Graham, then Tuck picked up the document box full of original ephemera and we took off. There really wasn't anything else we could do.

Just like on our way to Graham's house, I got the honor of driving. Kala rode in the back with Sandra while Tuck sat in the shotgun seat with the document box on the floor beneath his legs.

"What do you think our next move should be?" he asked as we pulled away from the cul-de-sac.

I slid my hand along the steering wheel. "I'm not sure. But it's pretty clear the thieves—however many there were—had been to Graham's house before. They knew how to get into the backyard unseen, and that he wouldn't turn on his alarm system until he went to bed."

Tuck said, "Are you thinking a girlfriend?"

"Maybe, or someone who's been to his backyard soirees."

He laughed. "That's everyone in the Vermont Chamber of Commerce and on the local Who's Who list. Not to mention most of the upper end art and antique dealers and collectors on the East Coast."

"I vote for a girlfriend," Kala said.

I glanced in the rearview mirror. She was barely visible, thanks to Sandra, who was sitting on her lap. I smiled. "Looks like someone's comfortable."

"She might be, but I'm losing the feeling in half my body. She's as heavy as an elephant." Kala leaned to one side, peering around Sandra. "There is something else we should add into the whodunit equation."

Tuck looked back at her. "What are you thinking?"

"Not everyone has access to drugs, but they did."

At this point, it went without saying that drugs, not a medical event, were behind Graham's condition when we found him. Still… "That's assuming the substance wasn't over the counter."

"I doubt that. It was something nasty, but probably not intended to kill him." She shoved Sandra off her lap, then took out her phone. "I'm going to check if Pinky's heard anything from Bill."

As she sent the text, I focused on the road ahead. We passed the entrance to the golf course and a vegetable stand. The stand's sign boasted early apples and local sweet corn.

Tuck's initial question came back to me. *What do you think our next move should be?* I glanced his way. "As much as I'm dying to dig through the ephemera, I don't think it's the first thing we should do when we get home." It helped that I knew the envelope with my grandfather's writing on it wasn't among the unstolen items.

Kala clapped her hands gleefully. "Whiteboard time."

"Exactly. We need to list what we know while it's fresh in our minds—who was at the auction, especially if they might've been to Graham's house at some point. And a timeline of what Graham did at the auction and afterwards."

"I'll set everything up in the dining room like usual," Kala said. Her phone buzzed. "It's Pinky. She says Bill should have the results for us by tomorrow morning."

"That's great news," I said. As Sandra wormed her way back onto Kala's lap, something she hadn't mentioned occurred to me. "Pinky or Bill didn't happen to ask how Sandra was doing?"

"Hmmm…Nope," Kala said.

Tuck chuckled. "Why am I not surprised?"

I shook my head. I wasn't either. In fact, I suspected the whole 'Bill's looking for a new apartment' ploy might have been concocted to get Sandra out of their hair, at least until the puppies were gone.

* * *

As soon as we got home, I left Tuck and Kala to their own devices and went straight to the downstairs library and locked the document box in the safe. Sure, the thieves had taken the Bible box and most of its contents, including the envelope my grandfather had addressed to Bucky. But one of Bucky's journals as well as a good variety of old pamphlets and papers had escaped theft. There was no reason these pieces—and not the stolen ones—couldn't hold clues to the location of the cache of missing Glass Widow bottles. That thought made my pulse speed.

I glanced at the bottom of the library's built-in bookshelves where the safe hid behind a decorative panel. *Bucky believed you had enough love of the hunt and smarts to find them. No one will miss you if you take a few minutes to look at the ephemera*, the voice of teenage me whispered.

I gritted my teeth. As tempting as it was to put treasure hunting ahead of unmasking the thieves for Graham, it wouldn't help free Mom from prison. And it was crazy to think looking at the ephemera would sidetrack me for just a few minutes. It would be more like hours, and I couldn't afford to waste that much time. To get want I needed from Graham, we had to figure out who committed the robbery before the police did. Because once they solved it, any information we uncovered would become redundant, giving Graham an excuse to not spill about my mom.

Before temptation could strike again, I turned my back on the safe and left the library, closing the door behind me. For additional temptation prevention, I took out my phone and texted Shane.

Changed my mind and took Graham's offer. We can talk later.

I wanted him to know what we were up to, rather than catching wind of it some other way. Details could wait until I talked to him in person.

He immediately texted back. *Working tonight. I'll call in the morning. XOXO.*

Disappointment that I wouldn't be seeing Shane mixed with

worry about the type of case that might require him to stay late, one that also had him so deeply involved that he hadn't responded to my comment about Graham's offer. I took a deep breath. Disappointment was okay. Worry was something I couldn't give into. It came with the territory when I'd chosen to fall for someone in law enforcement, and Shane would never not be a cop.

I let out a sigh and headed for the dining room where Kala was supposed to be setting up for our list-building session. When I stepped into the room, I came to a fast halt. A veritable wall of white boards ran along the far side of the room, just beyond the mahogany dining table.

"When did you have time to put all this together?" I said. I'd been in the library for maybe ten minutes, fifteen if you included a side trip to the bathroom. "What did you do? Teleport to Walmart for supplies and back?"

Her proud grin was matched by the sly glisten in her eyes. She tossed the brilliant ends of her hair back with a flick of her fingers. "I snagged the boards at a yard sale last week—ten for twenty bucks. I've been storing them and a couple of your mom's easels under the table, just in case. It's not like we eat in here."

She was right on both counts. We generally ate in the kitchen, on the porch, in the shop or car... anywhere except around the formal table, 'like civilized people', as my grandmother would have said. We also seemed to be making a habit of getting sucked into mysteries, a business where having a supply of whiteboards came in handy.

Kala made a sweeping gesture with her hand, showing off the headings written on the board in bright neon colors.

Timeline. Suspects. Motives. Alibies. Connections. Dirt.

Confused, I reread the last word. "Dirt?"

"The fun stuff—gambling, drug addictions, police records…infidelity."

She stopped talking as Tuck strolled in with Sandra on his heels. His gaze zeroed in on the whiteboards. "I was going to ask if you needed me for anything before I start supper. But it looks like you have everything under control, and then some."

"Before you leave," I said, "we should go over who we remember seeing at the auction." Something I'd nearly forgotten came back to me. "Frenchie Lefebvre videoed the auction. We should check to see what he posted on the *Gazetteer's* web channel."

Kala slid into a chair at the table in front of her laptop. Her fingers flew as she typed a string of words. "Bingo!"

Tuck and I rushed over, watching as she brought up a video. It showed people walking into the auction gallery and previewing items going up for bid. As the camera panned toward the auction house office, I caught a glimpse of Tuck, waiting in line to get his bidding paddle.

Tuck grinned. "Now there's one handsome gentleman."

"Best looking man in the whole place," I said.

Kala hit pause, then brought up a digital notepad on one side of the laptop's screen. "If you guys call out the names of people you recognize, I'll keep a running list."

"We should rule out Jules and Rosetta Ramone while we're at it," I said. "Pinky told me they're in Paris on vacation. Besides, they're fans of Graham."

Kala started a column with the letter 'D' at the top. She listed the Ramones below that. "D as in Doubtful they did it," she said. "I'm adding Albert Fisher to that list too, along with his employees, including Pinky, of course. We know she's not involved."

"Martina Fortuni was there," I said, "but ephemera and bottles aren't her thing."

"I'll put her in the M for Maybe column."

After Kala added those people, we began watching the video in earnest.

"Marissa Lavelle and Sparky Collins," Tuck said as the video slowly panned over Marissa in her white Cruella de Ville swing coat and the much shorter Sparky Collins, nodding at her every word.

"Joie Bascom," I said as the camera homed in on her flashing a smile. I bit my tongue to keep from mentioning that she was on the top on my personal suspect list. It was important to keep watching and not focus in on any one suspect, at least at this point.

As the voiceover recounted the historic significance of the Glass Widow, the video skipped ahead to the bottle coming up for bid. There were flashes of Albert Fisher at the podium and Joie Bascom standing in the audience, then Graham in the back of the house, and various auction house employees taking bids over the phone...

"Looks like at least an hour of the video was cut," Tuck said.

"Damn it." I huffed out a breath. Though the editing didn't surprise me, it was frustrating.

Kala paused the video again. "What's the big deal? We can get what information we can from this, tomorrow you can drive down to the *Gazetteer* and ask to see the uncut version." Her voice turned teasing. "You do have an in down there."

Tuck chuckled. "You can say that again."

My face went hot. I narrowed my eyes, shooting daggers to let them know they were treading on dangerous ground. *Scandal Mountain Gazetteer* was run and co-owned by three generations of Lefebvre men. They lived and worked together without any women in sight—Frenchie, his son, and an adult grandson, Tristan. Their journalistic zest, along with free obituaries and fiery Vermont news that couldn't be found elsewhere, had led to the *Gazetteer* thriving in print as well as online while other small-town papers floundered and died. The grandson, Tristan, and I had hung around with each other in high school. That was, until he wanted to go further than I was willing, and he swapped me out for a more eager girl.

I toughened my voice. "Tristan is just an old friend. He's barely even that now. And, in case you haven't noticed, I have a guy called Shane in my life."

"Since when did the presence of a boyfriend—or husband for that matter—deter a Lefebvre," Tuck said.

Kala swiveled in her chair to look at me. "We aren't suggesting you hookup with Tristan. Just use him to see the uncut video."

I squinted again to get my point across. "If I do, promise no razzing?"

They looked at each other and laughed. "You've got to be kidding," Kala said.

I folded my arms across my chest before I gave up and let them fall back to my sides. This was a war I'd never win. Besides, there was something more vital that needed to be said. I cleared my throat. "I think we need to talk about the stolen ephemera, the Bible box, and the Glass Widow—and what we're going to do if we find them. It's a real possibility."

Kala's eyes brightened. "I notice you left them out of your deal with Graham."

"You aren't going to suggest we keep them, are you?" Tuck said.

"Of course not." I hid my hands in my pockets, then confessed, "I'm not saying a certain envelope might not get opened before it's returned or that a journal or two might not be copied, but everything else gets given to Graham untouched." I looked down at the Persian carpet beneath my feet, dark blues, cream, and raspberry threads woven into a pattern as complex as I suspected the path to the thieves would prove to be. I looked back at them. "Above all else, when it feels like we're closing in on the thieves' identities, we need to take the utmost care. The last thing we want is for them to freakout and destroy the pieces to protect themselves—bottles are easily smashed, boxes and paper burn."

"I don't think we have to worry about that," Tuck said. "At least, not if they have their sights set on a big payout or if they're treasure hunters looking for the other Widows. They'll protect those things with their lives until they get what they're after."

"That's another thing I'm worried about," I said. "They drugged Graham. If they realize we're looking for them, they might be willing to do even worse to us."

CHAPTER FOURTEEN

M y phone rang bright and early the next morning. *Brrring! Brring!*

Suspecting it was Shane, I sprang for where it sat on the kitchen table next to my empty coffee mug. After all, he'd promised to call when we'd texted last night.

"Hey," I said. "How are things going?"

"Good." He sounded tired but upbeat. "Mostly, I wanted to let you know I'll be out of touch for the next few days..."

He continued, explaining that he and his partners were up to their eyeballs in a major case and on the verge of a much-needed breakthrough. He didn't say what the case was about, not that I expected him too. He did tell me it wasn't connected to Graham's robbery. I was glad he shared that much. I would've wondered if he hadn't, and I suspected he realized that.

In truth, as much as I longed to see him, Shane being snowed under at work was for the best. I really cared about him and our relationship, but things like me snooping around on Graham's behalf didn't mix well with his police detective job and his loyalty to it. I'd told him yesterday that I'd taken Graham's offer, that was enough for now.

Still daydreaming about Shane and how lucky I was to have such a considerate man in my life, I fixed a second coffee. Cradling it carefully, I went outside and up the walkway toward the shop.

Tuck and Kala were already there. After all, it wasn't like we could close the store and solely focus on unmasking the thieves. Electric bills, insurance…all those pesky things weren't going to stop flooding in. We were further from falling off the cliff into bankruptcy than a few months ago, but it wouldn't take much to return to that point.

That said, once Kala had listed a dozen or so items on eBay, her plan for the day included moving on to searching the internet for chatter about the stolen pieces. And, yes, none of us said it, but we knew that included her taking a trip to the dark side of the web.

As I reached the front of the store, I paused to admire the new window display Tuck was creating. He'd swapped out a collection of white ironstone dinnerware for antique baskets and wooden bowls filled with dried flowers and Murano glass fruit. He'd also included jars of honey produced by one of his garden club lady friends. Unlike the waste-of-space soap my mother had purchased, the rich-golden honey added to the autumnal look. It was organic. Local. And tasted wonderful.

Tuck appeared on the far side of the glass, readying to set a folk art crow into the display. I rapped on the window to get his attention. He glanced my way, and I gave him a thumbs up.

He smiled, set the crow down, then hurried to the doorway to meet me. "Glad you like it," he said. "I'm going to redo the book loft next. We'll be ready for the fall foliage tourists in no time at all."

"It really does look great," I said.

The rumble of a car engine echoed up from the bottom of the driveway. Sandra zoomed out from somewhere in the side yard, barking her head off.

I rushed to intercept her, snagged her by the collar. "Shush. You'll scare off the customers."

Tuck laughed. "You really think telling her off is going to amount to a hill of beans?"

"It's worth a try."

The car chugged into view, a Ford Escort with a smashed in front bumper. It parked in front of the shop doorway, a few yards from where Sandra and I stood.

Sandra wiggled free from my grip, and sped forward to greet the passenger. Pinky, I realized as she got out of the car. She spoke across the car's roof. "We thought it was better to give you the news face-to-face."

Bill emerged from the driver's side. Whereas the last ten years had transformed Tristan Lefebvre from a lanky teenager into a damn-good-looking man, it hadn't done any favors for Bill. He was nothing more than a super-sized version of the chipmunk-cheeked, weird little kid I remembered. The fact that he was wearing a plaid suit with a bright blue bowtie didn't help. I think he'd worn the exact same outfit to Pinky's high school graduation.

I plastered on a smile. "Hey, Bill. It's been a long time."

"Sure has." He took an old-fashioned briefcase from the car, then shut the door. As he started toward Tuck, Kala appeared in the doorway behind him. His eyes went to her. "You must be Pinky's friend."

She grinned. "Depends on what you mean by that."

"Best friends," Pinky clarified. Her rooster comb of hair swayed as she turned toward the shop door. "We should go inside. Bill brought samples."

"Samples?" I said, suspicious. He was just supposed to be testing the fluids on Kala's sweater for drugs.

Bill's eyes lit up. "You'll see."

I glanced at Tuck. He raised his shoulders in a shrug and grimaced as if to say he wasn't sure what was going on either.

Then we all followed Pinky and Bill inside with a super wiggly Sandra bringing up the rear.

Bill laid the briefcase flat on the front counter.

"Should we lock the door in case customers show up?" Tuck asked.

"Might be smart," he said.

My stomach tensed. "There isn't something illegal in there?"

"Not any more than usual."

That wasn't reassuring. Neither was Bill's silence as he fiddled with the case's combination lock. Neither was the odd way Sandra now sat stock-still, staring at the briefcase like a hunting dog pointing at a flock of gamebirds. The only sound in the place was the clip of Tuck's footsteps and the snap of the front door lock as he secured it. Pinky stood back, arms folded, an amused smile spreading across her lips.

As the briefcase's latches popped open, the tension in my stomach crept up my throat. What had we gotten ourselves into?

Bill lifted the briefcase's lid, then took out a laptop covered in stickers.

I blew out a relieved breath. Okay, so he wasn't going to show us physical samples of drugs, like test tubes of ketamine or heroin. Laptops were fine. Even if he was going to show us something on the dark web, we'd been there, done that. In Kala's case, done that quite often.

Out of the corner of my eye, I spotted a pint-size plastic bag resting against one side of the now all but empty briefcase. There was a foil wrapped packet inside the baggie, the size of a Tic Tac container. It was decorated with a casket shaped sticker that read:

Be nice. I know how to hide evidence.

That sick feeling returned. What the heck was in there?

Bill caught me looking and grinned, "That's the sample I mentioned. The real thing is always better than pictures."

"I suppose," I said. So much for a trip to the dark web being the most unnerving possibility.

The taste of bile flavored the back of my throat. Back in high school, Bill was known for his odd and unpredictable actions. One time, he'd picked up a dead raccoon on the roadside. He'd stuffed and mounted it on a piece of wood, dressed the poor thing like Rocket from *Guardians of the Galaxy*, and given it to our biology teacher for his birthday.

He opened the laptop, turned it on.

"Nice machine," Kala said.

"Thanks. You should stop by and see my lab sometime. I just got some great new equipment."

Kala beamed. "Really? I'd love to see what you have."

The screen came to life, displaying a myriad of folders and files. He clicked on one and a series of graphs and charts appeared. He tapped on another—a zigzag of lines, dots, and chemical formulas clustered along one side. "The test results were definitive," he said. He glanced once more at Kala. "Your body fluid samples were great—fresh and ample. After 48 hours a ketamine signature becomes almost impossible to detect."

Kala stood up taller. "So, he was roofied like I guessed."

"Yes"—Bill grinned again. He adjusted his bowtie, drawing out the suspense—"and no."

Tuck frowned. "What do you mean by that?"

"You might say he was roofied, but not the way I believe you're thinking."

"It wasn't slipped into a drink?" I asked. "But it was ketamine, right?"

He widened his stance like a teacher readying to lecture. "Ketamine is a registered drug, technically legal. It can be prescribed by clinicians or administered by people like veterinarians. The drug in the sample is similar, but it isn't registered or legal by any means. It's a synthetic street drug made in underground labs—methoxetamine, or mexxy as it's more commonly called."

"But it works like ketamine?" I asked.

"Ketamine is fast acting. It takes longer for mexxy to affect someone, but it lasts longer—maybe more than seven hours. Combine it with liquor, and a person could easily be as loopy as a zombie for twelve hours, maybe longer. Results in a killer hangover."

My thoughts whirred. Most likely Graham had ingested the drug after he got home, but with mexxy being slow acting, it might've happened sooner, like at the Jumping Café.

"You're frickin' sure about this?" Pinky asked.

"I'd stake my job on it."

I bit my tongue to keep from saying anything. He'd already done exactly that by doing the tests for us. At least, I couldn't see the State of Vermont being good with him playing freelance forensic scientist. I thought for a second. "Is there a lot of this drug around?"

"It's not getting the spotlight like fentanyl, but it's been a concern on college campuses for at least a decade."

"In New England?" I'd thought I knew what was going on in the world, but this was totally new to me.

He nodded. "More importantly, the sample from Kala's sweater wasn't garden-variety mexxy. The composition was very potent and pure. It took someone who knew what they were doing, and professional grade equipment."

"Like a college lab?" Kala asked.

"That's one possibility." Bill closed the laptop, then took the plastic baggie from the briefcase. "If anyone asks, you didn't see this."

Kala slapped her hands over her eyes, imitating her favorite wise monkey. "Call me See No Evil."

I shook my head and smiled. Tuck chuckled. But the levity quickly faded, as Bill took out the foil packet, and removed a glass vial from inside.

A slimy, cotton candy pink liquid swirled in the vial, speckled with what looked like gold glitter. "I recreated the chemical formula from your sample to make this," Bill said. "Methoxetamine—to the max—street name: Party Sparkles." He set the vial down, looked at us, his expression growing more serious. "This isn't the first time I've seen this exact chemical signature. About a month ago, another sample came from a police drug raid in Burlington. Whoever's making this, they're still out there, and most likely local."

CHAPTER FIFTEEN

After Bill and Pinky left, I promised to return with lunch for everyone, then set off for the *Gazetteer* office with Sandra riding shotgun. Tuck and Kala planned to keep an eye on the shop and finish their morning projects while I tried to get my hands on an uncut version of the auction video. I hadn't intended on taking Sandra, but she'd shoved past me and jumped into the car before I could stop her. I kind of felt bad for her too. Sure, Bill had fussed with her a little, but he hadn't mentioned missing her or when he hoped to have a new home for the two of them.

Anyway, by the time Sandra and I reached the village, she was merrily barking out the window, having the time of her life. Total brat dog.

I swung into Old Post Lane, a side street that ran behind Scandal Mountain's Congregational Church and the town museum. Across the side street from those buildings, *Scandal Mountain Gazetteer* occupied the front half of the old stagecoach inn building. The rest of the historic inn served as a home for Tristan, his father, and Frenchie. According to Tristan, the last woman to live in the place had been Frenchie's great-grandmother, Viola, who'd died in the 1970s after living there her entire life. It had been Frenchie's father who founded the news-paper back in the '50s.

I laughed at myself. Why did useless information like Lefebvre family history stick in my head, while vital stuff like computer passwords slipped away as fast as I created then?

As I neared the *Gazetteer*, I noticed something missing. The rust-bucket pickup Tristan had driven in high school and fully restored since then, wasn't parked in front of the business like the last time I'd stopped by.

"Damn it," I grumbled, but I pulled over alongside the curb anyway. The newspaper's open flag was out. Maybe the pickup was parked behind the building today.

Before Sandra could escape, I got out and shut the car door. The day was cool, so I didn't have to worry about her roasting alive in the car.

As I went up the walkway toward the *Gazetteer*, my mind went to when I was sixteen, riding home from school with Tristan: the squawk of his scanner always there beneath the blare of music from the radio. The scent of the sun-warmed upholstery: vinyl, vanilla, wool, and newsprint. Earthy, yet academic, sweet and heady. It was those rides in his truck and his flirtatious nature that cemented our friendship for as long as it lasted.

But I suspected it was our mutual lack of a parent that initially drew us together. My mom was married right after high school graduation. She soon got pregnant, but my father was long gone by the time I was born. Tristan's story was similar, only it was his mom that was absent from his life.

Taking a deep breath, I braced myself for the disturbingly-appealing sight of Tristan in his signature white shirt and open vest with his dark hair pulled back in a sleek ponytail, then I stepped into the newspaper's front office.

As always, the office reverberated with the yammer of scan-ners and the chatter of TVs. The thick scent of coffee and fresh newsprint hung in the air.

Seeing no one, I called out, "It's Edie Brown. Anybody here?"

"Hold your horses. I'll be right there," a masculine voice shouted from beyond an open doorway on the far side of the room. Not Tristan, that much I knew for certain. Perhaps his father, most likely Frenchie.

I waited a second, then two. A minute passed. I tapped my foot and glared at the doorway. What was taking so long?

Annoyed, I crept through an opening in the front counter, around desks and chairs, and various stacks of boxes to the doorway. The room beyond was long and narrow. Old-fashioned metal file cabinets lined the walls, except for where a Venetian blind-covered window stood partly open. Above the cabinets, hundreds and hundreds of antique and vintage toys were displayed on shelves and glass-fronted cupboards. Trains, planes, and automobiles, all metal and early with perfect paint, some still in their original boxes, some large, some small.... Frenchie's toy collection had at least tripled in size since I'd seen it ages ago. In the middle of it all, dressed in a mustard-yellow sweater and brown cords, he stood on a ladder with a toy biplane in his hands.

The plane was out of the 1960s, a Stanzel Electromic Flash. Battery operated. I wouldn't have been so sure, but I recalled my grandpa coming across one just like it in the attic of our house. Grandpa had gotten it for Christmas when he was young. He'd always loved planes. Judging by the way Frenchie cradled this one, he did too.

I knocked on the doorframe and stepped inside. "Wow! Your collection's really grown." I raised my voice just enough to be heard over the scanners and TVs.

Frenchie swiveled, smiled at me, then nodded at the biplane. "Just got this in the mail." He pressed a button on the remote, and a *whikity-wickity* noise filled the room as the plane's propellor spun. "I found it on eBay. I've been searching for this model for a long time."

"Looks like it's in great condition."

"Better than I expected." After he set the plane on top of a plastic storage container, he climbed down from the ladder. "Tristan's not here, if that's why you stopped by."

"Actually, it's about the video you took at the auction—"

Heat abruptly flushed my cheeks as the last time Frenchie and I had spoken rushed into my head. It had been four years ago, at the county courthouse the day I was sentenced for selling stolen property, to be exact. He had been there networking and searching for the latest news. We'd only talked for a few seconds, and he'd ended up barely mentioning my situation in his 'Day in Court' column—for which I was very grateful. For that matter, he'd always treated my family with respect. He didn't dwell on my mother's arrest like other news outlets had done. Likewise, he'd respected our privacy when my grandparents died, keeping the headlines about their plane crash to a minimum instead of sensationalizing the tragedy.

He studied my face, undoubtedly noticing the flush. "Is there a problem?"

I gulped a breath. "Ummm...not really. You posted snippets from the auction video online. I was wondering if it would be possible to see the uncut version?"

His brows lowered, shadowing his eyes. "Is there something specific you're looking for?"

For a beat I considered drumming up a lie to keep the real reason for my interests a secret. But with all their scanners and the Lefebvre's noses for news it was likely they already knew about the theft. "You heard about Graham, right?"

"You mean the robbery?"

"I told Graham I'd ask around for him. He thinks the thieves might have been at the auction and left either just before or right after he did." Okay, this time I did sort of lie, Graham hadn't actually said that. It was our assumption. I'd also violated my agreement with Graham to not let anyone know we were investigating for him. But half-truths and half-lies seemed the way to go at the moment.

Frenchie's voice sharpened. "If I had any information, I would have phoned the police."

"I didn't mean it like that." I retreated a step, back closer to the office doorway.

"We're aboveboard here at the *Gazetteer*. In fact, we're having a special Facebook live newscast at noontime, asking for people's help in bringing the thieves to justice. Those pieces are important to Scandal Mountain, irreplaceable parts of our town history..."

As he expounded on the newspaper's role in preserving local history—how they'd photographed and recorded events since the 1950s, how he personally devoted years to writing and publishing his magnum opus about the resort tragedy, *A Mystery in the Mountains*—my urge to defend myself subsided and I bit back a smile. Back in high school, when Tristan and I'd hung out together, I'd witnessed every one of the Lefebvre men go off like this on any number of occasions. Thunderous monologues and debates were a way of life for them, even the most innocent topics like replacing a toilet paper roll hadn't been immune to lively gestures and loud voices, nothing like my own family's restrained style of arguing.

Finally, Frenchie began to decelerate. I took a step closer, lowered my voice. "I wanted to watch the video to see who left the auction house around the same time as Graham."

He puffed out a breath. "Sorry I got so excited. Even the thought of thieves stealing irreplaceable pieces of history ticks me off."

"It bothers me too."

He wiped a dribble of sweat off his temple. "I'd be happy to let you look at the video."

"Thank you so much." I hesitated. "Do you mind not telling anyone, including the police, that I watched it? I don't need anyone wondering what I'm up to." There, I'd covered my back.

"Mum's the word. Total discretion." He glanced over his shoulder to where an antique schoolhouse clock hung among the shelves of toys, then back. "Unfortunately, I can't go over the video with you right now. Like I said, we have a special Facebook newscast coming up at noon. Maybe you could come back tomorrow?"

"Ah—" I looked once more at the clock. Its hands pointed to 11:35. I managed a weak smile. "I could come back later today."

"Tris has office duty tomorrow. I'll have him give you a call to set up a time."

His voice didn't hold any innuendo like Tuck or Kala's would've in that moment, and that made it easier to nod and go along with him. Besides, what else could I do? "Tell Tristan to call the house number. It hasn't changed," I said.

Frenchie wiped his palms on the sides of his pants. "If that's it, then I need to get going. I have lots to do before I jump on Facebook." He turned toward his desk but pivoted back. "One more thing."

"Yeah?" I said, puzzled.

His tone deepened, his concern plain to hear. "Take my advice and don't trust Graham. I don't want to see you or any of your family members hurt."

"Don't worry. I'm very much aware of what sort of person Graham is. And I wasn't particularly happy when he bought those pieces. But at least they were safe in his hands at that point."

"Just don't let him pull the wool over your eyes," Frenchie said.

CHAPTER SIXTEEN

As I walked back to my car, the concern in Frenchie's voice replayed in my mind. No question his distrust of Graham was deeply felt. That made me wonder if they'd had a run-in at some point or if Frenchie had come across dirt on Graham while chasing a story for the newspaper.

Lost in thought, I opened the driver's door—

Sandra wasn't in my seat or the passenger side. I glanced in the back. No dog. But the passenger side door was ajar. I stared at the door in disbelief. Sandra escaping once was a fluke, but twice...?

I scanned the *Gazetteer*'s front yard. No dog there or in the neighbor's yard either. Wheeling around, I looked across the street toward the town museum. It was a Gothic style building, red stone with a turret and arched windows. The parking lot was small and filled with cars. Near the museum's private rear entry, a woman and a beefy man stood close together talking.

That's when I spotted Sandra. She blasted past them, nearly knocking the woman over in the process. Without pausing, she rocketed between the lines of parked cars and across the thankfully traffic-free street. Still at top speed, she pushed past me and leapt into the driver's seat where she sat down like a queen on her throne, except this golden retriever queen's furry cheeks bulged with something.

I thrust out my hand, palm up. "Spit it out, bad dog."

She deposited a wad of slobbery crabapples onto my palm. I discretely let the mass drop to the pavement, then wiped my hands on my pants.

I pointed at the passenger seat. "That's where you belong."

Head low, she reluctantly retreated as instructed.

"That's better," I said, softening my voice. It was hard to be mad at her when she looked so dejected, though I suspected that was a total sham.

I was about to get in when I remembered the rear door on the passenger side was ajar. I closed my door—no way was I giving Sandra a way to slip out while I was busy. I walked around the car and closed the open door. As I headed back to the driver's side, the voices of the man and woman talking by the museum rose and carried my way. They sounded familiar.

I gave them another look. It was Joie Bascom and Sparky Collins. Seeing Joie wasn't a surprise, she was the museum director. But Sparky lived in central Vermont, several hours away. Sure, a blue van with his electrician logo on its side was parked nearby. Sure, he might've been doing a job for the museum. Still, this was way out of his home territory, and at the auction, he'd been chumming it up with Marissa Lavelle, not Joie.

I rubbed my bottom lip, thinking. Despite Joie being at the top of our suspect list, she'd always been courteous enough to me. Granted, she was a character with her wildly bright clothes and oversized necklaces, and she was known for being obnoxiously pushy. But she was also a devoted historian, and super proud of her Mayflower roots and Ivy League education. Her name on any charity event guaranteed donations would flow in from across New England.

Before I could talk myself out of it, I straightened my spine and strode across the street toward her and Sparky. Sandra had given me the perfect excuse for striking up a conversation. If I just happened to mention the burglary while I was at it, seeing their reaction could be very telling. Especially if their reason for being together had nothing to do with Sparky's profession.

As I made my way through the parking lot, their words became easier to hear.

"How about cash?" Joie said, voice taut.

Sparky said, "That would work better."

I slowed my steps.

"It's settled then. I'll have it for you tomorrow."

"I'm sure the doctor will appreciate that."

The doctor? Cash? The only doctor I could think of was Stanhope. What did he have to do with the robbery?

Joie must have noticed me out of the corner of her eye because she turned to look my way. I hurried my pace, then grimaced as if embarrassed as I reached them. "I wanted to apologize for my dog."

"Dog?" Her nose wrinkled. "You're talking about that old golden retriever. You do know the town has a leash law."

"She's not really mine. I'm just babysitting. She escaped from my car. Promise, it won't happen again."

Sparky jutted his chin at a cluster of decorative crabapple trees. He smirked. "I saw her filling her face over there. She'll probably have the pukes later."

"I'll be lucky if that's all," I said. I leaned in, lowered my voice. "You heard what happened to Graham, right?"

Sparky folded his arms across his chest, hands tucked out of sight. "Joie and I were just talking about that."

I nodded to keep from smiling too broadly. *Cash. The doctor.* Maybe Stanhope was involved.

Joie's mouth pinched into a sour expression. "Graham, that stupid fool. He didn't have courtesy enough to let us buy the pieces for the museum, then he didn't have the sense to keep them safe.

He deserves what he got." Her sour expression darkened. "I heard the thieves waltzed in and took them while he was passed out—no alarms, doors unlocked. No security measures whatsoever."

Once more, I restricted my reaction to a bob of my head. These details hadn't been on the news. Did Joie know them because she was involved in the robbery? Or had she learned them from someone like Police Chief Ovitt? I'd seen the two of them having coffee at Quickie's in the past and all the local departments might know the details. Whatever, it was probably smarter to not pry any further and make them wonder if I was up to something. I sighed. "I hope the pieces turn up. You're right, they do belong in the museum."

Joie puffed out her chest. "You can say that again."

The back door to the museum opened and a red haired, college-aged woman dressed in a historical outfit bustled out—pinstripe blouse and full-length black skirt, high collar, leg-o-mutton sleeves. She glanced my way, then smiled a greeting at Sparky before bending close to Joie and whispering something so low I couldn't make out the words.

"I'll be right in," Joie said to the woman. She looked at me. "I'd love to stay and chat, but duty calls." She turned to Sparky. "See you tomorrow."

"You can count on it," he said.

"I need to get going, too." I waved a friendly goodbye to them before walking back through the parking lot and across the street to my car.

Sandra had moved to the back seat and laid down, relaxing with her eyes half-closed. That was a good thing. I wasn't in the mood for any more antics, not with my thoughts whirring in every direction. At least it was clear neither Sparky or Joie knew Kala and I had found Graham, and that was a good thing.

As I drove toward Main Street, I remembered that I'd promised to return home with lunch. I could stop in a Quickie's for grinders—or I could kill two birds with one stone by picking something up at the Jumping Café.

I cringed at the awful saying, but my idea made sense. I hadn't learned a lot by talking with Sparky and Joie, but I might be able to add more information if I bought lunch at the cafe.

I kept going, out of the village and past the road to our house. A few minutes later, I turned into the Jumping Café's sizable parking lot. The Café was the town's most popular and largest gathering spot—restaurant, pub, and reception hall. The fields around it were used for the flea market and town celebrations, Little League fields, outdoor skating rink... You name it, it happened at the Jumping Café.

I parked, went inside and into the pub. The light was low. A few people sat in the booths, others around tables. My mouth watered from the smell of pizza and barbequing chicken. I spotted Jack working behind the bar. He was middle-aged, balding. His collection of rainbow-hued T-shirts belong in *Guinness World Records* for its endless variety and wild colors. Today's shirt was tie-dyed and sported a cartoon hippo holding a seafoam-blue martini. Next to Pinky, he was my favorite bartender.

As I claimed a stool at the bar, he smiled a greeting. "Citrus vodka with a twist?"

"How about an iced tea, nonalcoholic variety, and lunch to-go." I glanced at the daily special board, though my tastebuds had already made up their minds. "I'd like three orders of barbecue chicken with fries instead of mashed, and side salads. Better make one of those fries onion rings."

He winked. "Feeling a wee bit hungry today?"

I laughed. "The one with the rings is for me. The rest are for Tuck and Kala." I lowered my voice so it wouldn't travel. "Do you happen to know who was working Saturday afternoon?"

Wrinkles spanned his forehead. "I was. Why? Did you leave something behind? Gloves. Your phone."

"Not that. I was wondering if you remembered Felix Graham

being here." If Jack was the person who'd put Graham's leftovers in the to-go container, that ruled out the chance of a Café employee being involved with the drugging. Despite what any of his wild tees might suggest, Jack had a reputation for being squeaky clean, behind the bar and in his personal life. A total stickler for the rules. And, going by the timeframe Bill had given us, Graham had ingested or drunk the mexxy soon after he got home, not at the pub. But that didn't rule out the leftovers he taken with him.

Jack scooped ice into a glass, poured my tea. "I remember Graham being here alright." He nodded, indicating the booth closest to the dancehall entry. "He was down there, showing off that stuff he bought at the auction. Heather waited on him."

"Do you know when her next shift is?"

"She's here right now." He turned, looked away from me to a spot behind the bar that was hidden from my line of sight by an upright post. He called out, "Heather, can you come here for a sec?"

She appeared, walking quickly to join us. She was my age, with layered blond hair, slim fit jeans, and a Jumping Café tank top that was tight around the boobs and low in the neckline. I didn't know anything about Heather, other than that she was divorced, and had three or four kids to support.

"Edie wants to ask you something," Jack said to her, then he stepped aside. "While you ladies talk, I'll go put your order in, Edie."

"Thanks," I said. I smiled at her. "Jack said you waited on Felix Graham last Saturday."

"Oh, my gosh." She pressed a hand against her chest as if overwhelmed. "Isn't it awful what happened to him? Attacked and robbed in his own home, and he's such a sweet man."

"Yeah, as sweet as stewed rhubarb," I said before I could stop myself. Thankfully she didn't notice. Each to their own, I supposed.

"I heard he was taken to the hospital," she said. "I hope he's okay."

"He's home. Perfectly fine." I hadn't planned on embracing my connection to him, but clearly she was on team Graham. "Did you take his dinner order?"

"He had chicken Florentine. I went into the kitchen and dished an extra-large portion especially for him. Fresh grated parm on the side." The concern in her eyes faded, replaced by a momentary sharklike glisten. "He's a very generous tipper."

I smiled. Okay, so she wasn't totally taken in by Graham. I moved on to an even more vital question. "Was he alone in the booth?" In other words, who had access to his food.

"He was with Rene St. Marie."

"I know Rene. He's my family's neighbor." Graham had already mentioned Rene, and he'd been ruled out as a possible suspect.

"Felix talked to quite a few people, but that was before he ordered."

"Did you put his leftovers in the to-go container for him?"

"He did that himself." Her eyes went wide. "Don't tell me he got food poisoning. He left so quick after he ate, I was afraid something was wrong."

I leaned closer, elbows on the bar top as if about to share a secret instead of a fib. "Don't say a word to anyone. Graham would be mortified if it got out. He had one too many and doesn't remember most of that night. We're business friends. I'm asking around as a favor to him. You know, to make sure he didn't do anything embarrassing that he should know about."

Heather hunched closer. "He was fine when he left here." She closed her eyes. "Poor Felix. I should visit him. He told me to stop by anytime."

I clamped my lips together to keep myself from warning her off Graham. She was a grown woman, a woman with kids, and perhaps goals of her own. Some of which might include snuggling up with a man for financial security. Either way, I was positive she hadn't dowsed his leftovers with mexxy.

I sat back taller on my stool. "If you do go over to visit, a word of advice. I recommend calling first." So, you don't bump into one of his other *friends*, I thought.

"Good idea," she said.

Heather left me alone with my iced tea. I'd barely finished it when my to-go containers came out of the kitchen, steaming hot and smelling divine. Stopping here had proven to be a good move on several levels.

CHAPTER SEVENTEEN

F ive minutes later, I was home and parked in front of the shop. As soon as I let Sandra out, she zoomed off into the bushes. Considering I was carrying food, the only reason I could come up with for her disappearance was that perhaps the crabapples she'd eaten were taking effect.

I walked through the shop doorway, and called out, "I come bearing gifts."

Kala stood behind the front counter, hands on her hips. "What took you so long? It's almost two o'clock. I'm starving to death."

I set the to-go containers on the counter. There were customers browsing in the loft but no one else that I could see. "Where's Tuck?" I asked.

"All present and accounted for." His voice echoed from the nearby storage room. He appeared with plates and a roll of paper towels in his hands. "Just gathering weapons."

As we opened our boxes and got ready to eat, I glanced up at the loft to make sure the customers were out of earshot. They'd moved into the book room, even further away from us. Still, I hushed my voice before I told Tuck and Kala about my visit to the

Gazetteer. After that, I quickly went over my encounter with Sparky and Joie as well as what I'd learned at the Jumping Cafe.

Once I was finished, I ate a couple of bites of chicken, then looped back around. "I'm not saying for sure that Sparky, Joie, and Dr. Stanhope are the thieves, but we should group them together at the top of our suspect list."

Kala raised a finger, indicating for me to wait before saying anything else. She finished chewing and wiped barbeque sauce off her lips with a paper towel. "You might want to hear what I found out before you get any more worked up about them."

"Really? What is it?" I said.

"First of all, some of the stuff about the robbery—like that Graham went to the hospital and that his alarms weren't on—has leaked out online."

Okay, that explained where people I'd encountered had learned details. I was also pretty certain it wasn't Kala's big news. I took a guess. "Are people talking about who did it?"

"Negatory. No signs of the Glass Widow going up for sale either—not anywhere." She plucked a French fry from her box, dramatically drawing out the moment even longer by munching it down slowly before saying, "There was a huge wedding at the golf course the night of the robbery. "Moonlight in Vermont" theme. Ceremony at nine. Dinner at eleven. Toast at midnight. Dancing until dawn. And you'll never guess who the bride was."

As she once more drew out the tension by slowly munching another fry, I turned toward Tuck, hoping he'd spill the rest.

He shook his head. "I'm not breathing a word. Except, that it rules out the idea that the theft was necessarily premeditated."

I swiveled back to Kala. "No more torture. What's so important about this bride?"

She brought something up on her phone, then handed it to me. It was a post on a Facebook page featuring about a zillion informal wedding photos, clear despite them being taken with nothing more than candle and moonlight. The groom towered over the bride. She was my age, thirty at the most, dark hair pulled up into a stylish coil, simple but elegant dress. I enlarged her image, studied her face, and frowned. "I don't recognize her. Should I?"

"Not her," Kala said. "Check out her maiden name."

I flipped back to a closeup of a wedding announcement. Megan Lavelle. I shook my head, baffled for a beat. Then an image of Cruella de Ville's white swing coat flashed into my mind and I made the connection. "Oh my God. Marissa Lavelle. The New Hampshire dealer. The bride's related to her?"

"Marissa's her aunt." Kala beamed proudly. "I found the wedding announcement in the *Gazetteer*. It went on and on, listing friends and relatives. Maybe Marissa didn't plan on robbing Graham. She went to the wedding right after the auction. It makes sense for her to know where Graham lives. She's a big-time dealer, according to you and Tuck. She got drunk, grabbed a couple of friends, and snuck across the golf course to his house. No one would miss one or two guests once the celebration got rolling. Mexxy's a party drug. Someone could've had it at the reception. One time I went to a wedding and the groom was so high he passed out in the restroom."

I closed my eyes, letting it all soak in. This theory was nothing more than speculation, but it was sensible speculation none the less. Marissa had bid on the Glass Widow at the auction. She had plenty of clients with deep pockets. Taking the Bible box might've been a spur of the moment addition.

Opening my eyes, I looked at Kala and Tuck. "We need to get our hands on the golf course's security footage from that night. If it was Marissa—or her and some of her friends—they would've carried the pieces back to the club house and put them in their car before driving off. But—"

"I know where you're going with this," Tuck said. It was amazing how he could read my mind. "But—if they got interrupted or freaked out for some reason, they might've stashed the pieces right there on the golf course or in the club house."

"If they planned on going back for them the next day wouldn't one of them need to be a golf club member to get access?" Kala asked. "It's not likely Marissa is one. She's from out of state."

"That's true," I said.

Kala's expression brightened. "We need to go there first thing tomorrow. If I can get a little look-see at their security system, I'll be able to figure out how to access the feed remotely."

"I'm not sure that's a good idea," Tuck said. "The local police may have already come up with a similar theory. If they spot you two there, it could put you right back on their suspect list."

Kala blew a raspberry. "No problem. We won't use our real names. Edie and I can pretend we're two girls in love, looking for our wedding venue. I've always dreamed of having a big wedding —a moonlight ceremony followed by a country club reception like Megan Lavelle's sounds magical."

I scowled. Kala sounded way too eager about this fake wedding thing for my taste. Plus, I was pretty sure I'd fail at the lovey-dovey gay couple thing. "If we're doing this. I'm going as your maid of honor. That's it."

She harumphed. "Turning bridezilla already, are you?"

I laughed. "If anyone's a bridezilla, it's you."

Business taken care of, we all dug into our food with more vigor. My onion rings were fabulous but starting to go limp as they cooled.

Tuck set down his fork and looked at me. "Your mention of Joie Bascom and the museum got me thinking. There was another artifact connected to the Mountain House Resort tragedy that went missing."

"You're kidding," I said. "What?"

"According to rumors, not long after Joie was hired as the new museum director, they were setting up the new Mountain House

Resort exhibit when they discovered that the shirt from the old display had vanished."

"You mean, the bloody shirt?" I asked. It was locally infamous, though I only vaguely remembered it, more of a yellowed rag with dark stains on it than a full-fledged piece of clothing.

Kala did a double take. "Does this have to do with the story about the guy who killed his lover's husband, then burnt down the resort to cover up the murder?"

"Jeb Warner," I clarified. "The pharmacist who was hung for the crimes."

"The shirt didn't look like much," Tuck said, "but it was my favorite thing in the museum when I was a kid. That and the old crime scene photo of George Fielding's burnt body."

"Crime scene photos?" Kala shoved the remainder of her lunch aside. "I didn't know they took them back then."

"It wasn't common," I said. "They were mostly taken in big cities and of major crimes. The photographers took them for the police and also sold them to newspapers across the country—sensational stuff. They command big bucks nowadays. You should check them out online."

"I'll do that."

Tuck raised his eyebrows. "If we went to see the new exhibit, we could look at the crime scene photos and ask what happened to the shirt."

"Good idea," I said. I thought for a second. "I can't see Joie swiping the shirt, considering she was a relatively new director and in charge of setting up the exhibit—" I stopped talking as my phone buzzed. I glanced at the caller ID. *Tristan Lefebvre.* I'd totally forgotten about him and the auction video. I put the phone on speaker. "Hey, Tristan. Thanks for calling."

"Anytime, you know that." His voice was warm and upbeat. I could picture him sitting in the office, long legs stretched out, dark ponytail flopped over one shoulder. "Would around nine-thirty or ten o'clock tomorrow morning work for watching the video? I'll have coffee on. Fresh pumpkin muffins from Geoff's Bakery."

Tuck and I tended to go to Quickie's over Geoff's for pastries. But it wasn't because Geoff's wasn't good. In fact, it was excellent, trendy, but on the pricy side.

"Sounds great." I hesitated. "I totally understand if you don't have time to watch the entire video, or if it goes against journalistic ethics or something. We can speed through most of it. I just need to jot down who was there and left around the same time as Felix Graham."

"We can do whatever works best for you. I'm just glad I can help." His tone was more languorous now, husky even.

Kala leaned close to Tuck, and whispered just loud enough for me to hear, "'Coffee and video' sounds a lot like 'Netflix and chill' to me."

Tuck chuckled.

I gritted my teeth. Then took the phone off speaker and said, "See you tomorrow morning, Tris."

"Looking forward to it."

CHAPTER EIGHTEEN

Once evening came, I left Tuck and Kala to entertain themselves and went out to the front porch with the sole journal that had survived the theft. If we were lucky, it might contain the names of people who'd tried but failed to buy the Glass Widow and/or the ephemera from Bucky in the past. In other words, suspects.

The air was warm, slightly humid, and scented with the aroma of grass clippings and mint, a smell left over from when Tuck had mowed the lawn a few hours earlier.

I lit the kerosene lantern we kept on the coffee table, then settled down on the wicker rocking chair. I loved the lantern's wavering light. It made me feel as if I'd stepped into a world where time was suspended, the past coming forward to meld with the present. Sure, it only provided a soft circle of ambient brightness, but it was enough to read by.

Resting the journal on my lap, I stared out at the quarter moon peeking over the tree line. In another week or so, the temperatures would start to drop, and porch time would come to an end for the year.

My mind drifted to Tuck and Kala, and the plans we'd made

for tomorrow—first the *Gazetteer* and then a visit to the golf course. I hadn't admitted it to them, but they were right about Tristan. The chance of him wanting to turn our 'coffee and video' into something more was a real possibility. He hadn't hidden his interest the last time I'd seen him. It was flattering, kind of. Not that he'd make any headway. I wasn't about to do anything to jeopardize my relationship with Shane.

Shane. I pressed a hand against my upper chest. If he were here, I'd be telling him about what I'd learned and our plans. Well, most everything except about the mexxy and a few other details. What Shane didn't know, he didn't need to feel obliged to share with his law enforcement buddies. That was something he'd warned me about; a lesson I'd learned the hard way since we'd started seeing each other again. We both had to use restraint when it came to divulging certain aspects of our business lives to each other. Besides, the South Burlington police were investigating Graham's robbery, and undoubtedly they'd turn up the same information as we were. No way was I going to share anything that would put Pinky's brother, Bill's, job in jeopardy or reveal Kala's familiarity with the shadier side of the web.

Without stopping to think, I picked my phone up from the coffee table. Shane had told me he'd be busy for the next few days and out of touch. But what harm could a quick exchange of texts do?

I typed. *Thinking of you. Miss you.*

I hit sent, took a deep breath and looked back out at the tree line. The moon was gaining height, beautiful with the dark sky above and the hint of autumn color below.

My phone buzzed. It was Shane. *Miss you too.*

Busy day tomorrow? I asked.

After this is done, you and me, long weekend in the Adirondacks? I could use a getaway.

He sounded beyond stressed. I typed as fast as I could. *One hundred percent up for that. <3*

Got to go.

A shiver of fear ran the length of my spine. What the heck was Shane investigating? He usually was the epitome of calm and collected.

I typed. *Be careful.*

Will do. XOXOX

I traced his text with my index finger, as if the words on the screen were as personally inscribed as ink on paper. Then I picked up Bucky's journal and settled back in the rocker. Whatever kind of case Shane was tangled up in, I hoped it resolved soon and without issue.

Like the other two journals that had been in the Bible box, the one in my hands was a modern composition notebook with a black and white speckled cardboard cover.

I opened it. A date including the year was scribbled on the first page in pencil.

I froze, unable to breathe for a moment. The journal was from the year my grandparents' plane went down. The page I was staring at was exactly five months before the day of the crash. Bucky was close with my grandparents. The journal had to contain an entry devoted to that day. July tenth. The worst day of my life.

My fingers trembled as I vacillated between flipping ahead until I found July and not wanting to even see the date. Finally, I gritted my teeth and settled on starting at the beginning of the journal and reading forward. I was tired. I planned on only reading a handful of pages before going to bed. Maybe I'd come across some amusing interaction between Bucky and my grandparents. Bucky had loved to horse-trade and joke around. I'd be able to sleep after reading something lighthearted, but not if I read July tenth.

Taking a deep breath, I began:

February 3

Clear skies last night. Thirty below. Damn waterline into the base-

ment froze again. Used Doris's hairdryer to thaw it out. Bought new heater cables and a secondhand propane heater. Should talk to Gilbert about permanent fix when he gets back from Florida.

It was odd that the journal started in February instead of New Years. I could only assume it was continued from a previous book. For all practical purposes, the entry was boring, a common old house issue, though it did make me wonder if our own basement was adequately winterized. Since I'd been home, I'd already discovered my mom had failed to deal with a major septic issue. It was doubtful she'd checked the condition of things like pipe insulation. I added checking basement for potential freezing issues to my mental to-do list, before I moved onto the next entry:

February 7

Smith Auction Gallery in New Hampshire. Bought collection of post-Civil War era Vermont cabinet cards. Included a Beaumont Photography aerial view of Scandal Mountain. Had to pay up for them.

I read on. More day-to-day dry entries about weather and household chores. Food. His wife's health. Antique sales and shows. Purchases. His health. I went through the rest of February and into March before I called it a night, keeping an eye out for any potential clue to the thieves' identities. The whole time, a voice whispered in the back of my mind, urging me to flip forward to July tenth. But I couldn't afford to get sidetracked or overwhelmed by grief right now. I had to concentrate on the job at hand. I had to find anything that would help me unmask the thieves, so I could get the information I needed off of Graham.

This was about getting Mom out of prison, not about my grandparents' deaths.

CHAPTER NINETEEN

Tristan got a third mug out of the cupboard above the coffee bar and set it down next to a basket of pumpkin muffins. "Frenchie said you're looking into the robbery for Graham. That surprises me."

"Honestly, me too," I said.

Kala and I had arrived at the *Gazetteer* office right on time at ten o'clock—me in my standard business casual outfit, a tailored jacket, blouse, and slacks. Kala had dug a clingy, little polka dotted dress out from the depths of her closet, nothing like her usual overalls and graphic tees, but suitable for our upcoming information gathering at the golf course.

However, if Tristan was surprised by her presence or our overly dressy outfits, he hid it well. "Then why do it?" he asked.

Kala jumped in. "You know Edie—once she gets curious about something there's no turning back."

Tristan laughed. "Some things never change."

I wasn't sure I liked being thought of as obstinate. Still, I'd been called worse, and I had to give it to Kala for coming up with an answer on the fly. It wasn't like we could tell him the full truth.

I met his eyes. "The main reason is because I hate thieves even more than I dislike Graham."

"Can't argue with you there." He motioned at the coffee pot. "Pour yourselves a mug, then we'll get to the video."

While I waited for Kala to fix her coffee, the rich smell of the brew sent my mind veering away from thoughts of our deal with Graham and to my mom. What was she doing right now? She certainly wasn't about to drink top-shelf coffee like us. Instead, maybe she was spending her morning complaining to the prison officials about the side effects of her new medicine, at least I hoped so. Tuck hadn't heard about it either. What the heck was it for?

As Kala stepped aside and I took my turn at the pot, I focused hard on the trickle of the steaming liquid and willed the worries about Mom's medicine to the back of my mind. I couldn't afford to be distracted right now. Not if I wanted any hope of freeing her.

Tristan handed me a napkin-wrapped muffin, then Kala and I followed him into a side office. Between a pair of windows, a jumbo-size computer screen sat on a library table. The screen was swiveled around to face into the room. Two cushy desk chairs sat in front of it, like seats in a movie theater.

Kala dropped into the most front-and-center chair. I settled down on the other. Balancing his coffee and muffin in one hand, Tristan grabbed a chair from its place behind a desk and wheeled it up close to mine. He situated his snacks on the floor, produced a remote, then said, "So what's our plan here?"

"Easy-peasy." Kala pulled an iPad from her bag. "You and Edie are in charge of calling out names as you spot people in the video. I'll play the role of administrative assistant—you know, keep track of everything."

"Frenchie said there were at least a hundred people in the auction gallery," he said.

I nodded. "Our aim is to note just the most likely suspects. There's no way we could investigate everyone."

Tristan gave me a sidelong glance. "Ever think of becoming a journalist? You've got the makings of a darn good one."

"Nancy Drew, kid detective is more my speed." I took a sip of coffee, then pitched my voice lower. "We're looking for people who spent an overt amount of time previewing the bottle or the Bible Box. Plus, everyone who bid on either item, or people who look like they're watching Graham."

"Let's get cracking, then." Tristan hit play.

As the buzz of pre-auction chatter and the sight of people swarming between the stacks of antiques filled the screen, I was transported back to that day. But after only a few seconds, the muscles in the back of my neck grew taut and a dull headache pulsed in my temples. There really were a lot of people there. How were we ever going to sort out suspects?

I retrieved my coffee from where I'd set it on the floor beside Tristan's, took a long sip to steady my nerves, then refocused on the screen. There had to be something we could get from viewing this, there just had to be.

The video panned over Marissa Lavelle talking with Sparky Collins, like I remembered. The view moved deeper into the labyrinth of antiques. Joie Bascom in her autumn-orange leggings and yellow sports jacket posed for the camara.

Kala tapped her iPad. "Joie's already on our list, but I'm adding her again."

After that, things flowed more easily. It was like how buying antiques from a collector goes sometimes: First you can't make headway because they act like they don't want to part with anything. Finally, you manage to talk them into selling a low-end piece for a fair price, then they open up, showing you more items they're willing to let go. In this case, we managed to pinpoint suspects as they walked up to the showcase to look at the Glass Widow, either lingering or moving on quickly if they weren't that interested. Mostly the video reconfirmed the suspects already on the whiteboards back home.

Tristan abruptly froze the video on an interaction between Graham and a woman. His arm brushed mine as he leaned in close to me and whispered in full seriousness, "There's a likely culprit, if I ever saw one. Look how she's glaring at him."

It took a beat for me to realize the woman on the screen was me.

I teasingly shoved Tristan back into his own space. "Very funny, wise guy."

He laughed and shook his head. "I don't know what Graham was saying to you, but you sure don't look happy."

"I wasn't."

He started the video again, fast forwarding through an interview with Albert Fisher. After that, the video jumped ahead to Albert auctioning the Glass Widow. It panned from him standing behind the podium to Bucky's wife gripping the hand of her silver-haired gentleman friend, to Joie Bascom sitting in the audience a few rows in front of Tuck and me.

Joie murmured something to the younger woman sitting beside her. The woman's red hair allowed me to recognize her immediately. She was the woman in Victorian attire who'd whispered something to Joie in the museum parking lot.

I turned to Tristan. "Do you know the redhead?"

"Kaitlyn O'Connell. She works at the museum."

"Adding 'Kaitlyn the Whisperer' to the suspect list," Kala said.

On the video, Kaitlyn got to her feet and went up the aisle toward the back of the room. As the bidding on the Glass Widow heated up, she appeared on the screen again, stepping directly in front of Graham and blocking his view of the auctioneer as he raised his hand to bid. Had she done that on purpose, so Albert Fisher wouldn't see Graham's bid?

The video left them, panned to an auction house employee taking a phone bid, before returning to Albert Fisher and

Graham. Kaitlyn was no longer standing in front of him, and everyone was applauding Graham's winning bid. After that, the video once again jumped ahead, showing Pinky carrying the crate of bottles back to Tuck. Then it ended.

I sighed. "I wish the video hadn't cut off so soon. I really wanted to see who stayed in the gallery after Graham left."

"Sorry about that" —I jumped as Frenchie's resonant voice came from behind me— "I had to get to a little league game on the other side of town."

I wheeled around. "I didn't realize you were there."

Good humor twinkled in his eyes. "Blending in with the background is one of my charms."

Tristan smiled at me. "Watch out for the old flirt, he's worse than I am."

Frenchie leaned over Kala's shoulder, studying her iPad. "What you need to make is a spreadsheet. Names down one side. Details along the top."

"I've already done that," she said. "I've got a whole wall of whiteboards too."

"How do you plan on narrowing down the suspects?" he asked

Kala polished a fist on her sleeve. "A little cross referencing. Maybe a graph and timeline. I keep track of the prices we realize on eBay by date and…"

From that point on, the entire visit veered sharply away from the auction and suspects to eBay and vintage toys, and on to Frenchie giving Kala a more detailed tour of his collection than I'd gotten during my previous visit. It was hard to tell which one of them was more into it. If Kala hadn't been gay and Frenchie hadn't been old enough to be her grandfather, I might have thought they were flirting their way to a first date.

"We should get going," I finally said to Kala. "We do have another stop to make."

Tristan cocked his head. "Another lead?"

"Ah—we aren't exactly sure yet." I didn't want to be rude, but I didn't want to mention the golf course. They were journalists after all, and we'd already likely whetted their interest in the robbery.

Frenchie scratched his cheek, then looked at Tristan. "Since I know how much you love desk duty"—He winked to indicate he was kidding—"why don't I man the office while you give the girls a hand?"

I leapt in before Tristan could answer. "That's okay. We've got it handled." The idea of Tristan coming with us was even worse than us telling them where we were headed.

Frenchie's tone turned fatherly. "Getting information out of people is what Tris does every day. It wouldn't hurt to have him on your team."

"It might this time," Kala said. She set the antique camara she was holding down, and grimaced. "What we're doing is—girly."

Tristan laughed. "I'm not sure what you're talking about, but it does sound like something I'd rather avoid."

"Take my word for it. It's not something you'd enjoy," I said. "And we really do need to get going."

As we walked out of Frenchie's office and toward the *Gazetteer*'s front door, Tristan reached out and touched my shoulder. "I hope the video was at least some help."

"It definitely was," I said. "Thank you."

Frenchie spoke up. "I've been thinking about your thieves. It seems to me, they're most likely treasure hunters. There were a lot of diaries and papers in that old Bible box, things that might contain clues to the location of the lost bottles. We've written several articles over the past few years about illegal treasure digging around the old resort ruins."

"I do think that's likely," I said. When I was a kid, the vast mountainside resort ruins and mineral spring property had been owned privately. You had to ask the owner's permission to treasure hunt up there. But, if you got permission, it was perfectly legal to dig for bottles or whatever. However, eight or nine years ago, the town of Scandal Mountain had bought that entire side of the mountain and deemed it a recreation area. As town property, digging for anything was now illegal.

"We have a commercial drone equipped with a camara," Frenchie said. "If you want, Tristan could do a fly over for you. See if there's any recent signs of treasure hunting."

A tingle of excitement swept up my arms as I visualized a low, sweeping bird's-eye view of the mountainside, especially this time of year when there weren't as many leaves on the trees. What would a view like that reveal? Perhaps illegal digging. Perhaps even more, like traces of a hitherto undiscovered outbuilding's foundation, a place so overgrown it was invisible without a view from the sky, a foundation no other bottle digger had noticed or explored. A gateway to the long-lost cache of Glass Widow bottles.

I clenched my hands, hard enough to feel the sharpness of my fingernails against my palms. *No.* I couldn't afford to even think about looking for the treasure right now. This was about identifying the thieves and getting my mom out of prison.

I met Frenchie's gaze. "If our other plans don't pan out, we might take you up on that offer."

He smiled, a slow, pleased crook of the lips. "If you run into any roadblocks, don't hesitate to call. We've got a lot of resources and are happy to help."

The mexxy and who might be selling it popped into my mind. The Lefebvre's were known for not shirking from darker issues. But like Tristan coming with us to the golf course, even mentioning mexxy might send them on the hunt for information ahead of us, so I simply nodded. "Thanks a lot for everything. We really do appreciate it."

Tristan's voice deepened, sultry warm. "Seriously, don't be shy about calling. You don't even need a reason."

CHAPTER TWENTY

As we drove toward the outskirts of town, heading toward South Burlington and the golf course, I was grateful Kala didn't mention the inuendo in Tristan's voice when he made his last comment. Instead, she chattered about Frenchie. "Isn't his collection amazing, all those trains and planes? He still has the Royal typewriter his father used when he started the *Gazetteer*. It's from like 1949. Works perfect. He told me their original press is still in the basement. Can you imagine having a family business last that long?..."

I focused on the road ahead, resisting the urge to say anything. Our antique shop hadn't been around as long as the *Gazetteer* but rebuilding it and passing it on to a future generation was my dream. That was, if I had children and assuming they wanted to be involved.

Stepping harder on the gas, I sped up as we passed the Scandal Mountain Veterinary Clinic and the town limits. After a moment, I asked, "I wonder if Sandra's driving Tuck crazy?"

"He texted while we were watching the video. She stole a bag of peanut butter cookies from my room, scarfed them down, then puked in the shop—like a huge, slimy pile."

"I bet Tuck just loved that."

"He banished her to the outdoors for the rest of the day."

I laughed. "More like until she gives him the sad-eye treatment."

Talking about Frenchie's collection and Sandra's antics was a much-needed relief. If I thought too hard about how many suspects and how little information we had about the robbery, pursuing it any further was bound to start feeling pointless. How were we ever going to make any headway?

In what seemed like no time at all, I reached the turnoff to the golf course. I went down the long driveway, past the members' only parking area to the spaces near the clubhouse designated for visitors. The clubhouse itself was super classy, cedar-shingled gables and gray clapboard siding with a two-story wraparound veranda.

Kala flipped down the visor, studied her makeup. "This calls for a touchup."

"You look fine," I said.

"Maybe to you. I'm going for perfection. I'm also snagging an opportunity to check out the security set up without being obvious. You do want me to be discrete?"

I slanted another look her way. Sure enough, though Kala appeared to be dabbing on lipstick, in reality she was peering around the side of the visor and toward the clubhouse's roofline.

"There are a couple cameras there. Six on the light posts," she said. "One of them is trained on the clubhouse front door. I'd stake my favorite glitter-monkey sweatshirt that the whole place is covered just as thoroughly."

"Which means, the police probably have footage of the thieves sneaking toward Graham's house."

"Unless the thieves took down the system—which makes the theory of Marissa Lavelle coming up with the idea on the spur of the moment less likely." Kala pushed the visor back up. "Let's go. Your wedding venue awaits."

I frowned at her. "What do you mean, *my* wedding venue?"

She grinned. "Didn't I tell you? I've decided to remain single. You'll looked great in white. Actually, you'd look better in ivory. Your skin's awfully pale."

"Thankfully, dress color isn't something we have to worry about," I said.

"You need to get into your role. It's always classy when the table linens match the bride's gown." We got out of the car. But, as we walked toward the clubhouse, she slowed her steps and whispered, "Once we get inside, we have to look for a security room or office. I only need a quick looksee at the setup."

A group of golfers came out of the clubhouse front door and headed toward the member's parking area. A man at the back of the pack was short, thin blond hair—

Yikes! Dr. Stanhope.

I ducked my head, clamped my hand on Kala's arm, and steered her away from the entry to a walkway that ran along the side of the clubhouse.

"What is it?" she whispered.

"Dr. Stanhope. We can't risk him seeing us and wondering why we're here." The more I'd thought about that day at Graham's, the more I was convinced Stanhope had said something to make the cops suspicious of me and Kala.

Kala and I hurried along the walkway. A wall of trimmed cedars now partially hid us from Stanhopes view. A garden of hostas, as well as delicate maidenhair and tall ostrich ferns, ran alongside the hedge.

My breath bottled up in my throat as my mind went to the envelope with the dots of fern-spore like brown stains and my grandfather's handwriting on it. As much as I was determined to focus on unmasking the thieves, I couldn't deny I itched to get my hands on that envelope as well. Why had Bucky kept it after my grandparents' deaths? Why hadn't he opened it?

Kala hooked her arm with mine, towing me toward where a

flight of stairs led up to the overhanging veranda. She pointed upward and whispered, "According to the photos on the golf course's website, there should be a set of sliding glass doors up there that go into the clubhouse."

Taking the stairs, we didn't slow until we reached the top. The panoramic view from there was breathtaking —the swoops of the greens and sand traps, punctuated by groves of golden-leafed birch trees and scattered distant golfers and golf carts. Three men in slacks and polo shirts were in the foreground, strolling toward the clubhouse. But what held my eyes was the distant gleam of two houses, only their roofs and top stories visible along with a strip of mowed lawn between them. That strip led down to the golf course property.

"Is that Graham's place?" I whispered to Kala.

She nodded. "It's even closer than I thought."

My ear caught the swish of the sliding glass doors behind us opening, followed by the stucco-clip of high heels as someone marched in our direction.

I straightened my spine and turned to look. It was a woman dressed essentially the same as me, business casual slacks, blouse and jacket, dressy pumps, long brown hair pulled back in a ponytail. The only difference between our appearances was that she sported a name tag.

Leah Goldstein
Event Manager

She greeted my smile with one of her own. "Are you Denise? I wasn't expecting you until three."

"I'm afraid not. I'm...." My voice trailed off as I mentally fashioned a lie. "I'm Julie the maid of honor." I flagged my hand at Kala. "This is Dottie. She's the bride."

Kala scowled, I suspected not only at being foisted into the bride role but also at my name choice. Alright so I'd let her polka dotted dress influence me in that area, but it was the best I could do on the fly.

Leah pressed a polished fingernail against her bottom lip, thinking. "Dottie? I'm sorry, but your name doesn't ring a bell."

"It shouldn't," Kala said. "A friend of ours was at a wedding here last Saturday. She said it was fantabulous. I just wanted to take a quick looksee around."

I added, "Dottie's concerned about the golf course's security. There'll be a number of *important* guests attending her wedding. We don't want paparazzi sneaking in."

Leah's eyes glistened, probably at the thought of a posh guest list. "We offer the utmost privacy and security. We also extend the perks of membership to wedding guests. Tennis. Golf. Swimming. Guests are welcome to use the facilities throughout the wedding weekend."

Men's voices floated up from below the veranda, quickly becoming more understandable as they neared the bottom of the stairs we had come up. Most likely they were the men who'd been strolling toward the clubhouse.

"You do understand why we're concerned?" One of them said. His voice was all business—and perhaps familiar.

"I swear, it's the truth," a different man answered. "Like I told the officer on Sunday, there aren't any recordings. Not here. Not in the cloud."

A third man cleared his throat. "Your security just happens to go down during a wedding and all the recordings are missing—and no one notices until now? You expect us to buy that?"

The men stopped talking, but their footfalls began to sound on the steps, moving upward.

Leah's face went as milky-white as a glass of iced Ouzo. Sweat beaded her temples. Her gaze winged toward the stairs, then back at us. "How about if we go to my office? I have some free time to talk. It's more comfortable in there."

I widened my stance. "What were you saying about utmost privacy and security?"

"Please. Let's go inside." She stepped back, closer to the sliding glass doors. "I'll get you a sample plate of artisan cheeses and mimosas. Our mimosas are wonderful. Fresh squeezed orange juice. Petillant-Naturel wine from Snow Farm Vineyard in South Hero, Vermont's champagne."

Kala rested her hands on her hips. "Are your security camaras monitored here or off site?"

"Here." Her gaze again cut toward the stairs. "Don't worry about what they're saying. It's nothing, really. A onetime fluke."

As the men's heads came into view, I noticed one of them had an oddly bulbous forehead.

Oh crap. That's why one of the voices seemed familiar. It was the older officer who'd been at Graham's house. Sergeant Nelson. I couldn't be positive without seeing more of him, but what if it was?

I snagged Kala's hand and tugged her toward the glass doors. "Mimosas sound wonderful. Don't they, Dottie?"

"If you say so." Kala hurried along with me. The only one moving more quickly toward the glass doors was Leah. She positively zoomed, like Sandra leaving the scene of an apple theft, and just in time. Out of the corner of my eye, I spotted the men climb the last steps and walk onto the veranda. And one of them definitely was Sergeant Nelson. Talking wedding now sounded like the perfect idea.

Except—

As we started away from the glass doors and down a corridor, the contents of a large showcase stopped me in my tracks. The case contained a myriad of golf trophies and photos of people in golf outfits. I didn't care about the trophies. For the most part, I didn't recognize anyone in the photos. But two of the people stood out to me as unmissable as a gaping crack in a Ming dynasty vase: Dr. Stanhope and Joie Bascom, standing close together.

My gaze went from the photo and showcase to Leah. My voice faltered. "Is—is Joie Bascom a club member?"

Leah smiled. "She was our women's club champion three years running."

CHAPTER TWENTY-ONE

W hile Leah went to get the mimosas and cheese samples, she left Kala and me alone behind the closed door of her office. Actually, we were both there for only about a minute after Leah left, then Kala slipped out to case the nearby security office.

In less time than I'd expected, Kala returned. "Most of the security equipment is decades old," she reported. "Even you could have sabotaged it."

"Thanks for the vote of confidence."

"Just saying—tech isn't exactly number one on your skill set."

I ignored that and talked fast, "I think we should put Dr. Stanhope at the top of our suspect list along with Joie Bascom and Marissa Lavelle."

Kala wrinkled her nose. "You don't suppose Marissa slept with Graham? That would give her a reason to know Graham's habit of not turning on his alarm system early in the evening."

"I don't know, but that's something even this non-tech-savvy woman can find out." I pulled my phone from my jacket pocket. "I'm going to text Graham and tell him we need to talk. Who better to tell us if he's spent quality time with Marissa than the stud muffin himself?"

Kala snickered. "This is going to be interesting."

Only a second later the office door opened, and Leah walked in with the mimosas and cheese. But we barely had a chance to thank her and take a sip when a knock sounded at the office door.

I felt myself pale. *Crap.* What if it was Sargent Nelson? It seemed impossible that he wouldn't have planned on talking with Leah at some point.

As Leah rose to her feet and went to answer the door, Kala touched my hand and whispered, "Time to go?"

I nodded, though it was too late to escape unseen.

Leah opened the door. A slender young woman in a simple black dress, and an older man and woman stood there.

The tension drained from my body. The real bride. Leah's three o'clock appointment.

Leah glanced from the real bride to us. "I—"

I downed my mimosa, scrambled to my feet. "Don't worry. We'll leave. She's the one with the appointment."

"We'll give you a call," Kala said, as we whisked out of the office and past the newcomers without giving Leah our contact information.

In no time flat, we escaped out the clubhouse's front door. When we reached the safety of the Volvo, I collapsed onto the seat. "Thank heavens for real brides."

Kala pulled a cracker and square of cheese from the pocket of her dress. "Not a bad score either." She popped it in her mouth. "Yum. I bet this stuff is thirty dollars a pound at gourmet shops."

"I can't believe you swiped that."

"You're just jealous because you didn't think of it." She reached back into her pocket, produced more crackers and cheese, assembled a sandwich and held it out to me. "Don't worry, I got enough for both of us."

I took the cracker sandwich, bit off half. Sometimes I wondered about Kala—fast-fingering cheese, over-the-top internet related skills...security system knowledge—but I liked and respected her too much to pry into her past. Somethings were better left alone.

Munching down the snack, I started the car. I was about to put it into gear when my phone buzzed. A reply from Graham: *I'm at the antique shop. Do you have news?*

I answered: *See you in fifteen minutes. Tell you then.*

Only twelve minutes later, we arrived at the Golden Stag. Janet's look-a-like granddaughter, Alison, was manning the front counter.

I smiled at her. "Congratulations on getting the job."

She toyed with the top button on her cardigan. "It's on trial basis."

"Trial basis for who—you or him?" Kala said.

I softened my voice. "I'm sure Graham will hire you full time."

"I hope so. I'd really like to stay in the area." She lowered her eyelids, lashes fluttering as a flush crept across her cheeks. "My ex-fiancé lives near here. We're hoping to get back together."

"That's nice." Kala tried and mostly succeeded at sounding interested.

Alison sighed. "We were together all through college, which was a while ago now. Back then, all the girls were after him. I got this yeast infection and he…"

An expression of horror slid over Kala's face as Alison blasted past the TMI zone and into gynecology-land. I managed to block out most of the information she was revealing, and I really didn't want to hear what was coming next.

I looked toward where Graham's office lay beyond a partition made of antique stained-glass windows. I could see the outline of someone. Probably Graham. I interrupted her storytelling, "Graham's expecting us. Is it okay if we go right in?"

Her voice turned panicked. "You can't do that. I need to ring him first, please. It's protocol."

"Could you do that now, please?" Kala said.

"Umm…sure?"

I buried my hands in my jacket pockets, waiting with the patience of a melting ice-cream-cone as Alison went through a needlessly formal intercom conversation with Graham. Finally, Graham snarled at her, "Just bring them in."

"Yes, sir. Of course, sir," Alison said. She herded us to Graham's office door and ushered us inside.

Graham threw a look her way. "Shut the door on your way out."

Blinking like an awed schoolgirl, Alison backed out of the room and closed the door behind her. Though it pissed me off to see Graham treat her so dismissively, his snippiness was more understandable than usual. The last thing he needed on top of everything else was an inexperienced new employee with a penchant for sharing too much personal information with strangers.

"Did you find out who took my things?" he asked.

"We've got some solid leads," I said. More of an exaggeration than a lie.

He folded his arms. "You mean, *no*."

"I mean, we're close. But we need to ask you a few things."

"Like what?"

Kala sidestepped, moving to hide behind me. "Have fun," she murmured under her breath.

I squared my shoulders. "Has Marissa Lavelle ever been to your house?"

"I have parties. Holiday gatherings. What of it?"

I took a deep breath. "Let me rephrase. Have you ever slept with Marissa?"

The cords along his neck stiffened. "She's not my type."

"You mean she's too old?" Kala asked.

His voice hardened. "I prefer women with whiter teeth and fewer stretch marks."

Gotcha, I thought. I smiled, a slow, grin like the Grinch when he's feeling particularly evil. "When were you close enough to see her stretch marks?"

His jaw tightened. "All right, so I was with her once—or twice." He rejected the trajectory of the conversation with a flick of his fingers. "She isn't a thief. She's a clever woman, deals in quality art and antiques."

"You're saying clever and highbrow don't equal criminal? I seem to recall some dealers from Boston ..." I let the sentence trail off. He knew what I was referring to. Back in May, the decoy collection I'd appraised was stolen by a couple of bigwig dealers he was tangled up with. That relationship was just one of the reasons I'd become convinced Graham knew more than he was admitting about my mother being set up for the forgery charge.

Graham pushed off from his desk, paced across the room, pivoted once more to face Kala and me. "There are disadvantages to being seen as successful. People like the police assume the financial loss is all that matters to us, and that insurance will cover that. Frankly, I'm not convinced the South Burlington police are doing much of anything as far as my case goes." His eyes narrowed. "I'd wanted to distance myself from their investigation. Perhaps that was a mistake. The squeaky wheel gets the grease, and all that jazz."

Swallowing hard, I looked down. I didn't want Graham to lose faith in our ability to unmask the thieves and to turn to pressuring the police instead. I desperately needed his information, so I could help my mom. But I also didn't want to be foolish and share too much too soon. Still... I leveled my gaze on his. I had to toss him a small bone, something that he clearly was wondering about. "You're wrong about the police. We saw them today at the country club. They were asking questions connected to your case."

"Edie's telling the truth," Kala said.

His jaw remained clenched, frustration and anger visibly pulsing on the surface, then the tension loosened as if he were about to say something—

But I didn't give him a chance. "Marissa isn't our only suspect. We just don't think she can be overlooked, especially since she had the opportunity to see the layout of your home and learn your nighttime routine." I raised a hand to keep him quiet. "The last thing we need is for you to confront her about the robbery or mention her to the police or to tell them that we were at the golf course. If you want our help, hang tight a little longer."

"Easy for you to say," he muttered.

He went back to the desk, once again half-sitting on its edge. I gentled my tone and tossed him another detail, additional reassurance that we were moving forward. "We plan to use the Lefebvre's drone to see if there's illegal digging around the old resort ruins. If the thieves are treasure hunters and the ephemera they stole contains the final clue they need to locate the rest of the Glass Widows, then they won't waste time before going on the hunt."

He nodded. "Searching up there sounds like a good move. I'm going to assume you haven't told the Lefebvres too much?"

"Of course not," I said. The term 'too much' was open to interpretation.

Graham's gaze met mine. "The Lefebvres are astute businessmen. Shrewd. A while back, Michael Lefebvre and the old man interviewed me. They managed to weasel out a few things I hadn't intended to share." He tilted his head, as if to agree with himself and said, "I like the Lefebvres. Well, at least, I respect them on several levels."

"I'm glad you feel that way." I let out a relieved breath. Michael was Tristan's father. He was similar in age to Graham. It was likely they knew each other from school or the Vermont Chamber of Commerce.

Graham stood up again, walked forward until he could look down at Kala and me. If I'd grinned like the Grinch earlier it was his turn now. "I think it's time we put a firm deadline on our little agreement. Come back and see me first thing Monday. I expect by then you'll have the names of the thieves. That is, if you want that information for your mother."

CHAPTER TWENTY-TWO

"At least that gives us five days," I said as we drove away from the Golden Stag. *No need to panic*, I told myself.

"More like four," Kala said. "It's almost five o'clock already. Today's pretty much shot. You do realize, if we owned our own drone, we wouldn't have to rely on anyone else."

Sweat dampened my armpits. "I really wish I hadn't said anything to Graham about the Lefebvres." I wasn't even going to touch her sneaky comment about us buying a drone. This wasn't the first time she'd suggested it, and it was no small expense.

"I don't think your mention of the Lefebvres bothered Graham at all."

"I guess." Maybe she was right. I kind of wished I'd asked Graham what the Lefebvres had weaseled out of him during the interview. That said, he hadn't seemed that concerned by it, so I assumed the information was something fairly harmless, like the fact that most items in his shop were always open to a ten percent discount.

The rest of the way home, Kala and I batted back and forth everything that had happened and the foreshortened timeframe we were facing. By the time we reached the house, my panic had subsided, replaced by sheer frustration with Graham. Why couldn't he back off and trust us to uncover the thieves in as short of time as possible?

The shop had closed for the day, so we went straight to the house and into the kitchen. Tuck was at the stove, apron tried around his belly, unbaked pie in his hands. He slid the pie into the oven. "You're just in time. Supper's ready and waiting. Later, apple pie for dessert."

The sight of him took my tension down another notch. I sniffed the air. Chicken soup. Homemade, my grandmother's recipe by the smell of it: bay leaves, fresh lovage, and oregano from our herb garden. "Everything smells wonderful," I said.

"When did you have time to do all this?" Kala asked.

"Crockpot magic and store-bought pie crust. Now, wash up. I'm hungry as a bear."

We used the kitchen sink to do as he'd ordered, then lined up in front of the crockpot, bowls in hands like kids waiting to be served.

Maybe I hated being ordered around by Graham, but Tuck was a different story. His telling me what to do was a welcome relief, even if it wouldn't solve all our problems.

The bowl warmed my hands as Tuck ladled in the soup, thick with chunks of steaming chicken and vegetables and tender noodles. After I carried it to the table, I opened a waiting bottle of chardonnay. I was about to start pouring when the slam of a car door reverberated from the driveway.

Tuck groaned. "Please, don't be an after-hours customer."

I glanced out the window in the kitchen door. A dingy-black Ford Escape had pulled up beside my Volvo. The car was unfamiliar, but as the driver got out, I leapt to my feet. "It's Shane!"

"I didn't realize he was coming over," Tuck said.

"Neither did I." I dashed out the door and jogged down the walkway. Even before I reached him, I could see his white oxford shirt looked like he'd slept in it. There were dark circles under his eyes, and he needed a shave.

I threw my arms around him in a hard hug. He hooked one arm around my waist, gave me a kiss, lips pressing warm and soft against mine.

He released me. "Hope you don't mind that I came over without texting first?"

"You've got to be kidding. My castle is your castle. You're just in time for dinner. Homemade soup. Apple pie." I'd planned on eating, then spending the evening going over what we'd learned, adjusting the whiteboards with Tuck and Kala, and reading more of Bucky's journal. But taking a break would help me gain distance, and that would likely be of even more benefit than rehashing everything. Besides, I was surprised and thrilled to have a chance to spend some time with Shane.

Shane rubbed a hand across the back of my shoulders. "A homecooked meal, followed by about twenty hours of sleeps sounds like heaven."

I rested my head against his shoulder as we walked toward the house. "I'm glad you're here."

"I have to be back at work early tomorrow," he said.

"I assume that explains the car?" Usually, he drove his personal Land Rover, or a black Challenger for work.

"The Escape wasn't my first choice, but it's kind of necessary for the case."

As we went inside, I decided not to ask him how things were going. Shane looked beyond exhausted, and probably would benefit from a break as much if not more than I would.

After Tuck served Shane a bowl of soup, I offered him a glass of wine. He turned it down and asked for milk, which Kala bounced up and got for him. After that, Shane wanted to know how our investigation was going. I told him about Marissa's connection to the wedding and about Stanhope and Joie being members. I didn't bring up the clubhouse security system or Sargent Nelson's presence there or our talk with Graham. Shane had enough going on with his own job without taking on our problems.

After he was done eating, Shane stretched and yawned. "I hate to eat and run, but I should get home. I'm totally spent."

"Don't be ridiculous," I said. "I'm not letting you drive anywhere." I got up, nodded toward the hallway. "The only place you're going is upstairs to bed."

Amazingly enough, Tuck and Kala didn't snicker or make any comments as I marched Shane out of the room. While he showered, I threw his clothes in the washer and fetched his gym bag from the old Escape, then changed the sheets on my bed in record time. Not that the sheets were gross, but a fur-covered dent in the pillows made me suspect Sandra had spent part of the day napping there.

Shane reappeared in my bedroom, dressed only in boxer briefs. His skin felt smooth and warm when I pressed my palms against his chest.

He cupped his hands over mine. "Are you coming to bed too?"

Desire stirred low in my body, but there was a hitch of vulnerability in his voice that told me lovemaking wasn't what he wanted or needed. "It's been a rough case, huh?" I asked.

He closed his eyes. "I just want to forget about it for a while. Human trafficking. It's horrible what people do to—"

I pressed a finger against his lips. "You don't have to explain."

While he got settled in bed, I undressed. After that, I joined him, pressing up close against his warm body. He rested the side of his face against my breastbone, and I wrapped an arm around him, cradling him tight.

We laid like that, warm and motionless, as the leaves on the tree outside my window rustled and silenced with the rise and fall of a brisk wind. Shane's breathing slowed. His shoulders relaxed. After a while, darkness filled the room and the glow of the old-fashion alarm clock next to my bed became visible...

I'm not sure when I fell asleep. But I woke up feeling as squished as one of the cheese and cracker sandwiches Kala had assembled in the golf course parking lot. Shane was cuddled against my front side, arm thrown over me, snoring gently. Something pressed against my back, something warm and furry, and drooling. Sandra.

Wiggling out from under Shane's arm, I rolled onto my other side. Sandra's nose and wide-open eyes were inches from mine. She belched, loud and apple-scented. She grinned, her patented guilty smile.

"Out," I commanded, voice hushed.

Head low, she skulked backwards off the bed. I followed her. Shane needed his sleep, and I needed to take his wet clothes out of the washer and run them through the dryer.

I blinked to adjust my vision to the dark, glanced at the clock. It was only a little after ten. Not late at all.

I snagged my bathrobe, threw it on, then padded downstairs with Sandra a step ahead. A glow of light and the murmur of the TV seeped from the living room, as did the melodic sound of Kala's voice. It sounded like she was on the phone, chatting with someone, most likely Pinky.

Quiet as I could, I tiptoed past the living room, down the hallway and through the kitchen to the laundry room. As I'd assumed, Shane's clothes sat in a wet lump at the bottom of the washer. No surprise. I hadn't expected anyone else to notice them and finish what I'd started.

I pulled out his jeans, underwear, and t-shirt, tossed them into the drier. If Tuck had spotted the load, he would've admonished me for not separating Shane's whites and darks. But it had been a small batch and I'd been in a hurry.

I checked the washing machine again and discovered his damp Oxford shirt stuck against the side of the drum. Its sleeves were still rolled up, just as they'd been when he took it off.

My mind drifted back to the first time I'd met Shane. He'd

been assigned as my probation officer, and I'd been a quivering ball of nerves when I walked into his office that first day. Still, I'd caught myself staring at his delicious, muscular and tattooed fore-arms—a devil on his left and an angel on his right—bared by what I soon learned were habitually rolled up sleeves. What followed between us was a slow build of friendship and desire, culminating on Labor Day weekend when we gave into our mutual attraction. He'd risked his job, and I'd risked violating my probation for a few days of pure bliss.

I tossed his shirt into the dryer. As I started it, a slow thud filled the small room, gaining momentum as my thoughts returned to Shane. He was beyond attractive. He was smart. Good at his job. Good at a lot of things. A man of conviction, and heart. Whatever he'd seen during the last few days had to be beyond horrible to rattle him so deeply. *Human trafficking.* Certainly not something most people connected to supposedly idyllic Vermont.

With Sandra on my heels, I left the laundry room and retraced my steps. But instead of going upstairs, I went into the downstairs library and quietly shut the door. Last night, I'd lingered over every word in Bucky's journal. I'd told myself I didn't want to miss any clue that might be hiding in his trivial day-to-day entries, and that I couldn't afford to let myself get overwhelmed or sidetracked by grief and things I couldn't change.

But in truth, I was a fast and a retentive reader. I could've easily gotten through more pages if I hadn't given myself an excuse. I was not that emotionally tender. And, if Shane could face the very present horrors he experienced at work, I could deal with the retrospective pain of my grandparents' deaths.

I turned on a standing lamp, then retrieved the journal from the safe. As I'd done all my life, I made myself comfortable on the window seat with my back against a cushion and my legs stretched out. The light from the standing lamp cast a bright circle around me. Beyond the windowpane, the distant honk of night-flying geese sounded under the whoosh of the wind.

Sandra nudged my arm with her nose. She glanced at the cushioned seat and whined.

I pulled my legs up, making room for her. I'd never get any peace if I didn't. Besides, her furry warmth felt nice against my legs.

With her settled in, I let Bucky's journal fall open to the piece of napkin I'd used to mark where I'd left off reading:

March 17. St Patrick's Day.

According to the entry, Bucky believed the day was lucky and made for Irish whiskey, not green beer. His luck theory proved true that year when he uncovered a hidey-hole full of Probation-era, vanilla extract bottles while replacing floorboards in the mudroom of his house. The bottles were almost valueless, but the discovery, especially on St. Pat's Day, tickled him none the less.

My fingers itched to flip back a few pages and make sure I hadn't missed something the last time I'd read. Instead, I forced myself to push forward, reading faster from date to date, taking mental notes of people Bucky visited and antiques he purchased. Nothing stood out to me through the rest of March and the first week of April.

April 10

Drove up to talk with Rob Tuckerman again. He's more of a scholar than this old bottle digger will ever be.

I swallowed hard. *Robert Tuckerman.* My grandfather. I'd expected Bucky to mention him. It only made sense, yet somehow it felt surreal to see my grandfather's name in black and white.

I pressed my fingers over the entry as if by osmosis I might feel Grandpa's presence or be transported back to that day in April. Where had I been when that visit between Grandpa and Bucky occurred? At school most likely. Perhaps down by the airstrip digging for bottles. For certain, I wouldn't have been riding around in Tristan's pickup. Our relationship had ended the previous schoolyear.

Taking a shaky breath, I moved on to the rest of the entry:

I showed Rob the Bible box and ephemera I picked up last weekend, and various other things related to the resort. He was as intrigued by the discrepancies I pointed out as I'd expected. We shook hands on a deal. We aren't going to make friends with this.

I read the entry again. It was intriguing, and ominous. Discrepancies? Ephemera? No doubt Bucky was referring to the Scandal Mountain Resort, and likely the Bible box that Graham had purchased. The summer before this entry, Bucky had found the Glass Widow and shown it to me. Had he and Grandpa decided to work together to find the rest of the bottles? What else could it be? Them teaming up would've made other bottle diggers uneasy for certain.

The fast beat of my pulse sang in my ears as I speed-read the rest of April and into May. Mixed in with Bucky's day-to-day entries, there were cryptic mentions of my grandpa and references to research and Victorian-era records. But Bucky never outright said they were on the trail of the cache. I also didn't find a single mention of Bucky butting heads with any other dealers or collectors over the Glass Widow or the Bible box of ephemera, nor a single suspect to add to our list.

A headache began to pinch at the back of my skull. I closed the journal and leaned forward, scratching Sandra behind the ears as I mulled over the entry. I'd always believed my grandpa and Bucky had a friendly competition over who'd locate the missing bottles first. But I never recalled Grandpa mentioning them working in conjunction to find the cache. Still, it was logical that it might've happened at some point—like on April tenth of that year.

I sat back up, drumming my fingers on the edge of the journal, thinking deeper.

Bucky was gone. My grandparents were too. I could—and would—read the rest of the journal. Maybe at some point in my reading, I'd even find a clue to who Graham's thieves might be, though I was starting to wonder if Bucky had purposely left certain details out of his journal.

I swung my legs off the window seat, sat with my feet on the floor, and smiled. There was another way to find out what had gone on between Grandpa and Bucky that April. There was someone still alive who'd know for certain: Doris Sanders, Bucky's widow.

Sure, that handshake-deal between Bucky and Grandpa might've had nothing to do with Graham's robbery. Then again, perhaps there was a connection. Either way, I wouldn't be able to live with myself if we didn't pursue this avenue. A visit with Doris wouldn't take much time, and it didn't preclude me going to the ruins with Tristan and his drone—though, with luck, it might make doing anything with Tristan unnecessary.

No question about it, first thing tomorrow we needed to visit Doris. The only problem was, for years she and Bucky had lived in their old farmhouse out on the edge of town, past the Jumping Café and even Townline gas station, way out on the end of Hill Farm Road. But now the house was on the market, and she'd moved to—

That was the issue. I had no idea where Doris Sanders currently lived.

CHAPTER TWENTY-THREE

Some information is hard to uncover. Some isn't. Or maybe Kala's skills were starting to rub off on me. Anyway, after Shane left for work the next morning, I sat down at the kitchen table across from where Tuck was eating his breakfast and googled local real estate transactions. Though Bucky's old house was still on the market, it seemed Doris Sanders had already purchased a unit at Hawk's Nest Senior Housing in the nearby small city of St. Albans.

I caught Tuck's gaze. "Kala plans on spending the day researching online. You want to come with me to talk to Doris? I could use the support. She's a bit..." I let my voice drift as I searched for a polite word to describe her personality.

"Crusty?" Tuck suggested.

"That's putting it mildly," I said. On the rare occasions when I had spoken with her, she'd never done more than grumble a few words.

Tuck set his coffee mug down, dabbed the corners of his mouth with a napkin. "Maybe I should bring a gift to soften her up?"

"Couldn't hurt." Tuck's standard gift was African violets and various other plants. He grew them in a makeshift greenhouse that he'd created by outfitting the bathroom shower in his bedroom suite with grow lights and a hydroponic watering system. His plants were prizewinning, and people loved them, especially the garden club ladies. But Doris? I wasn't so sure the technique would work on her.

* * *

St. Albans was a half-hour drive from our house, depending on the traffic. It was where Shane lived in an Adirondack–style cabin he'd built himself. There were dozens of shops and restaurants on the city's main street as well as a hospital, across from which stood the three-story Hawk's Nest building Doris Sanders had moved into. Hawk's Nest was nice enough, I supposed, well-maintained, with little balconies for each unit. Still, living in an apartment had to be a major change for her after spending decades in a rambling farmhouse surrounded by fields and forest.

Once we arrived, Tuck retrieved his specially prepared basket of African violets from the back of the car, then we walked through the building's front door and into a small foyer. A bank of labeled buzzers spanned one wall. Ahead, a set of glass doors with a security keypad next to them prevented us from going any further.

Cradling the violet basket in one arm, Tuck pressed the buzzer labeled 'Sanders'.

"Fingers crossed that she's home," I said.

A crackling sound came from the speaker as if someone where about to say something followed by silence. One second passed, then another...

Tuck pushed the buzzer again.

More silence.

I folded my arms over my chest. I had a sneaking suspicion someone was there, and we were being ignored.

Out of the corner of my eye, I caught movement beyond the glass security doors. A silver-haired gentleman wearing a driving cap set at a jaunty angle was stepping out of an elevator. As he headed our way, I recognized him. He was the gentleman Doris had sat next to at the auction, gripping his hand as if it were a lifeline.

He reached the glass doors, they slid open, and I greeted him with a smile. "You're Doris Sander's friend, right?"

Not hiding his wariness, the man studied me and Tuck from beneath the brim of his cap. His eyes went to the violets, then he said, "Are you friends of hers?"

"Her husband was a friend of my grandfather's—Robert Tuckerman. We wanted to ask her about a project they worked on together." Considering he and Doris were apparently close, it seemed wiser to give the full reason for our visit.

Tuck added, "We brought her a housewarming gift. I'm sure the changes haven't been easy for her." He looked at the man more directly. "And you are?"

"Gilbert Vanderschmidt. Doris and I are cousins."

My mind went to Bucky's journal. Bucky had mentioned asking Gilbert to help with his freezing pipe issue. This had to be him.

Gilbert nudged his cap up, revealing a high forehead. "This isn't the best time. Doris has had a lot of visitors this week. News people. The police."

"About the robbery?" I asked.

"That and how much everything sold for at the auction. She's exhausted from all the hubbub."

"We understand." Tuck's voice was as warm and assuasive as a mug of hot cocoa on a cool morning, "I realize you were about to leave, but would you mind seeing that she got this?" He held out the basket of violets.

Gilbert hesitated, then took it. "I guess it couldn't do any harm."

"Thank you," I said.

Gilbert stepped to the panel of buzzers. "Let me talk to Doris. Maybe she is up for a short visit." Balancing the basket in the crook of one arm, he pressed the button.

This time Doris answered right away. "What's going on?"

"They're some nice people here to see you. They're—" Gilbert glanced back and raised a shaggy eyebrow in a silent question.

"Robert Tuckerman's son and granddaughter," I said.

Doris's voice crackled through the intercom. "Whadda they want?"

"They have a housewarming gift for you."

"Don't want 'em up here." The speaker silenced. Then it crackled again. "I'll come down."

Gilbert stepped away from the intercom. He glanced back at it and hushed his voice as if uncertain whether Doris was still listening or not. "Her reluctance isn't just because of the hubbub." He pressed a hand against his chest. "The other night, after the sale, Doris confessed she feels guilty."

"Guilty? About what?" I said. He couldn't be talking about the robbery. Doris feeling bad about that made no sense.

"I shouldn't say anything," he said. "She told me in confidence."

Tuck crossed his heart with a finger. "We won't breathe a word."

Gilbert took a fresh grip on the basket. "Bucky wasn't an easy man to live with—headstrong, drinking, always being gone to an antique show or flea market. I realize, a lot of people loved him…"

"And?" I prompted as his voice trailed off.

"He could be very frustrating."

I nodded. I could relate to that. Loads of people—especially men—thought my mom was the best thing ever. But she often frustrated me to the max with her self-centeredness. I could see how Bucky might've similarly aggravated Doris. But that didn't explain her feeling guilty.

Gilbert began to speak faster. "In the months before Bucky

died, Doris spent a lot of time at her sister's house. She wanted to teach him a lesson for leaving her alone so often, and for refusing to follow the doctor's suggestions. I'm not sure if you know, but Bucky'd had a series of mini-strokes. When he died, Doris was so angry with him for not taking care of himself." He looked down, silent for a moment. "She was so overwhelmed by his death that it took her five years to accept that she needed to sell the old place and move into a less isolated location. Even then, the grief and guilt hit her hard when she was cleaning out the house with the people from Fisher's Auction. She's still mad at herself for being away the day Bucky had his fatal stroke. She believes, if she'd been there to call an ambulance, he might be alive today."

I looked at the basket of violets in his hands, focusing on the plants' soft pink and lavender blooms as thoughts of my own culpability tossed in my mind. I could totally relate to the feelings that led Doris to walk away and leave Bucky to deal with his own problems. After my mom had been charged with art forgery, I'd been so angry with her that I'd stayed in New York and avoided even thinking about her situation. Truth be told, I'd wanted to punish Mom for her failings.

Gilbert's voice drew me from my thoughts. "Here she is."

Doris was emerging from the elevator—a slightly heavy woman in a rumpled fleece top and matching pants. Double chin. Short gray hair. Pretty much exactly as she'd appeared at the auction.

As she walked into the foyer, her mouth and eyes pinched. "What's this about?"

I stepped forward. "I don't know if you remember me—"

"Saw you at the auction. Tuckerman's granddaughter," she snapped.

It was clear Doris wasn't in a mood for pussyfooting around, so I didn't waste time on pleasantries. "Before Bucky passed away, do you remember anyone trying to buy the Glass Widow bottle or

Scandal Mountain ephemera off him—like the brochures in the Bible box?"

"Tons of people tried." She scoffed. "Most of 'em didn't even care enough about him to show up at his funeral." She hesitated. "You and your mother were there."

I nodded. She was right. We had gone to the funeral. "I liked Bucky. He taught me a lot." As my chest squeezed, I shifted the conversation back where we needed it to be. "Were there any people Bucky didn't trust? Someone who stands out in your mind?"

"That Bascom woman from the museum. Bucky told me to watch out for her. 'She can afford to buy what she wants' is what he said."

"Joie Bascom?"

"That's her. Just before Bucky died, she pestered him nonstop about donating things."

I wasn't positive, but I assumed that was around the time Joie became the museum director and attained financing for the new Mountain House Resort exhibit. It made sense that she'd wanted to buy local pieces, the cheaper the better. And, from what I'd seen, tactfulness wasn't part of Joie's style any more than it was Doris's.

I moved onto to other suspects. "How about Marissa Lavelle or Sparky Collins? Do you know them?"

"People like them were always in and out of our house, trying to buy this, dickering over that, asking where he found that Glass Widow bottle. We wouldn't have had any income if they weren't." She thought for a second. "That Collin's boy did 'lectrical work for us. He liked to trade doing a job for bottles."

Tuck spoke up. "How about break-ins? Did anyone ever steal odd things, like Bucky's record books or journals?"

She snorted. "Fat chance they would've found them. Took me six months to locate all the paperwork I needed for the tax people.

Receipts in the living room, notebooks and papers in the kitchen, the pantry, everywhere except his desk."

Gilbert smiled wistfully. "Do you remember the time he cleaned out that old jelly cabinet? There were old newspapers and open canning jars of this and that everywhere. Ketchup, peaches, tongue pickles…"

Doris scowled. "After he dumped the mess in the compost, every yellowjacket within a hundred miles moved in. I hate those nasty, stinging, good-for-nothing wasps."

I shuddered. Just thinking about a compost pile buzzing with yellowjackets gave me the heebie-jeebies.

Doris's gaze cut from Gilbert and the basket of violets to Tuck. "No sense leaving 'em. I kill plants."

I bit my tongue to keep from saying anything. I'd seen this coming.

"They aren't difficult to keep," Tuck said, voice soothing. "Maybe Gilbert could help you care for them."

Gilbert gave the basket a little shake as if to entice her into taking them. "I'd be happy to lend a hand."

Doris harumphed. "Whatever." Her eyes came to me. "If you don't have nothing more to ask, you might as well head out."

I slid my hands into my pockets, locked my knees. She might've been ready for us to go, but I wasn't done. Not without asking one more thing, something more personal to me. "Just before my grandfather died, he was working on something with Bucky. Do you know what it was?"

She went still. "That was a long time ago."

"Please, try to remember."

Fine beads of sweat appeared beneath her bottom lip. She wiped them away with the back of her hand. Her tone turned even more gruff. "Don't remember anything like that."

CHAPTER TWENTY-FOUR

When we arrived home, five cars with out-of-state license plates were parked in front of the shop, more customers than we usually saw at one time.

"Well, now. That's a good sign," Tuck said.

"For business, yeah. But I bet it put a damper on Kala's research time." I opened the Volvo's door and got out. As we walked toward the shop, Sandra appeared from behind a cast iron bench that sat nearby. She shot a few daggers my way, then trotted through the shop's open doorway ahead of us, nose in the air like a snubbed princess.

Tuck laughed. "Somebody's mad at you for leaving her behind."

"I'm not supposed to be her babysitter. Kala's the one who wanted a pet."

"Looks to me like Sandra's picked a different best buddy."

"That maybe, but she's going to have to learn the world doesn't revolve around her. Besides, Bill will be reclaiming her one of these days." Or at least, so I hoped.

Inside, we found Kala behind the front counter. One strap of her overalls had slid off her shoulder. The bandana holding back her hair was cockeyed. A customer stood in front of her, tapping one foot impatiently as Kala thumped her fist against the credit card machine.

Kala spotted us. "Thank goodness you're back. This darn machine is misbehaving—again." She jerked her chin upward, indicating the book loft. "There's a man upstairs interested in a pair of Bradley and Hubbard bookends. They're in the locked case. Could one of you take the keys up and give him a hand?"

"No problem." Tuck grabbed the shop keyring from under the counter and headed for the loft.

Kala grimaced. "And, before you ask, *no*, I haven't even opened my laptop. It's been busy the whole time you've been gone."

"Don't worry about that. I'll check and see if any of the other customers need help." I started toward where I could hear people talking at the back of the shop. Kala would have the credit card machine fixed in a jiffy now that she didn't have to split her attention between various people and jobs.

Not that I had a lot of patience for customers myself at the moment. On the way home, Tuck and I had agreed that Doris lied when she claimed to not know Bucky and my grandpa were working on something together. I really wanted to talk to Kala about that. But income producing business had to come before our pro bono work for Graham. I just hoped the entire rest of the afternoon wouldn't be a wash as far as our hunt for the thieves.

As I realized one way we could still make headway without neglecting customers, I did an about-face and rushed back to the front of the shop. Kala had already gotten the credit card machine running and moved on to wrapping the woman's purchases in tissue paper.

"I'll be right back." I dashed past her and out the door. It was vital that we found time for online research, but it was equally negligent to not comb through the ephemera we'd gotten from Graham, and that was something we could work on in-between customers.

Moving fast, I opened the library safe and whipped out the document box full of ephemera we'd gotten from Graham, leaving Bucky's journal behind. I'd read more of that later. Right now, we needed a project we could breeze through as a team.

When I got back to the shop, the customer Kala had been waiting on had left.

"Want to help me sort stuff?" I asked. "I'm thinking, we can start by separating things connected to the Glass Widow or the resort from nonrelated items."

She grinned. "Easy-peasy."

We cleared off the top of an old farm table by the front window, then piled the ephemera in the middle of it. Though we only had a portion of what I'd seen in the Bible box at the auction preview, there were more pieces than I'd expected—tons of newspaper clippings, invitations, calling cards…

"I'm putting definitely not important stuff here." Kala set a birthday card from the 1950s on the far end of the table.

"Perfect." I set a Victorian-era quack medicine booklet about a third of the way down the table. "This is the 'maybe' area."

"Look at this." Kala held up a cabinet card.

I glanced her way. "Is that an aerial view?"

She read the back. "It says, 'Scandal Mountain. 1883. Beaumont Photography.'"

My pulse jumped, hammering from excitement. "That's the year the resort burned!"

Snatching the card from her, I studied the surprisingly clear image. The mountain was less forested than nowadays. Not a shock, since the photo had been taken over a century and a half ago. Two thirds of the way up the mountain, the Old Coach Road meandered past what appeared to be a hill farm and a tiny cemetery. A little further along the mountainside, it passed a large building surrounded by smaller structures—the Mountain House Resort and the nearby Maiden Springs—before winding down toward the valley floor, Scandal Mountain village, the river, and the railway tracks, already established by that time.

The crunch of car tires against gravel drew my attention to the window. A blue van was pulling up in front of the shop. A van with a familiar logo and sign.

Sparky Collins
Master Electrician
Serving Central Vermont

My gaze darted to the ephemera on the table. My sorting plan was great, except I hadn't counted on one of our top suspects stopping by and discovering where the balance of the Bible box contents had ended up. Nothing good could come from that.

"Hide everything," I whispered to Kala. "I'll go slow him down."

I hurried out the shop door just as Sparky lumbered from his van. I skidded to a stop inches in front of him. "Hey, great to see you again."

He staggered back a step and grabbed hold of the van's doorframe as if my overeager entry had made him rethink whether to stay or flee. "Nice to see you too."

I thought fast. I had to keep him out of the shop. "I've a great old bottle in the house I'd like to show you. It's from Scandal Mountain Pharmacy. Spearmint green. No damage. Have you ever come across one?"

"Spearmint green?" His eyes widened with interest.

"I might sell it for the right price." I tilted my head to reinforce that it was inside our house and not in the shop.

He remained unmoving with his hand clamped on the van's doorframe. His eyes scanned the distance between us and the house's back door. What was taking him so long to decide? I'd just offered him a look at a rare piece and a chance to get inside our house, where there might be other treasures of interest to him.

Not that I really intended to sell him anything from our personal collections.

"Do you mind bringing it out here?" He glanced at his feet, clad in rubber boots big enough for a man twice his size. "I stepped on a nail about a week and a half ago. I'm not getting around so great."

A sore foot? I tried to bite my tongue but failed. "You looked fine when I saw you at the museum, and at the auction too."

"Damn thing developed an infection. Blew up like a balloon. It's still full of hot pus."

I cringed at the description. But if he really was in that much pain, how had he expected to get around in our shop? Plus, being hurt just before the robbery seemed like a mighty convenient defense.

Sparky let go of the van door, turned, and slid a cane out from beside the driver's seat. Balancing on it, he said, "I've been doing some work for the museum, that's why I was there." His demeanor was calm, but his need to explain came across as unnecessary, and, once again, perhaps defensive. Was that why he was visiting us? Had he discovered we were working for Graham and wanted to make himself less culpable? He continued, "I stopped to ask if you'd heard anything more about Graham? Is he doing okay?"

I forced my arms to stay loose at my sides and smiled. "I assume he's fine. Why? Did you hear something?"

"I stopped by the Golden Stag yesterday. Some ditzy younger woman was watching the store. She pretended like she didn't know anything about Graham's condition or the robbery, but I could tell she did."

"That would be Alison, Janet's granddaughter," I said. "She just started working there." I nodded at the iron bench Sandra had been hiding behind when we'd gotten home. "How about we sit while we talk?"

Without waiting for his response, I stepped in that direction.

I'd have preferred to stay entirely away from the topic of Graham and the robbery, but it didn't look like that was possible.

I glanced back to make sure he was following. He wasn't. He was galumphing straight toward the open shop door. "I haven't looked around your place in ages."

I veered away from the bench, rushing to head him off. "If you want to wait out here, I'll get that pharmacy bottle for you to look at. Spearmint green."

"I'll just poke around while you—" He stared at the open shop doorway as if frozen by the headlights of an oncoming train.

Sandra stood on the threshold, hackles raised, eyes trained on him as she lifted her upper lip in a silent snarl.

Sparky's Adam's apple bobbed. "Does—does it bite?"

I bit my tongue, holding back a snicker. "I'm so sorry. She's supposed to be locked in the office during business hours." I gestured at the bench more emphatically this time. "Sit. I'll ask Kala to secure her."

Sparky hobbled to stand beside the bench while I took Sandra by the collar and dragged her into the shop. I wanted to give her a huge hug and kiss. Instead, I said gruffly, "Kala, would you mind locking the dog in the back room?"

"No problem." Kala finished draping a tablecloth over the ephemera, then came over. She whispered, "Sandra's the best girl ever, isn't she?"

"Sure is," I said.

Sandra smiled, all her teeth showing.

As Kala led Sandra away, I went back to where Sparky was standing. "I'm sorry about that. Now where were we? Ah, yes, Graham's robbery."

"Have you heard any rumors about who might've done it?" he asked.

"Someone told me Marissa Lavelle might be involved." I watched closely for his reaction.

He blinked, blinked again and laughed, a nervous guffaw. "Whoever you've been talking to is nuts."

"Then who do you think did it?" I asked.

"One of Graham's ex-girlfriends. Could've even been that Alison woman." He took a fresh grip on his cane and rubbed his leg. "I'm going to have to take a raincheck on seeing that spearmint bottle. My foot's throbbing like a toothache. I need to get home, soak it, take something for the pain." He glanced nervously toward the shop door as if expecting Sandra to reappear at any second. "Guess I should get going."

I nodded. "I'll let you know if I hear anything about the robbery."

"Thanks. I'm just curious."

"Like everyone else," I said.

CHAPTER TWENTY-FIVE

As I went back into the shop, Sandra winged out from behind the front counter to greet me. I crouched, letting her wiggle and lick my face as I murmured, "You're the best old lady in the world. Yes, you are."

Kala walked over. "She's one smart dog."

"Definitely." I stopped hugging and got to my feet. As I helped Kala remove the tablecloth she'd used to hide the ephemera, I told her about Sparky's foot and his defensive reactions during our conversation. "All I know for sure, is that I'm glad he's gone."

We fell silent as Tuck came down from the loft with the last remaining customer. Tuck was carrying the cast iron Bradley and Hubbard bookends—a nice pair shaped like baskets of flowers and priced at just over a hundred-and-fifty, if I remembered right. The customer was holding a first edition copy of *Poems of Childhood* illustrated by Maxfield Parrish.

Parrish. I shuddered. Would I ever be able to think of him without remembering a replica of his work had sent my mom to prison?

While Kala went back to sorting the ephemera, I joined Tuck and the customer at the front counter, wrapping the book and bookends while he cashed them out. No sooner were they gone than Kala let out a squeal. I turned to see what was going on. She had a catalogue-size tourist brochure clutched against her chest and was wriggling like a kid in desperate need of a bathroom. "You won't believe what I found! Seriously, you won't," she said.

Tuck and I rushed over. "Better than the aerial view?" I asked.

Tuck frowned. "What aerial view?"

"While you were upstairs with the customer, Kala found an aerial view of Scandal Mountain from 1883. Done by Beaumont Photography."

Tuck's face brightened. "I believe they have one from that time period at the town museum. I wonder if the views are exactly the same."

"Forget about the aerial." Kala thrust the brochure at me. "Look what's inside this."

The brochure was notably heavier and thicker than made sense. I let it fall open to where a business size envelope was stuck between its pages. It was dotted with yellowish-brown stains, and Bucky's address was written on its front in cursive handwriting, large looping letters with an unmissable right-hand slant.

I gasped. "I can't believe it."

"Well, now," Tuck said. "That is a surprise."

"It is the one you've been going on about?" Kala asked.

"No question about it." I turned to Tuck. "You and Graham made photocopies of everything while Kala and I were searching outside his house. How could you have missed this?"

He shrugged. "I'm not sure. But we didn't actually go through everything with a fine-tooth comb. After we did a dozen or so items, Graham stopped being fussy and we started only copying the front covers. You didn't think we had enough time to go through every page of every brochure and journal, did you?"

"I guess I didn't think about it."

"As long as Graham was happy with doing an abbreviated job,

I wasn't about to argue." Tuck waggled a finger at the envelope. "What are you waiting for? Open it."

My hands trembled as I freed the envelope from the stray adhesive that had secured it to the inside of the brochure. As I cradled the envelope, my thoughts went back to Christmas mornings when I was a child. I'd sit at the top of the front hall stairs, waiting for permission to run down and see what Santa had brought. Mom, Tuck, and my grandparents would already be in the living room. The tree would be lit. The smell of coffee and bacon would hang in the air, and cranberry muffins, sweet and tart and melting with butter. Waiting on that stair had always been so hard, and there was always that knot of fear in my stomach. Would the gift I longed for be waiting under the tree? Or would I feel the sting of disappointment and have to pretend to be happy?

"Hurry up. Open it," Tuck said.

I weighed the envelope on the palm of my hand. "It's too heavy to only contain a pressed plant and writing paper. It feels like...cardboard."

Kala moaned. "Just open it, alright?"

"Okay, okay." I flipped the envelope over, ran a fingernail along the seal, breaking it open. I wiggled the contents out. It was a hand-tinted photograph mounted on card stock, a Victorian-era cabinet card. The dots weren't from spores. They were where chemicals from the photo had seeped through the paper.

Tuck bent forward. "What's it a picture of?"

"It's a man and a woman sitting on a wicker settee. There's an urn—" Uncertain I was seeing right, I studied it again. Slightly older man. A chubby woman with a long neck. "It looks identical to the photo we found in the crate with the bottles. George Fielding and Sophie Stebbins. *The Betrothal*. At least, I think it's the same image. This one's colorized."

Kala wheeled away. "I'll get the other photo from the office so we can compare."

In a second, she returned with the mouse-chewed cabinet card and a magnifying loupe. She set the photo and loupe on the table, and I set the other photo beside them.

"Looks like a match to me," Tuck said.

My entire body tingled, every cell screaming with excitement that the photos were both old and right. At the same time my instincts nagged at me. They were a match, but something was off.

I tilted my head, studying the cabinet cards like they were a 'spot the difference' puzzle. I'd loved those games as a kid. I suppose it was a predecessor to my love of spotting defects or the lack thereof in antiques.

The photo we'd found in the crate full of bottles was sepia-toned and raggedy. The one from the envelope was colorized, and essentially undamaged except for the few places where the photography chemicals had transformed into dots of stain.

The real difference finally jumped out at me. "I can't believe I didn't see that instantly!"

"What is it?" Kala asked.

I pointed to the urn. "What do you see?"

Tuck picked the loupe up off the table. Using it, he leaned close to the photos, examining one, then the other. He wiped a hand over his mouth, made a humming noise as if thinking. "In the un-colorized image there's roses, apple blossoms, bells of Ireland. There's an addition in the colorized one. Dark purply-blue." He straightened, stepped back from the table.

"Is it monkshood?" I asked. A chill traveled the length of my spine. Floriography, the symbolism of flowers, was a big deal to Victorians. Tuck knew more about it than I did, given his love for old floriculture books. All I was certain of was that monkshood was poisonous and generally had a negative connotation. "Why would anyone add those to a betrothal photo?"

"They wouldn't have been." He used the loupe to take another look. "Maybe they're meant to be purple gladiolas."

"They don't look like glads to me," I said.

Kala cleared her throat. She was holding the envelope. She gave it a meaningful glance. "You might've found the photo, but you missed something."

I snatched the envelope. A small, pale yellow Post-it clung to the inside. Unlike the moment I'd savored before opening the cabinet card, this time, I immediately took the note out. The handwriting on it was heavily slanted to the right, unquestionably my grandfather's.

I read it aloud:

"You're right. Altered. Just like the shoeprint card."

CHAPTER TWENTY-SIX

That evening Tuck, Kala, and I gathered in the dining room to go over the whiteboards. The burning question wasn't *how* all the information we'd compiled fit together, but *if* it did.

Kala twiddled a dry erase marker between her fingers as she studied the boards. "I added a couple of new suspects after we watched the video with Tristan," she said.

"Like who?" I asked. The whiteboards were so covered with names and notations it was impossible to tell what was older and what was added recently.

"Kaitlyn O'Connell for one," she said. "You remember 'Kaitlyn the Whisperer' from the museum? Red hair. Historical outfit. Blocked Graham's view when he was trying to bid at the auction."

I slapped my forehead. "I almost forgot about her."

"That's why we have the boards." Kala pointed to where Kaitlyn's name was written directly beneath Joie Bascom's. After that she moved on to the 'D' is for 'Doubtful' column. "I added Doris, Gilbert Vanderschmidt, and Frenchie Lefebvre. They were all at the auction."

I shook my head. "I can't see old Doris, Frenchie, or Gilbert tottering across the golf course in the middle of the night to steal back things Doris used to own."

"Stranger things have happened," Kala said. "What if Doris didn't realize Bucky's personal journals were in the Bible box until they went up for sale? What if she was afraid of something private coming to light?"

I shrugged. "I guess that's possible. But what about the mexxy? I can see Doris beaning Graham on the head with a frying pan. Slipping him street drugs? Not likely."

Tuck spoke up, "I wouldn't rule out any of those Lefebvres doing something underhanded to get a news scoop or a woman. But I can't see someone like Frenchie risking the reputation of his family and the *Gazetteer* by doping Graham with drugs, not to mention the robbery."

I rocked back on my heels, thinking and looking at the board for a moment. "We should add a note about Sparky's foot injury somewhere. If he was hurt before the auction like he claims, then we can rule him out as incapable of physically hiking to Graham's house."

"That doesn't mean he didn't take down the golf course's security system," Tuck said.

"I'd say he's the most likely suspect for that." Kala added Sparky's injury to the board. Then, she wrote *Alison* under the 'M' for 'Maybe' column.

"Alison? Janet's granddaughter?" I frowned. "Why would she risk stealing from Graham? She had a job interview with him the next day. Clearly, she plans to stick around the area. Remember— the local ex-boyfriend she's getting back together with?"

"You said everyone at the auction was a suspect and you saw her in the parking lot," Kala said. "You also said Sparky suspected her."

I countered, "Yeah, but Sparky could've been trying to throw us off the track."

Tuck hardened his voice. "We don't know anything about

Alison's background, and she could've found out about Graham's nighttime habits from her grandmother. Her ex-boyfriend could be a lowlife."

I huffed out a breath. "Alright. Alison's on the list, as well as her mysterious ex. I only wish we knew the motive for the robbery. That would make figuring out this suspect thing a lot easier."

"There aren't really that many possible motives," Tuck said. "Either someone wanted the Glass Widow and ephemera for their antique or historical value, or they're treasure hunters trying to piece together clues so they can locate the cache of missing Widows."

Kala set the dry erase marker down, looked at me. "My vote goes to treasure hunting thieves."

"There's one giant hitch in that theory," I said. "Assuming the ephemera and old photos can be used to find the cache, then why didn't Grandpa and Bucky locate it?"

Tuck's voice quieted. "Your grandparents' death was a shock to everyone. It might've thrown cold water on the whole venture as far as Bucky was concerned. They were good friends."

"Bucky was a hardcore bottle lover," I said. "He would have finished the hunt in Grandpa's name if anything."

"What's to say Bucky didn't find the bottles?" Kala asked.

I shook my head. "He would've told everyone if he did. He'd have even pestered the Lefebvres until the story ended up on the front page of the *Gazetteer*. Bucky had more than a little ego. Plus, the publicity would've led to more people wanting the bottles, which in turn would've driven up their individual value."

"I suppose you're right," she said.

I glanced at the whiteboards. "The way I see it. We need to divide and conquer." My gaze went back to Kala. "How about if you take a deep research dive into our buddy Sparky—and Marissa Lavelle, we can't let her slip between the cracks."

"We shouldn't forget Dr. Stanhope," she said.

"That's for sure." I rubbed the back of my neck, stalling for a second. "I'm not sure either of you are going to like my next suggestion."

Tuck's eyebrows lowered as he frowned. "That sounds ominous."

I laughed. "I'm not talking dangerous. I'm concerned it could be a rabbit hole to nowhere."

Kala eyes brightened. "I love rabbit holes. What are you suggesting?"

"I think we need to make a trip to Scandal Mountain Museum and check out the Mountain House exhibit."

"I don't know why you'd think that could be a waste of time," Tuck said.

"Because it doesn't make sense how a tragedy that happened over a hundred years ago could help us identify modern-day thieves, and that is our goal, right?" I blew out a breath. "It's just… My gut keeps saying there's a connection in there somewhere between the addition of what looked like monkshood to the cabinet card of Sophie Stebbins and George Fielding's betrothal, and Grandpa's note about it being altered like the shoeprint card."

"Don't forget the bloody shirt went missing from the museum." Kala pointed to where it was noted on a whiteboard. "Nowadays, DNA from that shirt might be able to prove whether the right or wrong person had been accused of the fire and George's murder."

Goosebumps peppered my arms at the thought of anyone being demonized and hanged for crimes they didn't commit. Still, why would anyone care if that truth came to life now? Everyone involved back then was long gone.

A voice inside me whispered—*because it could change history.*

I shook off that thought. The shirt had been gross and ratty. It might've been tossed in the garbage by mistake, or even thrown out on purpose by someone who didn't like seeing it on display.

I stood up taller. "Alright. It's settled. Tomorrow we'll jump down the museum rabbit hole."

CHAPTER TWENTY-SEVEN

My plan for the night was to finish reading Bucky's journal. There was no way of escaping what that meant. I'd be reading about the day my grandparents died. I thought I'd braced myself for this over the previous nights of reading. Still, a sense of dread weighed in my chest as heavy and cold as a mountain of broken glass.

As I turned away from Tuck and Kala, readying to leave the dining room so I could fetch the journal from the library, my phone rang.

Mom.

I frowned at the caller ID as the ring came again. She usually called the house phone number. Hopefully, depending on mine wasn't going to become a habit—

A voice murmured in the back of my mind. *Mom was living at home when Grandma and Grandpa died, and for months before then. She might remember Grandpa talking about the altered photo, and about his and Bucky's partnership.* Okay, so this call might be perfect timing, though I suspected mentioning the Glass Widow would only net me another conversation about how tragedy followed in the bottle's wake.

I waved to get Tuck and Kala's attention, then answered with the phone on speaker. "Hey, Mom."

"Last night's art class was fabulous!" She skipped right over any kind of greeting and started in mid-conversation. "It was so startling. Emotional." Her voice cracked. "I'm blessed. Most prisons wouldn't allow this. That's why my lawyer insisted on making this location part of the plea agreement. The women…"

I pulled a chair out from the dining room table and sank down into it as she chattered on. I longed to steer the conversation in the direction of Grandpa and Bucky, but there was no way to get a word in edgewise. She babbled about the paintings the inmates were creating and what she believed they symbolized, and what the women told her of themselves as they painted. She sounded buoyant and dizzyingly excited, which would've made me happy if her tone hadn't bordered on manic. Was her over-the-top mood caused by her new medicine?

I glanced at Tuck. His brow was wrinkled. He caught my eye and shook his head. I wasn't the only one worried.

Mom's tone dropped to a more normal level. "Not that I think any of the inmates have real talent."

I smiled and so did Tuck. That sounded more like Mom. Maybe she'd just had one too many coffees.

While I had the chance, I shifted the conversation. "Remember the other day we were talking about the Glass Widow?"

"Yes. I never liked that thing."

"Back before Grandma and Grandpa—before the accident—do you remember if Bucky and Grandpa were working on anything, maybe hunting for the other bottles?"

She made a little clicking sound with her tongue as if thinking. "I had lots of art shows around that time. I was out of the country some."

I pressed harder. "Did Grandpa ever mention doing research for Bucky?"

"Your grandfather was always interested in the resort's history. He must have taken you up there, right?"

"Yeah, lots of times." Though this wasn't the exact direction I'd wanted the conversation to go, I couldn't help but think back to hiking to the resort ruins with Grandpa, up the mountain trail, past Maiden Spring's stone grotto, and then down to where the remains of the burnt-out resort haunted an overgrown field, as eerie and picturesque as any abbey ruins in Scotland. It was on one of those hikes when Grandpa first showed me how to use a metal probe to test potential bottle digging spots, how to carefully wriggle the rod down into the soil, to feel the slight clink of reverberation as much as to hear when the probe's tip touched glass. That said, Grandpa and I never did any serious excavating at the resort ruins, back when we could've gotten permission to do so, or even afterwards, for that matter.

"Your grandfather took some wonderful aerial photos of that area," Mom said, wistfully. "He was planning on taking more once all the leaves were off the trees." She clicked her tongue a few times. "I seem to recall him and Bucky going over those aerials with a fine-toothed comb."

I smiled. *Aerial photos of the ruins and surrounding area.* For sure Bucky and Grandpa were using them in an attempt to locate the cache of Glass Widow bottles, it made total sense. And now that I thought about it, I did faintly remember seeing aerial photos, the same sweeping view of the mountainside and ruins that Tristan's drone would reveal. I just hadn't paid as much attention to them at the time as I should've. I asked Mom, "You don't happen to know where those photos are?"

"In with your grandfather's papers, I assume." Her voice hushed, hesitant even. "Tuck mentioned coming to visit me on the fifteenth. I'd love to see you, too."

I swallowed a lump in my throat. The prison she and her lawyer had negotiated for was in Connecticut. Not a short drive. Still, Tuck had visited Mom once a month since the start of her incarceration back in May. My excuse for not going had been that Kala was a newbie and needed help watching the shop. In reality, my reluctance—at least at first—centered on my belief that Mom was responsible for her predicament. But since then, my feelings had mellowed. Soon I'd hopefully have what I needed to get her released early. Truth was, if I saw her in person, it might alleviate my worry about her state of mind, including that new medication and its possible side effects.

I let out a quiet exhale. "Yeah, I plan on coming down with him."

"That's wonderful!" she said.

As I calculated how many days I had before the visit, the full ramifications of my promise hit me. Today was September ninth. The fifteenth was less than a week away. Graham had already given us a short deadline, and I'd just made sure begging him for an extension couldn't buy us more than a day or two, not if I had to be in Connecticut to visit Mom. I certainly hadn't made the world's smartest move.

CHAPTER TWENTY-EIGHT

I settled down at the dining room table, my elbows on its surface, Bucky's journal open in front of me. At the other end of the table, Kala tapped away on her laptop, searching for dirt on Sparky, Marissa, and our favorite doctor, Stanhope. Tuck had gone upstairs to hunt for grandpa's aerial photos.

Reading quickly, I went through May and into June. But as the end of June approached, my reading speed slowed, and my mouth dried. I glanced toward the hallway. If I went to the kitchen, I could get drinks for Kala and me, iced tea or beers. I could also make a side trip to the bathroom—

I clenched my teeth and forced myself to return to reading. Drinks or bathroom trips might put off the inevitable, but they weren't going to black out the upcoming entry.

A sick feeling gathered in my stomach as I read the rest of the page. Bucky had drinks at the Jumping Café with my grandpa. Grandpa was going to an antique show in New York state the next day. He had a lead on a Scandal Mountain cabinet card. The word: "altered" followed by a question mark was scribbled in the margin next to that mention, as if added at a later date.

I wiped a hand over my mouth, thinking. Was this cabinet card the one in the envelope? Maybe Grandpa addressed the envelope because he planned to mail it to Bucky from New York state, then decided to hand deliver it? Still, why hadn't Bucky opened it? And what did the Post-it Note included in the envelope with the photo mean—*"You're right. Altered. Just like the shoeprint."* It seemed more than likely that both mentions of altered referred to the same thing.

As I turned to the next page, closer to the day of my grandparents' death, the rustle of the paper in the silent room seemed as loud as the rumble of a crowded flea market.

July 1

Maine Antique Show. Bar Harbor. Perfect weather. Brisk sales. Arrived home to a stack of damn bills.

There was a possible answer to one of my questions. Perhaps, Grandpa dropped the envelope off at Bucky's house while he was away. It could've ended up at the bottom of that bill pile.

The tension in the pit of my stomach crept upward, gripping my chest. I looked up from the journal to stare at the dining room wall. There, a nineteenth century oil painting of our home hung beside a midcentury watercolor of Scandal Mountain Valley, and a charcoal of an ancestor in a carved oak frame...

Memories pushed into my mind. Grandpa. Grandma. Mom. Tuck. All of us, sitting around the dining room table. Laughing. Debating. In front of us, cut glass bowls of chilled pickles and black olives, and baskets of warm homemade rolls waited. There was always a golden-brown roast turkey at Thanksgiving. Mouthwatering prime rib on Christmas Day. Black pepper-crusted ham for Easter. And, ten years ago, all three meats laid out on ironstone platters when the crowd came to pay their respects after my grandparents' funeral. Tuck had been there that day, by my side through it all.

I squeezed my eyes shut and pressed my fingers against their lids. Without Tuck, I'd have had no support. Mom had been a drama queen the day of the funeral. Conspicuously absent at first, then making a sympathy-grabbing entry worthy of an Academy Award. I'd been so angry at her. Angry at everything.

Gritting my teeth, I opened my eyes and looked back at the journal. There was no time to wallow in the past. I had to keep reading.

The next two journal entries were about weather and household chores.

I turned another page. *July 10*

Tears dampened my eyes as I scanned the entry:

Robert and Mary's plane crashed this afternoon. Hard to believe they're gone. It's impossible to make sense of it. Robert was a good pilot. The weather was clear.

I wiped the tears away with my fingers as a sudden rise in curiosity overrode my grief. For me, the day of the crash and the weeks that followed were a blur of numb-nothingness interrupted by emotional moments acid-etched into my subconscious forever, like the hard lines of an Albrecht Durer print. Was it possible Bucky had recorded things I'd forgotten from that time; things that helped him make sense of what happened?

July 19

I blinked at the date of the next entry, then double checked.

Nine days later? That was strange. Up until then, he'd never gone any more than a day without making at least a short note.

Resting the journal against the edge of the table, I read that entry:

Hot as hell. Ninety in the shade. Basement remained cool. Bottled up some of Doris's dandelion wine. Robert and Mary's memorial service is tomorrow. Aviation investigation says they would have survived the crash, except a faulty carburetor caused the plane to explode on impact. The manufacturer had issued a recall notice for the part. Can't believe Robert didn't replace it. Can't believe they're gone.

I vaguely recalled the aviation investigator visiting our house. His report had made the *Gazetteer's* front page and gone viral on social media. I'd been so devastated. Why hadn't

Grandpa done the repair? Why hadn't Grandma pressured him into it?

July 21

Cooler, Seventy and partly sunny. Packed away papers and photos in Bible box. Don't need another funeral to tell me it's a road better not taken. RIP, old friend.

I thought for a moment. It sounded like Bucky had taken all the ephemera he and Grampa had gathered in their attempt to locate the bottles and simply put it aside. But giving up that easily didn't seem like the obstinate, Bucky I had known. It seemed more like him to do a couple shots of Wild Turkey in my grandpa's honor, and then press on harder with their treasure hunt. But perhaps I hadn't known Bucky as well as I thought. Perhaps, Tuck's suggestion was right: my grandparents' deaths had thrown cold water on the hunt as far as Bucky was concerned. Mom thought the bottles were cursed.

Still... Something didn't sit quite right.

I reread the entry. *A road better not taken.* A play on the line in Robert Frost's poem. What exactly did Bucky mean by that? It sounded like he was more than simply being disheartened. And there still was the unanswered question of why he hadn't sold the ephemera—if he'd decided not to pursue the hunt.

Scrunching my toes for luck, I went on to the next page. Hopefully, I'd come across answers to those questions.

August 15

Rainy. Mid-seventies. Scored big today. Grand Isle estate sale. Got in two days early. Purchased a pair of fabulous Lake Champlain decoys and an Iodine Springs bottle in attic-clean condition. Haven't bought either in more than a few years. Found a couple of good canning jars in the back of a not so wonderful jelly cupboard.

August 16

Sold the decoys. Solid profit. Keeping the Iodine Springs bottle for now. Took Doris out for lobster dinner to celebrate.

I hunched forward, flipping through the journal's remaining

pages, looking for answers... *September. October. November. December*. Months of day-to-day nothing. I'd thought I knew Bucky—a brilliant—albeit stubborn and eccentric—antique dealer and bottle digger who defined independent and determined. Then again, I'd been a teenager and a fan-girl of his at the time—

"Bingo!" Kala's shout shook me from my thoughts.

"What did you find?" I scrambled to my feet and went to look over her shoulders.

Kala was on the Vermont Judiciary Public Portal website. She tapped the screen with a glittery orange fingernail.

"Sidney James Collins—Sparky the Electrician—has a DUI on his record."

"Unfortunately, that doesn't make him a thief or say he's got drug connections," I said.

She swiped a finger across the screen and a new page appeared. "How about this? Misdemeanor possession—cocaine."

"That's more like it."

Kala picked up her phone. "I'm going to text Pinky and see what she knows about him."

"Great idea." In fact, I was surprised we hadn't thought of doing it to start with.

While she texted, I told her about Bucky's reaction to my grandparents' death, how he'd given up the hunt for the cache of bottles and, as far as I could tell, never returned to it.

She put her phone away, gave me a hug. "I can't imagine how hard it was for you back then. Losing your grandparents like that."

I rested my head against hers for a moment before wriggling free. I took a deep breath. "I need to take a break. Maybe have a cold beer. I don't know what I expected to find in the journal, but Bucky tossing everything aside wasn't it."

"Maybe this calls for nachos along with the beers?" she suggested.

I laughed. "Yeah, that would help."

We left the dining room and were almost to the kitchen, when the back door slammed opened and Pinky's voice called, "Anybody home?"

Kala bounced toward her like Tigger in *Winnie the Pooh*. "So, what do you have on Sparky Collins?"

"Slow down. You texted me what, two seconds ago?"

"More like five minutes."

While I preheated the broiler and set to work making the nachos, Pinky spilled the dirt, "From what I hear, he used to party a lot when he was younger."

"How about now?" Kala asked.

Pinky went to the fridge, took out two beers. After she handed one to Kala, they sat down at the cluttered kitchen table. "I'm assuming you want to know if Sparky could have access to mexxy?"

I slid the nachos under the broiler, waiting for them to brown as I listened to Kala and Pinky debate the likelihood of Sparky getting his hands on the drug. As an electrician he did have contact with a wide group of people. But, according to Pinky, mexxy wasn't a drug normally seen in blue collar circles, and if Sparky was anything it was blue collar.

I spoke up. "When I overheard him and Joie talking in the museum parking lot, they mentioned a doctor. I assume it was Stanhope since Joie's golf-buddies with him."

"If someone above suspicion like Stanhope were making mexxy," Pinky said, "he might be able to get away with it for a long time."

I took the platter of browned nachos out of the oven and set it on the table between her and Kala.

"Those look amazing," Kala said.

"They're super-hot, so watch out." I shook my head in amazement as she and Pinky attacked the snack like old ladies snagging jewelry off a church bazaar table.

I got a beer from the fridge for myself, then joined them, sipping my drink while they chowed down. Once the food was gone—and Sandra, who'd appeared out of nowhere, had claimed her plate-licking rights—Pinky sat back in her chair and told us what else she'd heard. It seemed Bill had learned via his job that the South Burlington police were turning up nothing, and seriously considering that Graham might've faked the robbery so he could collect the insurance money and sell the bottle and ephemera on the sly.

Picking at the label on my beer, I considered that possibility. I'd laughed off the very same theory way back when Shane and I were at the pond giving Sandra a bath, just after Graham called to say he wanted to talk to me. However, it was a logical conclusion, and it made as much, if not more sense than the mishmash of minutiae we were trying to piece together. Still, my gut, and that voice at the back of my mind, insisted Graham wasn't misleading us. He was furious about the robbery, suspicious of his own illicit connections, and willing to betray whoever'd setup my mom in order to discover who'd dared drug and steal from him. It also sounded like he had a right to be skeptical about the job the police were doing.

My mind went back to Bucky's journal. This time the whole line repeated in my head. *Don't need another funeral to tell me it's a road better not taken.*

What the South Burlington police were suspecting might have not rung true to me. But that line, it rang out loud and clear. It held the truth. If only I fully understood it.

CHAPTER TWENTY-NINE

The next morning it was raining, sluicing down, driving the autumn-bronzed leaves from the trees, and turning the parking area in front of our shop into a mudslide. We'd even put on full rain gear and boots just to walk to the shop.

Kala turned from where she stood looking out the shop's front window, coffee mug in hand. "I doubt we'll have many customers today."

"Maybe it'll get busy later," Tuck said. "The rain's supposed to stop by noontime."

I smiled, slow and devious. "Sounds like the perfect morning for a trip to the town museum. And that's number one on Kala's and my agenda, right?"

Kala tapped a finger against the side of her head. "My mental to-look-for list is ready to go."

The phone on the front counter beside me let out an old-fashioned *brrring*.

I answered. "Scandal Mountain Fine Arts and Antiques. Edie speaking."

"Any leads yet?" Graham's voice boomed from the other end, snarly as anything.

I motioned to Tuck and Kala. Mouthed, *Graham*. Then put the phone on speaker.

"Don't tell me you have nothing new," Graham said.

"Rumor has it the police suspect insurance fraud." No sooner was it out of my mouth than I regretted not biting my tongue.

"Who told you that?"

"None of your business," I said.

"Do I need to remind you that you're working for me."

My face went hot. Tuck rested a hand on my arm, a signal for me to calm down.

I took a deep breath. "I didn't say we believed it. The other day you said yourself that the police aren't putting a lot of effort into the case." Even without seeing his body language, I was certain Graham's anger was real, and that frustration was at its root. I could relate. I'd had false accusations flung at me before, and it wasn't any fun. "Why do you think the police are focusing on you?"

"Lazy, maybe. I don't know." This time a slight hesitation in his voice made his words less believable. He was avoiding telling me something, and I had a sneaking suspicion I knew what.

I kept my voice level. "The truth. Why?"

There was silence. Finally, he said, "I've got enemies."

Kala slapped a hand over her mouth, smothering a snicker. She whispered, "That's putting it mildly."

"Like who?" I asked. Graham had admitted before to not fully trusting his less than savory business connections. But it was time for him to give us names that might help us connect the dots.

Graham snarled. "What is that boyfriend of yours saying?"

"Shane's not involved at all." I rephrased my question. "Who's your number one suspect? If you want the thief's name by Monday, we need to know."

Silence again. A solid five beats of it. "Joie Bascom. The odious bitch confronted me after I bought the pieces. She was upset that I dared bid against her." His voice sounded strained, as if he spoke through clenched teeth. "I was still on the museum's board when they were hunting for a new director. I advised them not to hire her. The woman's not fit to clean the museum's toilets, let alone run it. Her so-called fancy degree's from some rubbish Podunk college. The only thing she has going for her is that one of her ancestors came over on the Mayflower."

The Mayflower bit jived with what I'd heard about her connections and ability to raise money, but the education part didn't. "I thought she went to some Ivy League school."

"That's what she'd like people to believe."

His voice ended on a slightly calmer note. I quieted my voice as well. "I'm glad you told me those things. Every little detail helps." Something occurred to me. If Graham was on the museum board of directors at that point, he might be able to verify Tuck was right about the timing of another vanished artifact. "Do you know when the bloody shirt from the resort tragedy went missing from the museum?"

"Must have happened after I left the board."

"When was that?" I asked, hoping to narrow the timeline.

"Not long after they hired Joie Bascom. Are you sure it wasn't deaccessioned? It was in horrid condition."

"All we know is that it happened around the time the Mountain House exhibit was updated," I said.

His tone sharpened. "Not on my watch, then." He huffed out a breath. "Enough of this chitchat. You have until Monday morning to get me the names of the thieves."

Clenching my teeth, I glanced toward the front window. As impossible as it seemed, the rain was sheeting down even harder. Sandra materialized out of the gray, streaking across the parking area and toward the shop door. Kala opened it and the dog raced inside. She shook, and water and mud drenched the floor and splattered onto a stoneware display.

"Damn mutt," Tuck grumbled.

I swiveled away, my back to them and voice toughening.

193

"Felix"— I'd never called him by his first name, and it sounded odd even as I said it—"We'll figure out who stole your things. I promise."

"Good. If I have to find someone else to locate the thieves, you won't get that information you want. That's my promise."

I ground my teeth. Jerk. Jackass...I longed to call him any number of names. But that wouldn't get us anywhere.

I pulled my shoulders back, straightened my spine. *Stand tall, Edie. You can do anything if you put your mind to it,* my grandma would have said. I took a breath, readying to reply calmly—

Graham hung up before I could say a word.

CHAPTER THIRTY

Kala had towel-dried Sandra in the shop. Still, she'd gotten rain-soaked again on the way to the car and an unmissable doggy odor wafted from the Volvo's backseat as we drove toward the museum. Sandra wasn't the only one who looked a bit scruffy. I glanced away from the slapping windshield wipers and at Kala. In her yellow rain slicker and old slouchy hat, Kala looked like she was headed off to work on a fishing trawler rather than to browse at a museum.

She caught me looking and scowled. "No judging. If yellow vinyl is good enough for Paddington Bear, then it's alright by me."

I laughed. "Whatever you say." I really shouldn't have picked on her. My hooded windbreaker and scuffed work boots weren't exactly high fashion.

Kala swiveled in her seat, facing me. "Do you think Joie and Kaitlyn the Whisper could be lovers?"

"No way. Joie's married to some muckety-muck banker guy. Besides, she's old enough to be Kaitlyn's mother."

"So? Married society queen, young lover. Happens all the time. Them being secret lovers was the first thing that occurred to me when I saw them together on Gramp Lefebvre's video."

"You've been watching too many *Midsomer Murders* episodes," I said. As a rule, Kala's taste ran to horror movies, but lately she'd been mixing in British mystery shows.

"Do you have a better theory?"

"Mentor and eager minion," I said, only half joking.

When we reached town, I turned onto Old Post Lane. As I slowed before entering the museum's back parking lot, I noticed Tristan's pickup in its usual spot in front of the Gazetteer office. I smiled to myself as I remembered how just the sight of it had sent my teenage hormones racing. It was weird how things like a truck or a mineral springs bottle could bring back such strong memories.

I steered into the museum parking lot. It wasn't particularly full, and I found a spot right away. After I pulled up the hood of my windbreaker, I jumped out of the car. Then, Kala and I dashed through the rain, up the museum's walkway, past the private rear entry and the building's castle-like turret, skirting rivulets of water until we reached the front steps and went inside.

A metal coat rack was set up in the entry. As I took off my windbreaker, I glanced through the entryway's inside doors. Kaitlyn O'Connell was behind the ticket counter. Her pale, waxy complexion combined with the gray and sepia somberness of her Victorian outfit made it looked like she'd stepped right out of a cabinet card. Her red hair provided the same colorful addition as the spike of purply-blue monkshood in Sophie Stebbins and George Fielding's betrothal photo.

"Vermont's a weird place," Kala whispered.

"How so?" I got my coat situated on a hanger.

"Most places there're hardly any gingers. Around here there's a ton of them."

"A lot of old families have Irish and Scottish heritage." I slid my coat in next to her slicker.

"I thought everyone was related to the Fishers or French-Canadian."

"My family isn't either of those things, and we've been in town since way back. We just—Well, we just haven't had as many babies."

Our footsteps echoed against the marble floor as we went through the inside doors and into the vaulted atrium. To our left, a stunning, six-foot-tall cow weathervane stood atop a reproduction cupola. A folksy mural of Scandal Mountain village spanned the opposite wall. Footsteps and the distant clamor of voices drifted in from nearby rooms and the floors above.

Kaitlyn smiled as we approached. "Welcome to Scandal Mountain Museum." The corners of her mouth arched downward as we walked closer. She looked directly at me. "I recognize you," she said. "You were at the auction the other day."

"Yeah, I only ended up buying a couple of things." I avoided her scrutinizing gaze by glancing at Kala. "I'll pay for both of us."

"Thanks," Kala said.

Kaitlyn rang up our tickets. "That'll be fifteen dollars. I gave you the Scandal Mountain resident discount. You both live in town, right?"

I nodded and thanked her. As I took out my debit card and let the machine scan it, I thought of the perfect excuse that would allow us to ask a variety of questions without making her wonder if we were up to something. "I'm working on a coffee table book about Vermont springs water bottles. I want to include a chapter on Maiden Spring and the Mountain House resort. I was hoping to talk to Joie Bascom. Is she in?"

"Ah—" Her gaze darted past me to a door near the weathervane. A sign beside it read:

Research Room
By Appointment Only
Archives and Library

Her eyes winged back to mine. "Sorry, Joie's not in today."

I pressed my lips together to keep from smiling. Kaitlyn the Whisperer was lying. I was certain of it. Then again, maybe I was overthinking her reaction. Maybe it was standard practice to not reveal if specific people were working. I sweetened my voice. "That's too bad. I guess we'll have to rely on the exhibit. I haven't been here in a few years. I hear it's expanded a lot."

"It's our pride and joy. You're in for a treat." She gestured at the elevator and the museum's grand staircase, offering a choice of routes. "It's on the second floor. The room at the end of the corridor."

Kala and I headed for the elegantly curved staircase. Halfway up, she glanced my way. "That coffee table book? Might not be a bad idea."

"You could be right." That was if we unmasked the thieves and brought this situation to a happy ending.

We reached the top of the staircase and went down a corridor. A room to our right was designed to resemble the interior of a Depression-era schoolhouse. A couple of families were gathered near a chalkboard, listening to a lecturing docent.

I tucked my hands in my pockets and kept walking down the hallway.

Kala leaned close. "I noticed a security guard in the room back there, but I haven't seen any others."

"I doubt you will. This isn't exactly a high budget place."

"I'm surprised more things haven't disappeared," she said.

We walked past a couple more exhibit rooms featuring quilts, antique clothing, railroad memorabilia… Straight ahead, the end of the corridor was blocked off by a twelve-foot-high, sepia-toned image depicting Scandal Mountain towering over the village. 'Murder in the Mountains: A Victorian-era Mystery' was written on the banner that spanned its middle.

"That looks a lot like the photo we found in with the ephemera," Kala said.

"I'd say it's identical to that cabinet card." I hurried my steps.

To the left of the giant blowup was a voluminously curtained entrance and a placard introducing the exhibit:

On May 10, 1883, the daughter of a wealthy New York glass manu-facturer stepped off the train in the village of Scandal Mountain. Along with her wedding trousseau, she brought a most unusual dowry. So begins the tragic story of the Mountain House Resort...

I snagged Kala's hand, pulled her through the curtains and into the enormous, but hazily lit, exhibit room. The air was cooler than in the corridor, fresh and gardenia scented. A soft recording of piano music and a woman singing *Comin' thro' the Rye* quavered in the background.

"Looks like we've got the place to ourselves," Kala whispered.

"For now," I said.

I scanned the room. Previously, the Mountain House exhibit had only consisted of the shirt, a couple of the amber-brown bottles, and a few of the crime scene photos crammed into a narrow cabinet that was shoved against a wall in the museum's turret. Now, a vast array of floor to ceiling, glass-fronted displays were devoted to the same purpose. Each display had a backdrop created from a blown-up Victorian-era photo. In front of the backdrop, realistic mannequins in historically correct outfits posed amid a setting overflowing with antique objects. The results were shockingly lifelike. If nothing else, Joie was a master when it came to bringing history to life.

"Wow!" Kala said, as we walked to the first diorama. It depicted a railway station complete with plank walkway and lampposts. A short, homely, plump woman in a bustled dress stood on the platform, surrounded by suitcases, trunks, and a stack of wooden crates stamped *Stebbins Glass Works*.

I read the placard. "Sophie Stebbins' arrives for her wedding. May 10, 1883."

Kala took out her phone and began snapping photos. I wasn't

sure if the museum allowed that or not, but I didn't care. They might come in handy later. And Kala was a much better photographer than I was.

I swiveled around to look at a freestanding display of bottles from various Vermont mineral springs. Near the top of the display, a trio of rare, amber-brown Mountain Resort bottles stood surrounded by warped shards of glass recovered from the resort ruins.

My chest squeezed. The very top of the display was crowned with a 3D mockup of a Glass Widow. It wasn't a bad reproduction, but it was easy to see why Joie Bascom had lost her cool when she'd confronted Graham. The lack of a real Glass Widow, a bottle that by rights should have been the exhibit's crown jewel, was painfully obvious.

"Look at this," Kala called out.

She'd moved on to the next diorama: a portrayal of a home wedding including several dozen elegantly dressed guests, plus the bride and groom: Sophie and George Fielding, a bewhiskered and paunchy older man.

My gaze went to the back of the scene, where a bespectacled younger man leaned heavily on a wolf-headed cane. According to the diorama's legend the man was Jeb Warner, the pharmacist Sophie was having an affair with.

While Kala photographed the wedding scene. I was drawn to the next diorama. Narrower than the previous two, it portrayed Jeb Warner behind the front window of his pharmacy along with an extensive display of Vermont medicine bottles. I rubbed an excited chill from my arm as I studied the bottles—some clear, some brown, some blue…embossed, paper labeled, mouth blown, machine made. I'd seen a lot of them before. I'd even unearthed some of them from my favorite digging spot down by my family's airstrip.

"I kind of feel sorry for all of them. Even Jeb Warner." Kala's voice tugged me back to the here and now.

"What I never understood was why Jeb Warner got involved with Sophie. There's no question she was unattractive. He was a single, successful pharmacist. Why go to the extreme of murdering your secret lover's new husband?" I said.

Kala aimed her camara, took a shot of the pharmacy diorama. "I vote for—horny, repressed woman messes up by bonding with an equally randy social outcast—who just happens to be a psycho."

"I can't see any other explanation," I said.

The next display featured local brochures and calling cards from that era, including some like those I'd noticed in the Bible box when I previewed the auction—only these pieces were reproductions, enlarged to make them easier to read. Along with them were a handful of actual brochures and local postcards.

The light in the room grew even more shadowy as we approached the next scene. The backdrop was a period photo of the charred remains of Mountain House Resort. The foreground depicted a parlor draped in black funeral bunting. Sophie stood alone, dressed in mourning clothes, next to a casket.

Kala took a quick photo of it, then rushed on to the last diorama: the likeness of the county courtroom. It was the largest of all the displays, packed with people in action—outraged townsfolk, a long-faced judge, an angry jury—and a visibly pregnant Sophie weeping as guards hauled Jeb Warner from the courtroom in leg irons.

A freestanding legend gave an abbreviated summary:

Jeb Warner was found guilty of murdering George Fielding and starting a fire to cover up his crime. The fire killed a dozen guests who'd stayed overnight after attending Sophie and George's wedding. The next day was scheduled to be the resort's grand opening where the guests would have received the Glass Widow mineral springs bottles as mementoes of the occasion. After the conclusion of the trial, Sophie was put on a train to Upstate New York where she and her child lived out the rest of their natural lives in isolation.

My gaze went to a heavily carved oak table set close to the

front of the diorama. On it was a display of the original crime scene cabinet cards, paired with modern enlargements. "Check this out," I said to Kala.

She leaned in, eyes wide. "You told me they took crime scene photos back then, but I haven't had a chance to look at any online. I never dreamed... They're really gruesome and fascinating."

She was right. Several of the hand-colored cabinet cards showed George Fielding's scorched remains laying in a charred bedroom on a semi-burnt Oriental carpet. Another was a close up of what appeared to be a gunshot wound to his head.

Kala shuddered. "They're surprisingly good. I'm also surprised anyone dared go into the building to take photos. It must've been ready to fall in at any moment."

"I suspect the notoriety was worth it," I said.

Curious, I check the attributions: *Original photograph by Louis Beaumont Photography*. The same photographer who'd taken the betrothal photo we found in the crate of bottles as well as the colorized one in the mysterious envelope my grandfather had addressed to Bucky.

A creeping sense of being on the cusp of a major discovery made my heartbeat quicken. But I didn't dare say aloud what my instincts whispered out of fear it would vanish into thin air.

Silent, I scanned the rest of the display, looking for one other infamous piece of evidence from the trial—the bloody shirt.

A modern photo of the rag-like, yellowed shirt fragment that Tuck and I had both remembered from previous trips to the museum was displayed next to an original cabinet card showing the same shirt at the time of the trial.

The placard that went with them read:

*Formal, blood-splattered shirt found by police
in storeroom of Jeb Warner's pharmacy.
*Note handstitched label identifying it as belonging to Warner.
(Original cabinet card photograph by Louis Beaumont Photography)*

I squinted through the glass. Only part of the shirt's label was visible in each photo, but it was there nonetheless, stitched to the inside of the collar. Condemning evidence.

To the left of the photos, a cabinet card showed a sooty shoeprint on a burnt carpet with a pattern identical to the rug where George Fielding's body lay. Next to the shoeprint was a mysterious second imprint, the size and shape of a silver-dollar.

Photos of imprints left by a shoe and a cane's ferrule (tip).
*Note lopsidedness of shoeprint.
Matched shoes and cane used by Jeb Warner,
whose leg was crushed in a childhood riding accident.

More condemning evidence.

Love affair with Sophie. Bloody shirt. Cane tip. Shoeprint.

Shoeprint.

My mouth dried and I could hardly breathe. I closed my eyes for a moment, thoughts whirring as I visualized the Post-it Note that had been stuck inside the mysterious envelope. *You're right. Altered. Just like the shoeprint card.*

"Kala," My voice rasped, "Do any of these crime scene photos look altered to you?"

"You're thinking about that note from your grandfather."

She'd caught on. "Exactly," I said.

She took a photo of the shoeprint cabinet card, enlarged the image, then scrutinized it. "I can't tell if anything's off. The show-case glass is distorting the image. But I don't see how it can't be the shoeprint your grandfather was referring to. Your grandpa wouldn't joke about something like this, would he?"

"Never. And especially not to Bucky when they were working together."

"Back then, the jury must've been totally wowed by these photos," she said. "They're pretty sensational."

Steepling my fingers, I pressed them against my lips and

scanned the cabinet card photos again. The burnt body, the shoeprint, the shirt…

There was one last photo in the diorama. It was a colorized image showing Jeb Warner lying in a coffin with bruises around his neck from being hanged for his crimes, and his wolf-head cane at his side.

I turned to Kala. "I can't help thinking Grandpa and Bucky stumbled onto something. The shirt going missing from the museum only adds to the mystery. Still, even if the shoeprint photo was altered as part of a setup, and even if DNA from shirt could now prove Jeb was innocent, who'd care about it a century and a half later?"

"One of Jeb's descendants?" Kala suggested.

"I suppose, but why steal the shirt? Even if you had a DNA test done and could match it to someone, stolen evidence isn't something you can wave around in public."

Kala bit her lip and smiled. "Did you notice anything interesting in the wedding scene?" She glanced back at the diorama of Sophie and George in the living room.

I grimaced apologetically. "I got distracted by the pharmacy bottles."

"Luckily, I didn't." She grinned. "There was a betrothal photo on display that reminded me of the cabinet card from the envelope—but that's not the weird part."

She had my full attention now. "What was it?"

"Beaumont took the betrothal photos. He took the crime scene photos too. But none of the wedding cabinet cards on display are labeled as being done by him. Isn't that strange?"

"Yeah, maybe. Who took the wedding shots?"

"Someone named Alonzo Harlow, from Montpelier, Vermont. It just seems odd—some swanky New York City photographer travels all the way out to rural Vermont to take betrothal photos, then returns to take the crime scene shots. But he didn't do the wedding, which took place the previous day?"

"Maybe Sophie and George didn't like the betrothal photos, so they hired Harlow to take the wedding ones." I was with Kala on this. It was weird, especially since the wedding happened only hours before the crimes.

"I'm adding look into Harlow and Beaumont to our to-do list," she said.

"That's a good idea. But I don't think we can afford to go down that rabbit hole right away. I can't begin to see how it could possibly connect to Graham's robbery—and that needs to be our focus." I nodded in agreement with myself. "I think our next step after this should be to go to the resort ruins and see if anyone's up there treasure hunting."

"Okay, Kala said, "but I still wish we knew who took the bloody shirt."

My gaze went to the courtroom scene in front of us, then down the line of dioramas, scanning back to the exhibit's beginning.

I thought for a moment. "Tuck never said he knew for certain that the shirt was stolen. He just said it 'vanished.' Graham thought it might've been deaccessioned. What if Graham's right? Or Joie could've put the shirt in storage because it was too fragile for display."

As another possibility seeped into my head, my eyes went to a door partly hidden by the velvet curtain framing the exhibit's entryway. If I wasn't mistaken, it hid the door that led to the turret room. What if the old display cabinet and the shirt were right where they had always been, simply deserted because neither was up to the quality of the new displays.

I took off at a sprint.

"Where are you going?" Kala called out.

The door to the turret was painted black to make it blend in with the surrounding wall. A small sign hung at eye-level:

Private. Do not enter.

I eased the door open. The space beyond the threshold was dark, except for faint light shafting in through the turret's narrow windows. As I stepped deeper inside, the floor was rough and gritty beneath my shoes, it definitely hadn't been polished and cleaned like in the rest of the museum.

My toe bumped something. *A loose floorboard*, I told myself. *Nothing to worry about.*

Kala's hushed voice came from beside me. "We shouldn't be in here."

I held a finger to my lip. "Shh…This won't take—"

A voice boomed from the doorway behind us. "This area isn't open to the public!"

Crap! It was Kaitlyn—apparently Not Always a Whisperer.

I swung around. "Sorry. We thought—"

"We thought it was the way to the restrooms," Kala said, as she slunk back toward the door.

I held my ground, met Kaitlyn's hard glare. "We wanted to see Jeb Warner's bloody shirt. Last time I saw it, it was back here in an old display case. It was always my favorite thing in the museum." Sometimes the truth gets you further than a lie.

"There are photos of that shirt in the courtroom diorama. Didn't you see them?" She rested her hands on her hips, "The shirt itself was actually stolen by some kids—three or maybe four years ago."

"Really, kids?" I said. I supposed the shirt was creepy enough that teenagers might've swiped it as a Halloween prank or maybe for some social media dare. Still… "Are you sure?"

"Who else would take something like that? It's not like it had any monetary value." Her scowled deepened. "This area's off-limits a good reason. It's not safe. Just over a week ago, a workman stepped on a spike back here. Drove it straight through his foot. You're lucky you haven't stepped on one, yet."

A workman? "Are you talking about Sparky Collins, the electrician?" I asked.

Her eyes widened with surprise, telling me I was right, but she said, "That's none of your business." She folded her arms. "If you're done snooping, perhaps it's time to go."

CHAPTER THIRTY-ONE

"So, Sparky didn't lie to us," I said to Kala as we whisked our raincoats off the museum coatrack and flung them on. "He was hurt before the robbery like he said."

We dashed out of the museum and toward the parking lot. The rain had stopped, but torrents of muddy water rushed every which way.

Kala slowed her steps. "That doesn't mean Sparky wasn't involved in the robbery. Even with a bad foot, he could've taken out the golf course security system and provided the mexxy."

"That's true. But it's unlikely he was physically involved at Graham's house." I stepped off the curb and into the parking lot. "Do you think I could have misunderstood the conversation I heard between him and Joie?" I stopped walking. "They were standing right here. I was coming across the street from the *Gazetteer* office."

"Refresh me, what exactly did you overhear them say?"

"Joie mentioned cash. Sparky said it was preferable, and the doctor would appreciate it. I assumed they were talking about Stanhope getting his cut for the robbery. But now we know for certain that Sparky got hurt while working at the museum.

Maybe it had nothing to do with Stanhope or the robbery. Maybe Joie wanted to avoid claiming his injury on the museum's insurance, so she offered him a cash settlement. She might've not wanted the museum to go through an OSHA safety review."

"That actually sounds logical," Kala said.

As we started toward the car once more, my eyes were drawn across the street. The *Gazetteer*'s front door was open. The flag was out. Tristan's pickup was still parked on the curb. "While we're this close, we should arrange a time with Tristan to take the drone up to the resort ruins. If we're going to see if anyone's treasure hunting, it needs to happen soon."

Kala plucked at the sleeve of her raincoat. "Fine by me, but I'm dropping off this nasty yellow tent in the Volvo first."

"What happened to, 'if it's good enough for Paddington Bear then it's good for me?'"

"Do I really look like the Paddington type?"

I laughed. Yeah, she was much more the See-No-Evil monkey type.

By the time we reached the car, Kala had already shed the raincoat. As she opened the door to toss it inside, Sandra bulldozed her way out and sped toward the crab apple tree where she'd previously feasted.

"Get back here!" I shouted after her.

To my surprise, Sandra made a reluctant U-turn, then slunk back.

"Poor, baby," Kala said. "It's not fair to leave her stuck in the car. Put her leash on. There's no reason she can't come with us to see Tristan."

Sandra looked up at me, her sad-puppy eyes matched by the pout on Kala's face.

I groaned. "Like I have a choice."

I ended up not only surrendering to their whims, but with leash-holding duty as well. Sandra dragged me through the balance of the parking lot and across the street. Seriously, how could one old, white-faced dog tug that hard?

As we started up the *Gazetteer's* walkway, a woman's voice screeched out from inside the building. "You wouldn't dare!"

Tristan's voice growled. "Just try me."

"I—I gave up everything." She sobbed.

I turned to look at Kala. She was already staring at me, eyes wide in dismay.

"Let's get out of here," I whispered, too late.

The sobs now came from right inside the doorway. The woman was about to come out. No way could we retreat to the car without being seen.

Grabbing Kala's wrist with my free hand, I yanked her and Sandra off the walkway and to a thick cedar hedge that ran along the side of the *Gazetteer* building. Whatever was going on between the woman and Tristan, I suspected it was something he'd rather not have overheard.

Thankfully, Sandra came along willingly. No sooner had we ducked behind the cedars than the stomp of high heels against wet pavement sounded, then stopped. The woman's voice rasped. "Haven't I proven anything to you?"

"Get the hell out of here or I'll call the police."

She huffed. "Fat chance of you doing that."

I leaned forward, peering between the cedars as the woman came into view: tossing her hair back, hips swiveling as she strutted down the walkway toward a compact car that was parked in front of Tristan's pickup. The way she was flipping her hair and strutting she looked like a scorned reality TV star, except for her clothes. At least from behind, it appeared she was dressed like a boarding schoolgirl. Long cardigan. Knee-length pleated skirt. A baby Miss Marple—

I clamped a hand over my mouth to keep from gasping. *Holy freakshow!* It was Janet's granddaughter Alison.

CHAPTER THIRTY-TWO

Hidden behind the cedar hedge with Kala and Sandra, I stood, pulse pounding, thoughts reeling. Tristan and Alison. It was hard to believe. No, it was impossible to see them as a couple.

"Was that who I think it was?" Kala whispered, as Alison flounced into her car.

I shook my head. "I just don't get it. She's not his type at all."

"Are you sure Tristan has a type? Some guys—and women, for that matter—aren't fussy."

The compact car's tires squealed and the stench of burning rubber filled the damp air as Alison took off, speeding down Old Post Lane.

"Maybe it had nothing to do with romance," I said.

Kala snorted. "Yeah, right." She glanced toward the Volvo. "Let's get out of here."

"What if Tristan sees us leaving? That would be awkward."

"Why? He was the one fighting with the crazy lady."

"I suppose." I licked my lips, rethinking the situation. "Let's just wait a second, then do what we came here to do."

"It's your call," Kala said.

I secured Sandra's leash to a cedar branch—I'd intended to let her come with us, but now it seemed wiser to not complicate the situation—before Kala and I emerged from our hiding spot and walked slowly toward the *Gazetteer*'s front steps.

To my surprise, Tristan was still in the doorway, glaring off in the direction Alison's car had taken. He jumped as if startled when he noticed us. "Where—where did you two come from?"

"We were on our way in to see you when"—I cringed—"when we overheard you and her."

He closed his eyes, jaw tensed. "I'm so sorry. I—"

The bang of a door slamming against a wall reverberated from the office behind him.

"Shit," he muttered.

Frenchie stormed into view, face red, madder than a wet hornet, as my grandpa would have said. "What the hell was all the shouting about! Your father and I were out back talking with the advertising rep we just hired. I won't be surprised if she quits after hearing that ruckus." His eyes went to me and Kala.

I held my hands up, warding off his anger. "Don't look at us. We just got here."

He turned back to Tristan.

Tristan cleared his throat. "She is—was..."

Frenchie glared at Tristan. "Spit it out."

I looked down, face hot with empathy for Tristan.

"She...I went out with her two maybe three times—back in college," he said.

Kala poked me in the back. I had a good idea what she was urging me to confess, and it was only fair to put what we knew on the table. "Yeah, we know her too. Alison. We met her at Felix Graham's shop."

Tristan stared at me, dumbfounded. "You're kidding. What was she doing there?"

"She works for Graham, and so does her grandmother," Kala said.

Tristan put his hands over his face and groaned. "I can't believe this."

Frenchie smirked. "I told you to stay away from the crazies."

"It's not like that. I never knew her that well, and it was years ago."

I gentled my voice. "Alison told us she moved here because of some guy she'd dated all the way through college—her ex-fiancé."

"It wasn't like that. She's delusional."

"If it makes you feel better," Kala said, "she didn't mention you by name. It's just—once we saw her here—the connection seemed kind of obvious."

Frenchie fast-walked to the coffee pot, snagged a mug. "Don't tell me she's the woman we banned from the letters-to-the-editor column."

Tristan scrubbed his hands up and down his arms as if chilled. "It was senior year. Some of my so-called friends thought it would be funny to fixed me up with her. I didn't know it then, but they knew she called campus security like every other day to claim she was raped. Each time by a different guy."

"She accused you?" I asked.

He nodded. "I never even slept with her."

Kala snickered. "Malicious slander. The trope that launched a thousand stalker movies. She probably has a shrine devoted to you in her bedroom."

He shot a dagger at Kala. "It wasn't funny."

"Sorry," Kala said. "You're right, people like that aren't a joke. Not to mention the difficulties false accusations create for people who really have been raped."

His voice quieted. "She'd accuse guys of knocking her out with date rape drugs. She even had stuff in her system when they tested her. Luckily, a girl came forward and admitted to selling the stuff to her."

The hairs on the back of my neck stood on end. *Date rape—aka: knockout drugs?* "You're not talking about mexxy, are you?"

"GHB, I think. I never even heard of mexxy until more recently." He let out a loud breath. "I thought she'd given up hounding me for good. It's been years since I've seen her." He looked at Frenchie. "And, for your information, she wasn't the woman we banned from the editor's column."

I shifted my weight from one foot to the other. This was all very interesting, but time was sliding away, and Kala and I hadn't come here to discuss the not-so-glorious side of Tristan's love life. I raised my voice, "Kala and I've been thinking about the drone idea and decided you were right. Do you happen to have any time this coming weekend when we could go up to the ruins? The sooner the better."

Tristan smiled. "Of course." He scanned me from my damp windbreaker down to my scuffed work boots. "How about we do it right now? Looks like you're dressed for hiking."

I was about to say *no*, when I realized it made perfect sense. "That would be great."

Frenchie grimaced. "I hate to ruin your plan, but there's a major glitch. The number one drone isn't currently up to snuff, and the backup's in my workshop in pieces."

"Why didn't I know about that?" Tristan said.

"Yesterday, the drone and I had a run in with a goose. Scared the bejesus out of the bird. Didn't do the drone any good either."

Damn it. I mustered a smile. "That's okay. We've got lots of other angles to look into."

Frenchie waved off my comment. "Why not hike to the ruins anyway? Tristan can go with you and help look around." He grinned at Tristan. "After that girl's visit, you could probably use a break."

Tristan turned my way. "I wouldn't mind lending a hand. What do you think?"

"Um…" I hesitated. The birds-eye-view the drone would give us of the area was really the only reason to get Tristan any more involved with our business than he already was.

"An extra set of eyes might not hurt," Kala said.

I clenched my teeth, wishing she'd kept her mouth shut. But it was too late to take it back.

"Then it's settled—" Frenchie abruptly stopped talking and stared open-mouthed as Sandra thundered in through the open front door, flew past us, then crisscrossed through the room, sniffing desks and chairs like a bloodhound scenting a rabbit, before vanishing into his office. "I'm assuming that dog belongs to you?" he said.

"Unfortunately." I took off after her. Hopefully she wouldn't knock something over or get into his trash.

I found her sitting in front of his desk, spine straight as a rod, ears perked as she gazed fixedly at the middle drawer. Crazy dog.

Frenchie laughed. "What is she? A retired drug-sniffer." He gave her a cautious pat on the top of the head. "Found my stash, did you?"

Kala picked up Sandra's dangling leash. "Only if it's peanut butter cookies. She stole a whole bag of them from my room the other day."

"Well, if that's what she wants, maybe we can make her happy." He opened the drawer, took out a plastic bag of mini-donuts and held it up as if it were evidence in a drug bust.

Sandra grinned—teeth showing.

"Is it alright if she has one?" he asked.

"Go ahead," I said. "You see that white on her muzzle? I'm starting to think it's powdered sugar, not old lady fur."

CHAPTER THIRTY-THREE

K ala, Sandra, and I rode in the Volvo, while Tristan
followed us in his pickup. He was far from a germaphobe,
but thanks to Sandra my backseat wasn't exactly a welcoming
place for anyone.

I drove down Main Street, past the road to our house, and the
Jumping Café. The next right-hand turn was Maiden Lane. It was
a dirt road with clusters of new homes sprouting up on both
sides. While I drove along, Kala texted Tuck to tell him what the
three of us were up to and that we'd fill him in on what we'd
discovered at the museum once we got home.

After a few minutes, the scattered homes, fields, and stone
walls gave way to the darkness of dense hemlock forest, and the
roar of a nearby brook, then the road became narrower, muddy
and potholed. As much time as the drive was taking, I was glad
Kala, and I had shared a few tidbits with Tristan and Frenchie
about the mysteries we'd run into during our investigation
before we'd left the *Gazetteer*. We hadn't shared much, we just
told them about the monkshood being added to the betrothal
cabinet card and the missing shirt being odd. Frenchie didn't
have anything to say about the monkshood, but he agreed with

Graham's belief that the shirt might've simply decayed to the point it was thrown out. I still wasn't convinced it hadn't been stolen by kids, like Kaitlyn the Not Always a Whisperer contended. After all, she worked for the museum and was privy to the inside scoop.

As a sign announced we'd entered Scandal Mountain Wilderness Area, I tapped the brakes and slowed. A minute later, the road dead-ended in a muddy, crude excuse for a parking lot.

Three vehicles were already there, pulled up close to where the Old Coach Road—now nothing more than a wide, grassy trace—meandered away from the parking area and into a brushy field. From previous visits, I knew the Old Coach Road trace led straight to the resort ruins.

I eyed the vehicles. The Corolla had a New Hampshire plate and the other two were from Vermont—a pickup with an empty gun rack in its back window, and a Cherokee with a stick figure family on its tailgate window: a man, woman, five large dogs. *Five dogs?* Just what Sandra didn't need.

I turned and parked in front of a dirt trail that went into the hemlock forest. The path led steeply uphill to Maiden Spring's stone grotto—an area as vital to our search as the resort's main ruins.

I looked at Sandra. "Want to go for a walk?"

She flung herself forward between the seats and onto Kala's lap, leash lashing out behind her like a whip. Kala threw her door open. "Alright, all ready. I get the idea. You want out."

Sandra flew from the car, rocketed past a 'dogs must be leashed at all times' sign, did a quick loop around the parking area, and returned just as Tristan's pickup pulled in next to us.

He jumped out, gave Sandra a pat on the head. "Where do you want to look first?"

"I was thinking the spring." As I nodded at the other vehicles to indicate their owners had most likely hiked along the trace of the Old Coach Road, something occurred to me, and I gave the

Corolla another once-over. "That car's from New Hampshire," I said to Kala.

She squinted at it suspiciously. "Are you thinking—Marissa Lavelle?"

I nodded. "I wish we knew what she drove."

Kala took out her phone, snapped a photo. "I'll search the plate number when we get home. I should probably check all the cars."

"Good idea," I said.

Tristan grinned. "I can do you one better. I'll have them checked while we're hiking in." He snapped a few photos, sent them with a text.

Kala narrowed her eyes. "You've got a friend at the DMV?"

"Us journalists have our ways."

She rested a hand on a hip, studied him. "Skills, cool truck, good looking...If this girl was into guys, you'd be in trouble."

He laughed. "Same goes for you."

I eyed them both. "You realize if it is Marissa, she might recognize my car and think we're spying on her."

Kala blew a raspberry. "There's like a million old Volvo's in Vermont. Besides, it might not even be her car."

"You're right," I said, and I did agree. Still, worry tumbled in the back of my brain.

After I retrieved a pair of binoculars from the car and hung them around my neck, I grabbed hold of Sandra's leash, and we started up the Maiden Springs trail.

The path rose steeply away from the parking area into the hemlock forest. It was crisscrossed with roots and layered with rock.

"Break time," Kala announced when we reached the top of the first rise. She stood with her hand pressed against her waist as if she had a stitch. "If I hadn't seen the old aerial photo of this place, I'd never believe it was ever farmland. I mean, it's freaking mountainous. Must've been a hard life back then."

"I'm sure it was," I said. "I can also imagine that when George

Fielding started buying up properties for the resort, the farmers jumped at the chance to sell." My chest squeezed. George Fielding's money might've saved the hill farm owners from lives of poverty. Still, giving up their land must also have been heartbreaking for them and their family. At least, it would've been for me.

Tristan's phone buzzed. He answered, "Hey, Frenchie." He listened for a second. "Can you repeat that? You're breaking up. Cell service's bad up here." He looked at Kala and me. "The pickup belongs to a William Calder, and Joyce Stone. Megan Meyer owns the Cherokee. The New Hampshire Corolla belongs to Terry Zalins."

I let out a relived breath. "That's good news." Marissa wasn't here.

"What about the Cherokee?" Kala said excitedly. "Don't you remember who Megan Meyer is?"

I frowned, uncertain for a beat. Then it came to me. "Oh, my God! The golf course bride!"

Tristan tucked his phone away. "You want to tell the guy who just got you the information what's going on?"

"Megan Meyer is Marissa Lavelle's niece," I said. "She was married at the golf course near Graham's house the night of the robbery." I bit my tongue to keep from saying more, like that Marissa had slept with Graham and gone to his parties, so she'd had the opportunity to learn his habits and the layout of his house. I liked and trusted Tristan, but he was a journalist. The last thing we needed was for him to piece together the identity of the thieves and announce it in a *Gazetteer* headline before we had a chance figure it out and tell Graham. If that happened, Graham wouldn't give us the information we needed to help Mom.

Kala hugged herself. "I wish I'd brought Taz—just in case." Taz was the nickname of her industrial grade Taser.

"We'll be okay. We just need to play it safe by making sure

Megan doesn't see us. Besides, it's her honeymoon. Marissa's probably not even with her, or guilty of anything for that matter."

We started up the trail again, Kala and me in the lead with Sandra sniffing along beside us, and Tristan a step behind. After a few minutes, the trail leveled off but became a whole lot muddier. We went through a thick swarm of black flies. Normally there weren't a lot of them this time of year, but it had just rained and that had most likely brought them out.

Kala swatted them away. "Next time, remind me that I hate hiking. To heck with the lions and tigers and bears, oh my. I'm rewriting the song: blackflies, mosquitoes, and bugs by the hundreds, yeah no."

"The mineral spring's just around the next bend," I said.

"You better not be lying."

"I'd never do that."

The path once again became steeper. The air cooled and took on an unmissable mineral and sulfur odor. After a few more steps, the spring's stonewalled grotto came into view, set deep into the evergreen-covered mountainside. In the center of the grotto, ginger-colored water gushed from a faucet-sized pipe before cascading into a shallow pool.

Kala rushed ahead. "Now, that's cool. It looks medieval."

"The water's supposed to cure anything that ails you," I said.

Tristan added, "If you can get past its smell."

Kala looked away from the spring and the trail we'd climbed, off to where the hemlock forest gave way to an open grove of autumn-hued maples. I followed her gaze. Between the maples' trunks, the resort ruins were visible in a hollow below, an eerie conglomeration of crumbling stone relics holding court in the center of an overgrown field.

Kala's voice went breathy. "This is the perfect setting for a gothic movie. The only thing missing is a governess in a flowing white negligée."

Tristan laughed. "Maybe we should have come here at night."

"Thank you, but no thanks," she said.

A growl reverberated from Sandra's throat.

I rested a calming hand on her head. "What is it, girl?"

Tristan whispered, "I hear voices."

Now that I listened more carefully, I could make out the murmur of people talking. It came from the evergreens above the grotto, moving closer. Men? Women— Marissa and Megan? I couldn't tell. But there were at least two of them. And they were headed our way. We needed to get out of sight.

"Follow me." I shortened Sandra's leash and hurried away from the grotto, down a steep secondary trail that led toward the ruins.

"Yikes!" Kala screeched as we hit a spot where the trail turned slick with mud. I felt her hand on my shoulder for a half-second, then she went down, landing on one hip in the middle of the trail. In a flash, Tristan grasped her arm and pulled her to her feet.

"This way." I veered into a thicket of waist-high cinnamon ferns. Thankfully it was early autumn, and the frost hadn't killed them yet. Another week and we wouldn't have had their cover.

A few more steps and we were scooting down into the hollow of an old cellar hole. Rusted stovepipe and decaying bricks lay nearby, perhaps exhumed and tossed aside by a long-gone bottle digger.

I crouched low, holding Sandra close, one hand clamped around her muzzle to keep her silent as I peered over the cellar hole's foundation, back uphill in the direction we'd come. If the people were headed this way to hunt for digging sites, we were sunk. Especially if Marissa was among them.

"My hip hurts," Kala grumbled.

"You're okay though, right?" I whispered.

She nodded.

Two men in camo caps walked out of the evergreens above the grotto. As they hiked down past the spring, the muscles along my shoulders tightened, then relaxed as the duo turned onto the main trail and went in the direction of the parking area.

I let go of Sandra's muzzle. "Phew. That was close."

"Close and unnecessary," Kala snapped. "It wasn't Marissa or anyone from the auction."

"I'm just glad you're okay," I said.

While she wiped mud off her jeans and gave her hip a massage, Tristan and I searched around the area for a few minutes. It quickly became apparent no one had been digging recently or even testing for possible dig sites. Mostly, I was grateful Kala was okay and that she didn't bring up how much easier this would have been if we owned a drone. At that point, I might not have argued against the idea despite the cost.

As we continued down the secondary trail toward the overgrown field and resort ruins, the sun came out, shining brightly from a now clear sky. The air warmed and took on the scent of crisp autumn leaves. Kala stopped grumbling about her hip and talked lightly with Tristan. Sandra left off pulling, heeling by my side instead. Still, an ever-increasing sense of foreboding coiled in my stomach. It was as if the improving weather had been sent, not as a good omen, but rather to lull us into a false sense of security.

"Wait a second," I said as we reached the edge of the field. "I want to take a look before we go any further."

I raised my binoculars, scanning what lay ahead for people as well as possible dig sites. There was no one in the area around the crumbling chimneys and archway, or the stone staircase to nowhere that marked the location of what once was the resort's extravagant main house. I widened my search. As well as that unmissable building, there'd originally been guest cottages, privies, well houses, stables, storage sheds...tons of small buildings scattered all over the property, and hidden now beneath weeds, grass, and layers of soil. Many of those spots had been dug by people like my grandpa and Bucky, but signs of those efforts would be long gone. After all, digging had been illegal here for nearly a decade.

"I don't see anything," I said. The cars in the parking area guaranteed there were people around somewhere, though it was possible Megan and anyone with her were simply hiking to the mountain summit and not hunting for the cache or even visiting the ruins. It was possible, but my gut refused to believe it.

I felt the warmth of Tristan's hand on my shoulder as he leaned close and pointed beyond the main ruins. "What about over on the tree line? Is that a person?"

I saw what he was talking about now, a narrow shadow—*no*, two distant shadows—walking into the field and toward the main ruins. "You're right. Two adults, for sure." I passed the binoculars to Kala. "Do either of them look like Marissa or Megan to you?"

Kala glanced through the glasses. "They're pretty far off. Might be—only the short person looks like a man. Megan's husband was taller than her, wasn't he?"

I thought back to the photos we'd seen of them on Facebook. "Yeah, quite a bit taller." Dr. Stanhope leapt into my head. He was short. He and Marissa were both friends with Graham and went to his parties. It was more than likely they knew each other. She could've borrowed Megan's car.

"We need to get a closer look," I said.

Hunching low, we zigzagged through the waist-high weeds toward the main ruins, hiding behind bushes when we came to them, trying to move noiselessly—which would've been easier without a leashed dog, crashing back and forth like an overexcited yoyo. Why had any of us thought bringing Sandra was a good idea? I could blame my lack of foresight on the fact that I never had a pet, but what about Tristan and Kala? Hadn't either of them had a dog as a kid?

Sandra's ears picked up. She growled, louder than back at the grotto.

I flicked her butt with a finger. "Hush. Bad dog."

She glared at me but fell silent.

I motioned for Tristan and Kala to hurry, then made for what looked like a mound of bricks, piled in the shadow of the tallest fireplace and chimney. If we wanted to stay out of sight and get a good look at the people, it was vital that we get as close as possible to the main ruins before they reached them.

As we slid in and crouched behind the mound, I realized it was not bricks, but an abandoned cast iron cookstove, on its side and mostly decayed, not bricks. I threw an arm around Sandra, forcing her into a sit as I knelt. Tristan crouched beside me. Kala was on my other side.

Tristan whispered, "Can you see who it is?"

Keeping a tight hold on Sandra's collar with one hand, I retrieved the binoculars from Kala, then rested them against the edge of the stove to keep them steady as I took a look. I could see the people better than before. But between the tall weeds and the shadow from the chimney, it wasn't good enough. "The woman has a backpack on, I think," I said. "They aren't carrying any tools or buckets." No shovels or probes, no metal detectors. Nothing to indicate they'd been bottle digging or testing possible sites.

I closed my eyes, trying to remember exactly what Marissa looked like. But all I could recall was her boniness and Cruella Deville–style swing coat.

Something tickled the hand I had clamped around Sandra's collar. I glanced to see a yellowjacket wasp walking across my knuckle, moving toward my index finger.

A nauseous feeling clogged my throat. I hated yellowjackets. Sure, it was only one right now, but they never traveled alone for long. They came in swarms—massive swarms.

Sweat rolled from my armpits. Their stings were hideously painful. I'd learned that when I was five years old, and ten, and twelve… My eyes darted from the wasp to the rusted out cookstove. It was hollow. Yellowjackets built nests in places like that.

As if to prove me right, another wasp emerged from a hole in the stove. A second one wiggled out.

I tilted my head, listening. A distant, sickening buzz came from inside the stove. All it would take was a single pheromone alarm from the one on my hand and the troops would rally to its defense. Yeah, I'd learned about yellowjacket pheromones and troops the hard way too, and also from the movie *Swarmed*.

I glanced at Kala. She was kneeling, gaze trained on the slowly approaching people. I needed to warn her about the yellowjackets. I wanted to tell Tristan too. But if I panicked them, and they jumped up to get away from the stove, the people would see us and our chance to find out who they were and what they were up to would vanish.

The yellowjacket on my hand reached the end of my index finger and flew into the air. Relief went through me, then crashed as the evil creature landed on Sandra's forehead, right between her eyes. It raised its butt, baring its stinger.

Holding tight to Sandra's collar, I slapped her between the eyes with my free hand, squashing the wasp against her fur.

Sandra stared at me in shock.

Tristan's widened eyes mirrored hers.

Kala whispered, "What the heck?"

For a beat, I considered telling them the truth. But I couldn't chance them bolting. I had to ignore their dirty looks and the rest of the yellowjackets until we'd gotten a good look at the people, and they'd moved on to somewhere else.

I pasted on a smile and shrugged, then craned upward, not resting the binoculars on the stove this time as I glanced toward where I had last seen the people.

They were gone.

Pulse hammering, I scanned the area directly in front of us. They hadn't walked closer while I was distracted by the yellow-jackets.

I looked further away and spotted them. With their backs to us, they'd reached where the trace of the Old Coach Road went past the ruins and were walking down it in the direction that led back to the parking area.

"Where are they now?" Kala whispered.

I held up a hand, silencing her and watching several more yellowjackets emerge, until the people were not only out of sight but also earshot. Then I released Sandra's collar, jumped to my feet and ordered in a hushed voice, "Don't ask questions. We need to get away from the stove. *Now.*"

I fled away from the stove and chimney into the center of the ruins. Panting, I struggled to catch my breath as they joined me. I glanced from Tristan to Kala. "There—there was a yellowjacket on Sandra's forehead. That's why I hit her. There's like a zillion more of them in the stove."

"Yikes," Kala said. "We're lucky they didn't swarm."

I gulped another breath. "Did either of you get a good look at the people?"

"You were the one with the binoculars," Tristan said.

Kala smiled. "Even if we didn't see them, we know who owns the Corolla, and that's pretty condemning."

I glanced toward the tree line where we'd first spotted them. "We should go see if they were up to something over there."

"Good idea," Kala said.

Backtracking the route the two of them had taken from the tree line proved easy, thanks to a trail of flattened grass and weeds that their passing had left behind. On top of that, Sandra had turned bloodhound again, nose to the ground as she ran off-leash ahead of us. I'd be lying if I said I wasn't impressed by her tracking skills in that moment. But when she came to a screeching halt and began gulping a mysterious something off the ground, my forgiveness evaporated.

"Don't eat that!" I shouted as I jogged to catch up with her.

Lunch leftovers were scattered everywhere—sandwich crusts, coleslaw, a half-eaten pickle. Sandra's current target was the contents of a crumpled potato chip bag.

Kala laughed, and so did Tristan. I shook my head. No question, Chowhound Sandra had found where and what the couple had been doing, but it was picnicking, not hunting for treasure.

I laced my hands behind my head, looked up at the sky. I didn't know whether to laugh with Tristan and Kala or to growl because this entire trip had been a monumental waste of time. Even if it had been Marissa and Stanhope picnicking after scoping out potential dig spots they'd discovered thanks to Graham's ephemera, we'd never know for sure.

The hum of a single-engine plane reached my ears. A few years ago, my mom had leased our airstrip to the owners of the Drunken Turkey Inn. Around this time of year, they hosted sky-view foliage tours. Most likely that's what this plane was doing.

It came into view, silver above a slight veil of clouds, descending in the direction of the airstrip—

Descending.

My mind flashed back. My grandparents plane descending toward our airstrip. Me waiting on the ground to greet them. The crash. The explosion. The flames. I'd relived those moments, so many times. Running, not being able to save them. The flames.

As I watched the plane—bright in the sunshine—the familiar sense of helplessness and anguish clenched my chest. Panic rose, my pulse pounding—

My thoughts screeched to a halt.

Then, as if witnessing this plane had triggered a reshuffling inside my head, those horrific moments began to replay again, but for the first time ever, the explosion came a second before the plane crashed. Not after it hit the ground.

My body went hot as I tried to make sense of what my mind was showing me. This wasn't right. It wasn't the way I'd recalled those horrific moments for the last ten years.

Before the crash, my brain insisted. Before the wheels hit the ground.

A recent discovery pushed its way into my thoughts. Bucky's journal mentioned a recalled carburetor that Grandpa had failed to replace. Bucky had questioned my grandpa's lack of follow through. Truthfully, I found it hard to believe as well. Grandpa always prided himself on going above and beyond when it came to maintenance of his vehicles and plane.

A touch on my shoulder brought me from my contemplation. "You're thinking about that day." Tristan's voice was low and filled with sympathy.

Kala was busy wrestling the potato chip bag from Sandra's mouth, paying no attention to us.

I nodded. "I don't think I'll ever forget."

"I was such an ass," he said. "I should've been there for you. You meant a lot to me." His voice turned husky as he slid his hand down my arm until it reached my fingers. "I shouldn't have treated you the way I did, pressuring you and..."

As his voice trailed off, I stepped away from the intimacy of his touch and turned to face him. "You were a kid. So was I. It was nothing."

"It still wasn't right for me to act that way. You were—are—an amazing woman, Edie Brown."

I puffed out a breath. The conversation was headed toward a place I had no interest in returning to. I lightened my tone. "A woman who also happens to be currently dating an amazing guy."

He closed the space between us, touched my fingers again. "I don't see a ring."

Heat flooded my face. I wanted to give a smart-ass comeback, but my mind had gone blank.

A teasing smile cocked his lips, and I was no longer certain if the ring comment had been a joke or serious. He said, "Boys can be idiots."

I found my voice and laughed. "You aren't kidding. Your current Alison issue is pretty much proof of that."

CHAPTER THIRTY-FOUR

After Tristan noticing my emotional reaction to the plane, and after his ring comment, I made a point of keeping what distance I could between us. I wasn't interested in romance with anyone other than Shane, and I really didn't want to talk about my grandparents and the crash. I was fairly certain the plane had triggered some kind of memory breakthrough, but I needed time to contemplate before I talked to anyone about it.

For the next half hour or so, we scouted the field for signs of treasure hunting, but the only excavation we found was where an animal had rooted up the grass.

"I should get back to the office," Tristan said. "I'm supposed to be working on an article for the Sunday edition."

Kala nodded. "I've got stuff to do, too."

"Alright. Let's get out of here," I said. It was clear we weren't going to find anything more at this point.

With Sandra loping a few yards ahead, we followed the trace of the Old Stage Road back down to the parking area. All the vehicles were gone, except my car and Tristan's truck. Not surprising since everyone we'd encountered had been headed in this direction.

"I'll text you once my grandpa gets the drones up and running," Tristan said. "You do still want some photos from the air?"

I wasn't enthusiastic about spending time with him. Still, there was a strong possibility we'd missed something, and the drone's-eye-view might provide the puzzle piece we needed to identify the thieves. I drummed up a smile. "Sounds good. Let me know and we can make plans."

"Will do," he said, a little too cheerfully.

As he drove off, Kala turned to me. "Where's Sandra?"

I glanced around. No dog in sight. I shouted, "Sandra. Come, bad doggy."

She flew around from somewhere on the far side of the car, looked me in the eyes, then did an about-face and took off back the way she'd come.

"Get back here!" I pushed all the authority I could into my voice.

Her bark resounded, definitely just on the other side of the car.

"She's found more potato chips," Kala said.

I rolled my eyes. "You really think she'd tell us about that or just gobble them down?"

We dashed to see what she was up to. She sat a few yards from the car, spine as straight as a rod, ears perked, panting like it was a hundred degrees in the shade. She glanced at me. Her gaze swung to a brownie-size lump of gunk on the ground in front of her.

"Yuck!" Kala snatched Sandra's collar and towed her toward the car. "No more free-range snacking for you."

Unable to believe Sandra hadn't instantly eaten the gunk, I took a closer look to see what it was. There were bits of apple, peanuts and peanut butter, part of a cookie... My stomach heaved. It looked like fresh puke glazed with something glittery and cotton candy pink.

Cotton candy pink. Gold glitter.

My mind rushed back to the contents of the glass vial Pinky's brother Bill had taken from his briefcase: a slimy, cotton candy pink liquid speckled with what looked like gold glitter. He'd said, "I recreated the chemical formula from your sample to make this. Methoxetamine—to the max—street name: Party Sparkles." He'd set the vial down, looked at us, his expression growing more serious. "This isn't the first time I've seen this exact chemical signature. About a month ago, another sample came from a police drug raid in Burlington. Whoever's making this, they're still out there, and most likely local."

"Sweet Jesus," I muttered. The apple-peanut gunk was coated in Mexxy. What would've happened if Sandra had gulped it down?

I took out my phone, snapped a photo of the stuff.

"What the heck are you doing?" Kala shoved Sandra onto the backseat of the car, then shut the door and hurried back.

"Look at it," I said. "Does it remind you of anything other than puke? Look at the color."

Nose wrinkling, she craned over it. Her eyes went as round as Oreos. "Holy fruitcakes. It's laced with mexxy."

"We need to call the cops—and Shane," I said.

"We can't do that. How can we explain knowing what mexxy looks like? We technically shouldn't even know it's connected to Graham's robbery. It's not like Sandra ate it and got sick."

"She could've been poisoned," I said.

Kala gave it another look. "I didn't notice it there when we arrived. Did you?"

"No. But I don't think it being left next to our car was an accident. Someone recognized the Volvo or saw us—like the couple who were at the ruins. They counted on Sandra finding it."

"You think they wanted to kill her?"

"I don't know. Maybe not. They didn't make any attempt to disguise the drug's color. Maybe they wanted us to see it. Maybe it was intended as a warning for us to back off."

"But that means they'd have to know we're working for

Graham, and assumed he told us what drug was used on him, and that we know what Mexxy looks like."

"Exactly," I said. I added, "We should save some for evidence in case we're right."

"What do you want to put it in?"

I smiled as the perfect container came to mind. "I don't have any plastic bags, but there's spoons and a sugar bowl under the driver's seat—remember Sargent Nelson found them when he searched the car at Graham's house?"

"How could I forget?"

In no time flat, Kala fetched the bowl and a spoon, handed them to me. I said, "This whole thing is getting pretty scary. But it doesn't seem like anyone would risk openly threatening us like this unless they were starting to feel cornered. We could be closer than we thought."

"Considering where we are, it also kinda points to treasure hunting being their motive, wouldn't you say?"

"For sure." I scooped most of the gunk into the bowl before scuffing what remained into the ground to make sure nothing was left for another animal to find.

Kala rested back on her heels. "I was planning on researching the stuff that came up at the museum when we got home. The two photographers were at the top of my list. Do you think I should switch and look into Megan since we know for a fact that her car was here?"

"How about a shallow dive into both areas?" I pressed a hand against my chest, feeling the rapid pound of my pulse. "Before, it felt like we were just poking down a whole bunch of rabbit holes to nowhere. Now I'm starting to think we've been poking down a bunch of connected tunnels. We just need to find where they intersect."

CHAPTER THIRTY-FIVE

W hen we got home, I was surprised to find Shane's Land Rover parked by the walkway to the house. He and Tuck were in the living room sipping whiskeys and snacking on pretzel chips and dip. A rerun of *Wicked Tuna* was on the TV, volume turned low.

Sandra galloped into the room ahead of us and plopped down on the floor without even glancing at the pretzels.

"What's wrong with her?" Tuck asked.

"You're not going to believe it. Someone tried to poison her." I collapsed onto the sofa next to Shane.

A frown darkened his face. "Please tell me you're kidding."

"I wish we were. Luckily, she didn't eat any of it. The smell or something must've spoiled her appetite."

Kala poured herself a whiskey. "It was in the parking area by the resort ruins. She just sat there and stared at it like a drug-sniffer dog. Her favorites—apples, peanuts, cookies—coated with mexxy."

"Mexxy. How do you know?" Shane asked.

I bit my lip. There wasn't an easy answer for that.

"I've seen pictures of it on the internet," Kala said. "Pink with gold sparkles, right?"

Shane nodded. He looked at me. "That's not just any methoxetamine. It's called Party Sprinkles. From a local underground lab."

If Shane was anything it wasn't a pushover. He knew something was up. I raised a hand to warn him to tread lightly. What he didn't know, he wouldn't feel obliged to report to his superiors.

His frown deepened. "You sure it was intended for Sandra?" He added, "I'm assuming you didn't call the police?"

"It was right next to our car." I brought up the pictures on my phone and handed it to him. "We took a sample. Well, actually we brought ninety-nine percent of it home. It's out in the kitchen. She wasn't poisoned, and we didn't see who left it there. We thought...I figured calling the police would be a waste of everyone's time."

Shane ran a hand over his chin, darken by five o'clock shadow. "Tuck said you were up there with Tristan Lefebvre."

My throat tightened. Whether I had an interest in Tristan or not, that was something I'd just as soon Shane hadn't known. "We were at the museum, looking into things. Tristan had offered to use one of their drones to take aerial photos of the ruins, so we went over to the *Gazetteer* to set up a time. Their drones were down, but we decided to go have a look anyway. Tristan left before we found the mexxy laced—"

Kala interrupted, waving her arms. "Oh, my God." Her gaze pinged from Tuck to Shane. "We assumed this was related to the robbery investigation, like the thieves warning us to back off. But when we first arrived at the *Gazetteer*, we overheard an argument between Tristan and a girl he knew in college. She was—is—a real psycho-stalker type. She probably saw us there—and she knows Tristan likes Edie."

"What's this woman's name?" Shane asked.

"Alison," I said. "She's Janet from the Golden Stag's granddaughter. We know she used date rape-type drugs in college. You don't think she could've followed us to the ruins?"

"Jealousy's a powerful motive," Tuck said.

Shane picked up his whiskey glass from the coffee table, took a sip. He cleared his throat. "Normally I'd agree. Except the case I've been working on"—He fell silent as if rethinking whether he should share more—"I've got a strange feeling there's a connection between my case and what you found in the parking lot. As in, it's connected to Graham and not this woman." His voice deepened. "It's time for all of you to back off. Let the police do their job."

I narrowed my eyes. "I thought the case you were involved with was about human trafficking."

"It was—and the results are probably on the news by now. This morning, we raided several homes across the state. We found what we expected, plus a large quantity of Party Sprinkles and stolen property."

Stolen property? "Are you saying, you found Graham's things?"

He shook his head. "ATVs, computers...items like that. My point is, I think it's time for you to drop this."

Kala got to her feet. She snatched a handful of pretzel chips. "This girl thinks it's time to start doing more research."

Shane shot a hard look her way.

She shrugged. "I'm not doing anything major. Just a little looksee at some history. Innocent stuff."

His lips twitched as if holding back what he wanted to say. Instead, he finished his whiskey. Once Kala had vanished down the hallway, he looked me in the eyes and lowered his voice. "When you and Kala walked in, I was about to tell Tuck something. I shouldn't be sharing it with anyone, at least not yet. I heard it through the law enforcement grapevine. But it's important to both you and Tuck."

Important to both me and Tuck? I had the feeling it had

nothing to do with Graham or the mexxy. I took a guess. "Does it have something to do with Mom?"

He shook his head. "It's about your grandparents' plane crash."

I went numb. He could've said anything else, and it would've been less shocking, especially after what happened when I'd seen the plane earlier in the afternoon.

Shane continued, "Caleb McMahon, the senior air safety investigator who did the field work and was in charge of your grandparents' case, has been indicted for taking bribes, tampering with evidence, and a long list of other crimes. It's a major federal investigation."

I blinked at him. "Are you saying they're reopening my grandparents' case?"

Tuck had gone as pale as opalescent glass. He stammered, "I always thought there was something fishy about the investigation."

Shane quieted his voice. "There is no proof at this point that case was compromised. It might be years before the Feds can say one way or the other, unless McMahon confesses..."

His voice faded into the distance as my memory went back to the unbearably painful days and weeks after my grandparents' deaths. I remembered with absolute clarity eavesdropping outside the living room when Tuck and Mom talked with the crash investigator. Caleb McMahon.

"The plane exploded on impact," he'd said to them. I recalled those words now as if I'd heard them yesterday. Had those words —spoken by someone I thought was an expert—stamped a false memory in my mind? Had I chosen to not trust the horror I'd seen with my own eyes because it was at odds with what everyone else said and believed? Or had I simply repeated that false scenario so many times that it became the truth in my head.

Tuck's voice drew me back to the room. "I should've questioned his findings back then. My father took such pride in that plane. He'd never have neglected a recall." He pressed his hands over his face, voice cracking. "It's my damn fault. I should've said something."

"No, it's not," Shane said. "You were in shock. You'd lost both your parents. You're supposed to be able to trust people in positions like his. They're sworn to protect the public."

Tuck looked up, his face now blotched with red. "That doesn't matter. I didn't do a damn thing, and I was in charge of the family."

Shane gave an understanding nod, then his attention turned to me. "You're being awfully quiet. Are you okay?"

I shook my head. "At the ruins, I was watching a single-engine plane, and I remembered something—" My throat clamped shut.

"What was it?" he asked, voice gentle. The voice I loved.

"I had a flashback. I think I've been remembering the crash wrong. The plane exploded a second before it landed. I think...I don't believe Grandma and Grandpa died because a faulty carburetor exploded on impact."

CHAPTER THIRTY-SIX

Before Shane left, I told him about Bucky's journal, how he and Grandpa had been working on a mysterious project that we assumed involved using ephemera and aerial photos to locate the missing cache of Glass Widows. However, after the plane crash, Bucky appeared to have stopped pursuing the hunt.

I also gave Shane the sugar bowl full of mexxy-coated gunk, and the photos of it on the ground, as well as the pictures Kala had taken of the license plates. We went over other unsettling things we'd come across, like the bloody shirt missing from the museum, details from Graham's robbery.... The only thing I didn't reveal to Shane was the part Bill had played in our investigation.

Like it or not, the time had come to give law enforcement information that might lead to them identifying the thieves before we were able to give their names to Graham. I was risking not getting what I needed to help my mom in hopes that the police might uncover clues connected to the truth behind my grandparents' deaths. I didn't say it out loud to Shane, but two words sat in my gut and chest, and on the tip of my tongue:

Sabotage. Murder.

If my grandparents' plane hadn't exploded on impact, then what had happened?

One thing was certain, one thing I couldn't ignore: Grandpa had been searching for the Glass Widows around the time his plane crashed. And now, our investigation had led to someone setting out drugged food for Sandra while we were poking around at the ruins. Something was going on. It involved the Glass Widows and, apparently, air safety investigator Caleb McMahon was tangled up in it.

I woke up the next morning at a little after seven, dragged myself out of bed, showered and then plodded downstairs. To my surprise both Tuck and Kala were already at the kitchen table, talking or more likely plotting, judging by the sly looks on their faces. They were both already dressed, Tuck in slacks, casual shirt, and a tweed jacket, Kala in a rosy cashmere pullover and her favorite carpenter jeans. They were up to something for sure. I just hoped it didn't involve razzing me, I didn't have the patience for that this morning.

I frowned at the empty coffee pot, sitting under the maker. Household rule number one: first person up makes coffee for all. And, as Kala pointed out to me the other day, they don't hog it all.

"Sleep okay?" Tuck asked.

"Not really." I squinted at him and Kala, trying to figure out what was going on.

Kala grinned. "What you need is a good breakfast." She pushed up from her chair. "Brunch at the Jumping Café? Tuck and I are starving."

"My treat," Tuck said. "You could have a veggie frittata, cinnamon rolls, fresh OJ…We can be back before it's time to open the shop."

Kala whipped her quilted vest off the wall hook where it hung.

"I found out something interesting when I was researching. I'll tell you about it on the way."

I managed a smile. Yeah, this was what they'd been plotting. It was way better than being razzed, and something in my stomach probably was what the doctor ordered. "Alright. But I'm not driving this time."

In no time flat, we were all in Tuck's Suburban, except for Sandra, who'd been left behind to eat dog food for a change. The weather was bright and crisp, the air refreshing when it hit my lungs. Overnight, the maples had taken on more color. Backlit by the morning sun, their orange and scarlet colors shimmered like stained glass.

As Tuck drove down the driveway, he glanced in the rearview mirror at Kala. "Tell Edie what you discovered."

"I'm assuming it's vital?" I asked, totally curious.

Kala scrunched forward, closer to the front seats. "First of all, I looked into Megan. She couldn't have been driving her car yesterday. She's honeymooning on a cruise ship. Could've been Marissa. I couldn't find out if she's in New Hampshire or here."

"At least that rules out Megan." I shifted in my seat, so I could see Kala more clearly.

Her voice sped up, full of eagerness. "Once I was done with them, I started to look into the Victorian photographers. Alonzo Harlow from Montpelier, Vermont—the guy who took Sophie and George Fielding's wedding photos—is an open book. Native Vermonter. Worked here, then moved to Boston at the turn of the century and became a real estate clerk. Nothing noteworthy. On the other hand, Louis Beaumont, who did the betrothal and crime scene photos, is much more interesting. He lived in Paris and, of course, New York City, photographing the Who's Who—"

She paused dramatically as we reached the end of the driveway. The airstrip was across the way. I'd dreaded driving past it, expecting my emotional hangover to only worsen. But instead, thanks to Kala's impending reveal and my new suspicion that the crash had been a case of sabotage, my usual grief and remorse was replaced by an unshakeable determination. My grandparents had done so much for me, taken over my care when my mom went off to art school, given me a childhood that was unique and beyond amazing, filled with opportunity. For once, I was in a position to repay them, not just by reviving the business they'd built, but also by helping solve the mysteries behind the Glass Widows and their deaths.

I prodded Kala to go on. "So, what did you find out about Beaumont?"

"Okay. Here are the deets." She held out for one more beat, before she continued. "I was searching Louis Beaumont's crime scene photos—he took a lot of those, by the way—when I came across a Victorian-era article about the Mountain House tragedy. As you would say, I jumped down that rabbit hole—and wow!"

"Yeah?" I sat immobilized, waiting to hear the rest.

"*Scandal Mountain Gazetteer* wasn't around back then, I double checked. It wasn't founded until 1950. But all the Victorian big city papers covered the resort tragedy, and some of them have archives online."

I moaned. "Tell me, already." I looked at Tuck, planning on asking for assistance. His gaze was focused on the road ahead. I'd been so wrapped up in myself earlier that I'd failed to notice the dark circles under his eyes. Of course, what we'd learned about the crash last night was as emotionally hard—if not harder—on him. My grandparents were his mom and dad. Why was it so easy to forget about other people's feelings when it came to things like grief?

Kala leaned even further forward, her hand on the back of my seat. "I was up until almost three in the morning, digging into those newspaper archives. You won't believe it. The guy arrested for arson and murder—Jeb Warner? He wasn't actually hung."

I shook my head. "That's not right. He was tried and hung.

Remember the photos at the museum of him in the casket with his wolf-head cane and the bruises around his neck?"

"According to the Victorian-era newspapers, the trial was terminated due to Jeb Warner's death—from tuberculosis. He contracted it in prison."

"What about the photos? I mean, Jeb being hung is a huge part of the story."

Tuck interrupted. "Kala thinks the colorized bruises around his neck are an addition, like the monkshood in the betrothal photo."

"You're kidding," I said, stunned.

"I can't say for sure when the addition happened," Kala said, "but that same photo of Jeb Warner in the coffin with the wolf-head cane was on the front of newspapers across the country in the 1880s—and there weren't bruises on his neck in any of the images. At some point, someone got creative and changed the story."

"But why would anyone want to make it look like Jeb Warner was hung?" I said.

Tuck slowed the car, then pulled into the Jumping Café parking lot. "All I know is, whoever it was, they screwed up our local history."

Tuck parked not far from the entrance. When we got to the front door, Kala held it open, letting Tuck and me walk inside first. She said, "Can you imagine how upset the Scandal Mountain Museum people are going to be when they find out their fancy new exhibit is wrong?"

I lowered my voice to a whisper. "You don't suppose this is what Grandpa and Bucky uncovered when they were researching?"

"Could be," Tuck said. "This whole thing could be about a coverup and not about treasure hunting."

We scored a table next to a window. The view was of the dumpsters near the end of the parking lot. Still, it was brighter than anywhere else, cheerful with a checkered tablecloth and a vase of wildflowers.

I ordered the veggie frittata. Tuck and Kala went for the 'Vermonster Waffle Stack' special. I might've been hungry, but they had to be starving.

In no time at all our coffees and food arrived. No sooner had the waitress left than my phone rang. *Mom.*

Surprised by such an early call, I looked at Tuck. "Wasn't Mom scheduled to phone this afternoon?"

"You better answer it," he said. "It must be important."

I put the phone on speaker, volume low enough that her voice wouldn't travel. "Hey, Mom. What's going on?"

"I'm waiting to see the nurse, so they let me use the infirmary phone."

The infirmary? "What's wrong?"

"Nothing, really," she said.

My pulse jumped to lightspeed. Mom never played down medical issues. "Did you have a reaction to your new medicine?"

"I—sort of passed out."

"You're alright now, right?"

"I guess," she said.

Tuck raised his voice. "Tell the nurse we'd like a call from her."

"I'm not sure she can do that. I'll ask." Her tone shifted to a confidential whisper. "Edie, those aerial photos your grandfather took of Scandal Mountain that you were asking about the other day, I think I put them in the library window seat. After the crash I couldn't stand to look at them. They reminded me—" Her voice cracked. "I wish your grandparents were still alive."

"I do too." It was strange to think I'd sat on the window seat the other night, reading Bucky's journal, none the wiser that the photos I'd wanted to locate were only inches from my derriere.

Mom's voice lightened. "You're still planning on coming to visit—" Her voice muffled as she stopped talking to us and spoke with someone in the room with her. She came back to us. "The nurse is right here. She'd like to talk with you. I have to go have some blood drawn."

Before I could say goodbye, a stiff voice came over the speaker, replacing hers. "This is Gabriela Torres. I'm your mother's nurse."

"Thank goodness," Tuck jumped into the conversation. "We're worried sick about her. Is she okay?"

Gabriella's voice turned soothing. "She had some blood pressure issues. We're working them out. She said you're visiting on the fifteenth. Perhaps we can set up time to talk in person?"

"We'd love that," I said. "She's okay, right?"

"We're fairly sure her issues are stress related. Some people adjust to life here better than others. Your mother is…"

As her voice trailed off, I took a guess, "High strung?"

"She mentioned a mental breakdown when she was younger. Is that correct?"

Tuck answered, "She was a teenager. Nineteen—twenty, maybe. She was married and divorced in less than a year."

The nurse was silent for a beat before she continued, "Thank you for the information. Rest assured, she's doing fine for now. We'll talk in a few days. I'm glad I had a chance to touch base with you."

"Same here," I said.

My hands shook as I put the phone away. Fine for now wasn't exactly comforting.

"I'm glad you're going to see her soo—," Kala didn't finish her sentence.

Her attention swung away from us and across the room like a metal detector drawn to a stash of coins. Pinky was strutting toward us.

I was grateful to see her. There was something I'd been meaning to ask her. On top of that, we couldn't afford to be totally sidetracked by Mom's health issues right now. Mom would be okay. She was being supervised 24/7. *The nurse will call if she gets worse*, I told myself.

Pinky pulled out the fourth chair at our table and sat down. "Why didn't you guys tell me you were coming for breakfast?"

"We didn't know until the last minute." Kala nudged her towering plate of waffles toward Pinky. "There's more here than I can eat. Want to share?"

"You don't have to ask twice." As Pinky picked up a fork, she lowered her voice. "So how goes the search for the thieves?"

I took a quick sip of coffee to wet my throat, then asked my question, "You didn't happen to notice if Sparky Collins was limping the day of the auction?"

"Yeah, for sure. He was bitching about stepping on a nail at work. He said it hurt like hell. I asked him if he'd been to a doctor. He said no."

"Do you know when the accident happened?" I asked.

"Few days before then, maybe. I didn't pay that much attention. I told him to get a frickin' tetanus shot."

I nodded but kept my thoughts to myself. Sparky being in pain and limping at the auction confirmed our theory that he hadn't hiked to Graham's house later that evening—

Kala interrupted, nose wrinkling, "Do you guys smell something stinky—like burning garbage?"

I sniffed the air. She was right. It smelled like the café's dumpster was on fire.

The front door of the café flew open. A man rushed in. He shouted, "Where's the fire extinguisher."

Pinky was on her feet. "Behind the door!"

He grabbed the extinguisher and rushed back outside. Pinky was a step behind him. I took off with Tuck and Kala on my heels.

In the parking lot, close to the front of Tuck's Suburban, smoked billowed, and flames leapt skyward, tall and bright.

"Jesus Christ." Tuck rushed ahead.

The man pulled the safety pin from the extinguisher, started spraying. The flames retreated, smothered by the foam. The fire might've been as high and fierce as if fueled by gasoline, but its source appeared to be nothing more than an average-size card-board box stuffed with papers and set up close to the car.

"Isn't that your rig?" Pinky said to Tuck.

Ignoring her, Tuck said to the man, "Did you see who did this?"

He shook his head. "I didn't see no one. I just heard a little bang—like a firecracker exploding. Then I saw the flames."

I rubbed a chill from my arms. I didn't need to catch Tuck's eyes or Kala's to know they were thinking the same thing I was. Another warning, like Sandra and the mexxy-coated bait.

As Tuck and everyone else went to see if the Suburban had suffered any damage other than it being coated with smoke and soot, I was drawn to the box of still smoldering papers. Smoke-darkened shards of a bottle lay in the middle of the mess. Consid-ering how fast the fire started, I couldn't help wondering if they were the remains of a Molotov cocktail.

Near the glass, a few thick pieces of black and white cardboard were singed but not burnt beyond recognition—

"No!" I gasped as I realized what I was looking at.

Remains of a composition notebook.

And not just shards from any bottle. Not a cardboard box.

Shrieking in horror, I ran to the smoldering pile and kicked the shards out where I could see them clearly. "It's the Glass Widow! They smashed it. They burnt the Bible box. The ephemera, the journals. They destroyed everything they stole."

CHAPTER THIRTY-SEVEN

Roger Ovitt, our local police chief, was first on the scene. He looked disappointed by the seemingly innocuous burnt box and nonexistent damage to Tuck's truck. That was, until we told him the bottle was a Glass Widow, then his attitude changed.

While Tuck and Kala went into details about Graham's robbery, reiterating that the case was currently in the hands of the South Burlington Police Department, I walked out of earshot and called Shane.

"It's just horrible," I said, holding the phone close. "The Glass Widow, the Bible box—they're totally destroyed. Can you imagine someone doing something like that?"

Shane's voice was gentle, filtered by a firm shot of detective reserve. "You need to call Graham right away. I'd do it for you, but—"

"You're right, I'm the one who should tell him."

"And, Edie, it's more important than ever for you—all of you—to stay out of this. Go home and stay put."

I swallowed hard. Forcing a measure of resignation into my voice, I said, "Don't worry. Once Chief Ovitt's done with us, we're headed home." It wasn't exactly a lie. We were going there, but no way was I done looking into this. We were close, so close the thieves had felt compelled to go to this length. No way was I letting go now.

My call to Graham was nowhere near as pleasant as the one I had with Shane. Graham yelled at first. Then, he screamed. I explained we weren't giving up yet, that he'd get the names of the thieves as soon as we had them. I also confessed that we'd shared everything we knew with Shane. I couldn't tell how he felt about that.

"All right," Graham said as our conversation wound down. "I want their names. They're the worst kind of scum. Forget what they did to me and the value of those pieces. Those items were irreplaceable, historically significant."

"I know," I said. "I just don't get how someone could simply destroy them."

* * *

When we reached home, I went straight to the downstairs library and switched on the overhead light. Kneeling, I pushed the window seat's cushions up so I could access the lid of the bin that formed its base. The hinges resisted my tug and creaked as they relented.

The compartment inside was the size of a toybox—which was exactly what it had been when I was little. Now it was piled to the brim with dog-eared magazines, and forgotten boardgames— Candy Land, Hungry Hungry Hippos, Monopoly... loads of vintage goodies Kala could get money for on eBay.

I started pulling things out and piling them on the floor beside me. About a third of the way to the bottom, I found a pair of identical, framed aerial prints. Perhaps Grandpa had planned on giving one to Bucky as a gift, but never got the chance.

I picked up one and tilted it so the light from the overhead fixture shone directly on the glass. The image was clear and bright, not faded at all thanks to spending the last decade in the dark. Grandpa had taken the photo from the same angle as the Beaumont Photography cabinet card. However, whereas the Beaumont photo showed the mountainside as pastureland, the much more recent shot showed the forest and overgrown fields we'd walked through yesterday. The main ruins were easy to spot —the crumbling chimneys and archway, the stone staircase and even the faint outlines of umpteen small cellar holes were visible.

My eyes went to the edge of the photo and the roofline of the Jumping Café, a place with no direct connection to the resort mystery, but none the less impossible not to note after what had happened earlier.

With my finger, I followed the path we'd driven yesterday from the main road to the Wilderness Area parking lot, down the trace of the Old Coach Road, past the ruins and to where the people had been picnicking. I vaguely recalled hiking further along that route, long ago, perhaps bird watching with my grandmother.

In the photo, the faint trace of the old road continued on, disappearing where the brush grew thick and then reappearing behind a tiny cemetery and a farmstead—sheds, a large barn, and small house.

A strange feeling came over me and my fingers tingled as if I were holding a piece of antique Vermont stoneware, my fingers sliding over its glazed surface, detecting slight dents left behind from the potter's fingers, a physical reminder of people who'd lived long before me: potters, loggers, ambitious men like George Fielding who hoped water from a mineral spring would draw in tourists and make them rich, and the hardscrabble farmers who'd surrendered their land to him for much needed cash. It must've been heartbreaking for those farmers and their families to give up the land they'd planned to pass down through the generations. It would've been for me, if I'd been in their shoes.

I studied the farmstead again. Now that I thought about it, I knew where it was. The current road—Hill Farm Road—that led up to the barn and small house started on the very outskirts of Scandal Mountain, past Townline Gas. The farm was one of the oldest homesteads in town, a place that predated the building of the resort by at least fifty years. The house now sat on a tiny portion of what had once been a vast landholding, reduced in size back when George Fielding bought up the mountainside, at least that was the farmstead's history according to Bucky Sanders—and he had every reason to know. For as long as I could remember the house had belonged to him and Doris.

Clutching the framed photos, I sprinted out of the library and to the shop. Tuck had opened for business, though I doubted he felt like being there any more than I did. Kala was keeping him company, sitting at the front counter with her laptop open in front of her.

As I dashed in, she turned the laptop to face me. A photo of the burnt Bible box and the smashed Glass Widow was on the screen. She said, "Tuck and I noticed something odd. Can you see it?"

I set the aerial photos on the counter, looked at the screen. My instinct whispered an answer, but it still eluded me.

"The box's lid is missing," Tuck said.

I looked again. No mistaking it, he was right. "Why would someone go to the effort of removing a lid if they were going to burn the piece? Why keep something that could incriminate them?"

Tuck shrugged. "Maybe it meant something to them personally?"

"But the rest of the box and the ephemera didn't—and the Glass Widow didn't?" I said. It didn't make sense.

My thoughts went to the auction preview. When I'd opened the Bible box's lid, there'd been a painting of sheep and a farmhouse on its interior, a nice, unexpected addition but not notable for its skill.

It came to me in a rush. Why hadn't I recognized it then? It seemed obvious now.

I nudged one of the aerial photos closer to the laptop, pointed at the tiny image of Bucky's home and said, "There was a painting of this house on the interior of the lid."

"That's Bucky and Doris's place, isn't it?" Tuck said.

My smile became a grin. If the thieves were looking for the cache of long-missing Glass Widows, like we thought, and assuming they kept the box's lid for a reason, then perhaps, just maybe....

"I think we might've found where the rabbit holes connect. Bucky and Doris's house. We need to talk to her again. She might know something, even if she doesn't realize it."

CHAPTER THIRTY-EIGHT

The obvious first step was to check the farmstead's history by looking at its deeds. Unfortunately, only the most recent were available online. Not unusual for a small town founded in the late 1700s like Scandal Mountain.

Kala closed the laptop. "I'm going to run down to the town clerk's office and ask to see the property's records."

I gave her a thumbs up. "I say divide and conquer. You go there. I'll head for St. Albans to have another chat with Doris." I turned to Tuck. "Why don't we close the store for the day. You can come with me."

Tuck folded his arms and frowned. "What happens if Chief Ovitt shows up looking for more information or if Shane stops by? He said for us to stay put."

"He meant for us to not do anything dangerous." I looked down at the floor. We both knew full well that wasn't what Shane meant, and Tuck deserved better than lies from me. I raised my eyes. "Honestly, after discovering Caleb McMahon lied to us about the crash, I can't not keep digging into this."

His lips pressed into a firm line. But after a second, he unfolded his arms. His chest rose and fell as he exhaled a long, relenting breath, "Alright, you two go. I'll stay here and hold down the fort." He added, "I keep thinking if only I hadn't been so focused on my own grief after the crash, the investigation might've been brought into question back then."

"No one's going to get away with anything this time," I said.

* * *

I can't say I wasn't uneasy as I drove toward St. Albans and Hawk's Nest. All the way there, I kept one eye on the rearview mirror to make sure I wasn't being followed. Clearly, someone had been keeping tabs on us. How else would they've known we were having breakfast at the café and burned the Bible box there, as opposed to some place like in our driveway at home?

When I turned into the apartment complex and parked, I waited until I was certain no one was trailing me before I got out and walked to the entry. Now my only problem was, would Doris be willing to talk to me?

Scrunching my toes for luck, I pressed her buzzer.

"Whatda want?" Doris' voice came through the intercom.

I straightened my spine. "Hi, it's Edie Brown. I just have another couple of questions."

She harumphed. "I might regret this but come on up—apartment 220. Don't be bringing any more plants. I've already got my hands full with them violets you brung the other day."

The entryway's inside door buzzed; I pushed it open before Doris could change her mind, then took the elevator to the second floor. Her apartment door was the third on the left. It was gray and unornamented except for the number, a sharp contrast to the door across the hallway which sported an enormous placard shaped like a rainbow trout. The name Vanderschmidt was painted across the fish, a not too subtle hint that the apartment was likely Doris's cousin Gilbert's place.

Doris opened her door and grumbled, "Come in."

"Thank you." I hurried to take the invitation.

Unlike the stark welcome offered by the exterior of her door, the inside of her apartment was colorful, packed with decorative pieces that took my breath away: blue decorated stoneware, early ceramics, antique Vermont furniture... Oil paintings hung on the walls. Tuck's basket of violets sat on a bar between the living room and a kitchenette.

Like the other day, fine beads of nervous sweat shone beneath her bottom lip. "Can't imagine what else you could want from me," she said.

I took a breath, then gave it to her straight. "The other day you said you didn't think Bucky was working on something with my grandfather. I don't believe you. Not only do I think you were lying, I think you'll feel better once you tell me the truth."

Defensive anger shone in her eyes, but patches of red crept across her cheeks like she was embarrassed. "I—I might recall something."

To clarify just how important her answers were I added, "The inspector that was assigned to my grandparents' plane crash has been indicted for taking bribes and tampering. I've read Bucky's journals. After the crash he immediately stopped working on the project. Please, tell me what you know."

As I followed her into the living room's sitting area, the red faded from her face. She slumped onto a rocking chair.

I half-sat on the arm of a couch beside her, putting us eye-to-eye and her within my reach. I touched her arm. "I need your help. I—" My voice clenched as I readied to confess my own guilt. "I regret not speaking up—or doing anything—back when the crash happened, and so does Tuck. We both suspected something was off."

She rang her hands, looked down and murmured, "They were workin' on a book."

"A book?" I blinked in surprise, though a nonfiction book seemed like something either one of them might've done on their own—given the extent of their personal knowledge on any number of subjects.

"They were researchin' the resort's history," she said. "It was all Bucky talked about for months. Until the crash."

"So, they weren't hunting for the cache of Glass Widows?"

She began to ring her hands harder, as if by doing so she could squeeze my question out of existence.

A suspicion I'd first had when I was sixteen years old, and Bucky'd shown me the Glass Widow at the flea market pushed its way to the forefront of my mind. I took a guess, "Bucky wasn't looking for the cache of bottles because he didn't find just one Widow like he always claimed. He found all of them, the year before the crash, didn't he?"

Her hands stilled. "Remember the last time you was here, the story Gilbert told 'bout Bucky cleaning out an old jelly cabinet filled with canning jars?"

I shuddered. Gilbert had said something about Bucky dumping the contents of the jars in the compost pile, and the sugary mess attracting every yellowjacket within a hundred miles. I looked her in the eyes. "Was that when Bucky found the cache?"

"That hundred-thousand dollar bottle had homemade ketchup in it. Been down in our cellar with the canning jars since who knows when, longer maybe than Bucky's folks owned the place before us."

The day at the flea market once more came to mind. When Bucky showed me the Glass Widow there'd been a trace of red crust on its lip—ketchup. Still, she was talking about the Widow that had sold at the auction, and that didn't entirely answer my question. "Are you saying he found one bottle with the canning jars or the whole cache?"

"I only ever seen that one." Her voice lowered to a confidential whisper. "That day, Bucky didn't let Gilbert *or* me help carry anything upstairs, and he made a big deal out of cleaning the canning jars and bottles himself. He never said nothing 'bout there being more of them Widows, but I wondered."

"You think they're still in the house?"

"Before the auction, Fishers went through the place with a fine-tooth comb. They was real thorough." She clenched her hands again, but not before I saw their trembling. "Bucky and I never wanted no highfaluting, rich-person life. Ask me, he kept the rest 'em secret, so we'd have something to fall back on in case of an emergency. Then he went and died all of a sudden with no one around to tell where he'd hid them."

My chest squeezed. Hiding the cache of Widows as a rainy-day fund did sound like something Bucky would do. Still, I couldn't afford to spend any more time going down this rabbit hole. This conversation was supposed to be about the project Bucky and Grandpa were working on before the crash. I steered the conversation back on track. "Why did Bucky stop working on the book about the resort?"

"He never would tell me." Her voice tightened. "One time, not long after your grandparents' funeral, I came home early from shopping and overheard Bucky talkin' on the phone. It sounded like someone was threatening to do something to me. You know, make an accident happen. When I asked Bucky 'bout it, he never flat-out said I was right. But after that day, he kept a gun by our back door, and all our income on the down-low."

My mouth went dry. "No one's threatening you now, right?"

"Nope, nothing. Truth is, I'll never know if I was right about that phone call—or about Bucky finding the rest of the bottles mixed in with the canning jars."

CHAPTER THIRTY-NINE

After I left Doris's apartment and got back to the Volvo, I sat with the door open, breathing in fresh air as I sorted through my spinning thoughts.

Grandpa and Bucky were working on a book about the mineral springs resort. The crash happened, then someone started threatening to hurt Bucky's wife. Was the crash investigator, Caleb McMahon, behind both these things? It didn't make any logical sense. Other than the investigation he had no connection to my family, at least as far as I knew. It seemed more likely the person behind the crash had paid McMahon to cover up the sabotage, and that the same person had threatened Bucky when he got suspicious.

My phone vibrated. I answered, "Hello."

Kala's voice said, "I'm at the town clerk's office, but I wanted you to know I took a detour to the museum on my way here."

I swallowed hard. I wasn't all that thrilled that she'd wasted time on a side-trip, but worse than that… "Don't tell me you had a run in with Joie or Kaitlyn."

"Not a chance. They weren't there." I heard a crinkling noise like a potato chip bag opening and several munches. Finally, she said, "Some of the photos I took yesterday were blurry, so I decided to have another in-person looksee. I'd been thinking— maybe the person who added the neck-bruises to the coffin photo of Jeb Warner got the idea from looking at the colorized Beaumont cabinet cards."

"I'm assuming you called because you discovered something?"

"Yeah, big time. I think all the Beaumont crime scene cabinet cards were altered."

"All of them?" This was huge.

"They'd have to be analyzed by a professional image forensic specialist to prove it, of course. But I'd stake money on it."

"You're really that certain?"

A few more munchy-crunchy sounds came over the phone before she continued, "I'm not suggesting the crime scene photos were altered at a later date, like the coffin photo. All the crime scene images are identical to how they appeared in newspapers around the time of the trial. But—and this is the major point I didn't notice the last time we were at the museum—every single crime scene photo was embellished."

"You're losing me," I said.

"Every incriminating detail in the cabinet cards that were taken by Louis Beaumont and used at Jeb Warner's trial—the round imprint of his cane's ferule (tip), the darkness on one side of the shoeprint as if the shoe had worn unevenly because the wearer was disabled—each and every one of those details were hand-colorized. Back then, there would've been no way to tell if Beaumont's embellishments had ever so slightly changed the details. And those alterations happened before the photos were presented at trial."

I thought for a second, then played devil's advocate, a job that usually fell on Kala's shoulders. "You're saying all the crime scene cabinet cards at the museum are colorized, but they also look identical to the photos that appeared in the Victorian-era newspapers? How can that be? Didn't newspapers just have black and white photos back then?"

"Mostly," she said. "But that doesn't mean the newspapers didn't use the colorized cabinet cards. The photos just appeared black and white when they came out in print. Any changes to the shape of a cane's ferule or darkening along the edge of a shoeprint that occurred because of the colorization would remain part of the image."

I gripped the phone harder, steadying my hand and voice as what she was implying sank in. "You're thinking Louis Beaumont intentionally created fake evidence against Jeb Warner." I hesitated. "Which means Beaumont was likely protecting the real murderer."

"Or Beaumont *was* the murderer." She started speaking faster, words flowing into one another in her hurry to get them out. "All the pieces fit. No photographer would risk their professional reputation by adding a malevolent flower like monkshood to a betrothal photo—unless they vehemently hated someone. Next thing you know, the groom's dead and a fire is started to destroy the body, and Jeb Warner is conveniently accused of the crimes. If you ask me, Louis Beaumont was one nasty, unscrupulous dude."

I took my travel mug from the cup holder. The water inside had gone lukewarm, but it soothed my dry mouth and throat as I sipped and swallowed. If the evidence against Jeb Warner in the crimes scenes photos was faked, then that raised another question —and not for the first time. What about the only piece of physical evidence at Jeb Warner's trial—namely, the bloody shirt? Was it a fake as well? And why had someone stolen it decades and decades after the trial?

* * *

I made good time on the way home. Okay, so I might have been even more lead-footed than usual on the accelerator. I couldn't wait to get home and talk to Tuck about all I'd learned from Doris and Kala.

As I pulled up in front of the shop, I frowned. The open flag had been taken in. Tuck had said he was going to stay open all day, so that was weird.

Sandra galloped across the lawn to greet me. I gave her a scratch behind the ears, then we went inside the shop. Tuck was taking the cash out of the register drawer as if readying to close.

"What's going on?" I asked, studying him.

"I'm glad you're back. A few minutes ago, I got an interesting call from Gilbert Vanderschmidt."

"Doris's cousin? What did he want—does it have something to do with why you're closing early?"

"I'll tell you while I finish up." Cash in hand, he headed into the office.

I tailed him. "I've got some things to tell you, too."

"Later. First we need to get going." He opened the safe, tossed the cash inside. Tugging on his tweed jacket, he turned to me. "Gilbert wanted to know if we were the antique dealers he met at Hawk's Nest the other day, Doris's friends. I reassured him we were. He's up at Doris and Bucky's old house right now. He was in the basement fixing something when he came across a box of old bottles stuck way back in the coal bin."

I gaped at Tuck. "The Glass Widows? But Doris just told me the Fisher's went through the place with a fine-tooth comb."

"He's not sure that's what they are. He wanted to know if we'd come up as soon as possible and take a look at them."

Adrenaline spiked into my blood. So did wariness. I found it hard to believe Fisher's crew would've neglected to search a coal bin. "Doesn't the timing of this feel a little too good to be true, especially after the threats we've been getting? Are you sure it was Gilbert on the phone?"

"I wondered the same thing. Honestly, I couldn't tell if it was his voice or not. There was a lot of static on the line. After he hung-up, I redialed the number to be sure. I got an 'out of range' message, then it went to his voicemail—Gilbert Vanderschmidt."

"So, it was him," I said. When I'd been at the ruins, Tristan had trouble hearing Frenchie when he called back with the license plate information. Bucky's house wasn't far from the ruins. It was quite possible they had similarly spotty service.

Plus, there was something else to back up Gilbert's claim that he might've found the cache. "One of the things I learned from Doris was that she believes Bucky found all the Glass Widows and stashed all but one of them." I told Tuck the rest, "Doris also said Grandpa and Bucky were working on a book about the resort. She suspects he put the project aside after the plane crash because someone was threatening to hurt her."

"Sounds like we should err on the side of caution, then." He patted where a pistol-shaped lump sat in his jacket's pocket. "Good idea?"

I nodded. "I've got pepper spray in the car."

CHAPTER FORTY

While Tuck made a fast trip to the bathroom, I called Shane to let him know what we were up to. Like Tuck had said, it was better to cover our bases, in case something went sideways.

Shane didn't answer, even after I let the phone ring a few extra times. I sent him a text.

Tuck and I are headed to Bucky Sander's old house on Hill Farm Road. Doris's cousin, Gilbert Vanderschmidt, is there. He may have found the cache of Glass Widows!

I waited a beat, then another. Shane still didn't respond. With a text like that, the only reason he wouldn't get back to me was if he was in the middle of something pressing at work. It was frustrating not to touch base with him, but probably a good thing. He would've told us to stay home and have Gilbert bring the bottles to us. That might've been a smart move, except—even if those bottles weren't the Glass Widows—the fact Fisher's had missed something made it possible the Widows were still in the house. Maybe deeper in the coal bin or somewhere nearby it. I wouldn't be able to live with myself if I didn't check out the lead in person.

"Let's go," Tuck said, returning from the bathroom. He added,

"And, before you ask, I'm not worried about Chief Ovitt stopping by. He's had his chance."

"I totally agree," I said.

When we reached the Volvo, he went around to the passenger side. As I opened the driver's door, Sandra leapt in before I could stop her. She hurdled over the front seats and into the back. I groaned but let her stay. It was faster to give in than to spend precious minutes wrestling her out of the car.

Once we were on the road, I glanced at Tuck. "Do you think we should call Kala and tell her what we're up to?"

He shook his head. "The town clerk's only open until noon today. She's got a lot to do on a tight timeframe. Let's wait until we know if this is anything or not."

"Yeah, no distractions is a good idea..." I went on, telling him about the side trip Kala'd already made to the museum. By the time I finished recapping what she'd seen there and her theory that the crime scene cabinet cards had been altered to make Jeb Warner look guilty, we were past the Jumping Café and driving around Dead Man's Curve.

I glanced in the rearview. Sandra was leaning into the curve and grinning like a kid enjoying a tilt-a-whirl ride. She certainly was a strange dog, but I was going to miss her if and when Bill came to take her back. Maybe he'd let us be on-call babysitters.

I took the first turn after Townline gas station. Hill Farm Road was narrow and dirt, no homes, just fields and sugar woods, and lots of blind curves. There was no way to go fast, even after Bucky and Doris's clapboard house and outbuildings appeared in the distance, nestled partway up the mountainside, looking very much as they had in the painting on the Bible box lid.

"There's a car out front," Tuck said as we passed a realtor sign and started up the winding driveway. It was an older Toyota RAV, nothing fancy.

I pulled in beside it, retrieved my pepper spray from the glovebox, and pocketed it. I glanced at Sandra, "You're staying here.

And, this time, I'm double-checking the doors. There won't be any escaping, hear me?"

Her ears lowered.

Yeah, she'd been hoping for a ride and maybe another apple scrounging adventure like she'd had when we'd visited the *Gazetteer*. Dream on, crazy dog. None of us get what we want all the time.

Hoping similar disappointment wasn't what Tuck and I were headed for, I took a deep breath. What if Gilbert really had found the Glass Widows? They wouldn't be ours to sell. They belonged to Doris alone. Still, playing even a small part in the recovery of a long lost treasure would be amazing.

"Is that a realtor's lockbox on the front door?" Tuck asked as we got out.

The house had been repainted since the last time I'd visited Bucky six plus years ago. Now the front door was a shade of country blue instead of scabby-brown. A lockbox indeed hung from the knob. "Looks like we need to go around back," I said.

We circled toward the rear of the house, past an abandoned chicken coop. At the point where the driveway went on to a large barn and a cinderblock garage, we veered down a path that led to the home's back door, centered with windows grouped on either side.

The door stood open.

Perhaps Gilbert had left it that way to welcome us inside. Still, the silence around us combined with that beckoning door raised a red flag in the back of my mind, like the warnings Nancy Drew shouldn't have ignored in pretty much every book.

"Wait a second," I whispered to Tuck.

As I crept off the path toward the closest window—to the living room, I recalled from past visits—the murmur of soft country music reached my ears, emanating from somewhere inside. I peeked through the glass. The room was dark, except for a haze of light in the doorway to the kitchen. All the furniture was gone, and the floorboards were spic and span clean, but lovely white birch logs sat in the fireplace, no doubt a realtor's touch. Doris was far too pragmatic to leave a quick-burning wood like birch for a fire.

I was about to retreat when the shape of a person passed the hazily lit doorway—an average size man wearing a driving cap like Gilbert had worn the other day at Hawk's Nest. Stooping slightly, he set down a laundry basket-size box.

My stomach began to bubble with excitement, and the mental red flag disintegrated. Sure, lots of bad things had happened and they were all real and well worth my fear, but they didn't mean evil lurked around every corner. Good things did happen. And we were overdue for a lucky break.

Still, I didn't want Gilbert to catch me spying, so I jogged back to Tuck. "Looks like Gilbert hauled the box up from the coal bin," I said.

He smiled. "Fingers crossed."

"And toes," I added.

Tuck moved ahead of me, swaggering a bit as he went up a plywood ramp, through the open back door and into a small mudroom that led to the kitchen.

"Hello, Gilbert?" he called out. "It's Tuck and Edie."

My phone vibrated. I glanced at the ID. *Kala*.

I thought about not answering. But, intoxicated by those bubbles of excitement, I needed to share what was going on with her. I stopped half-way up the ramp and turned my back to the doorway, so my voice wouldn't travel into the house, and answered. "Hey, Kala. You won't believe what Tuck and I are about to look at."

"Yeah, well, you won't believe what I uncovered." Her voice was a full octave higher than normal. "Seriously, I hope you're sitting down."

"What is it?" I said, totally curious.

"It's shocking. Bucky's property? Guess who owned it before Bucky?"

My vanquished worry returned, knotting hard in my stomach. "His parents, right?"

"Yup. And before that?"

"Kala, I don't have time for games, just spit it out. We're at Bucky's house right now."

Her voice went stiff. "Ah...that might not be so good. In the 1950s Bucky's father bought the house from Jean-Louis Lefebvre —Frenchie Lefebvre's father."

I frowned. "Tristan's great-grandfather?"

"Exactly. And there's more." She started speaking faster. "We totally missed something big. I'll actually take the blame. Jean-Louis Lefebvre? *His* father got married in 1906 when he was close to fifty. Viola, his bride, was like seventeen. I know old guys marrying much younger women wasn't uncommon back then, but the difference between their ages messed with my mental timeline."

My thoughts jumbled. "You learned all this from searching deeds?"

"And marriage certificates. This town clerk's office's got a boatload of stuff. Their own records. Archives from some church that closed..." Her voice trailed off as she took a breath. "Jean-Louis, Frenchie's father, inherited the house from Viola. She didn't die until the 1970s, though she didn't live in the house after the 1950s. The important part is: the guy Viola married in 1906? He was none other than Louis-Francois *Beaumont* Lefebvre."

It took me a second to get it. When I did, the implications chilled me to the bone. "Louis Beaumont the photographer? The guy we suspect altered the crime scene photos?"

"He shortened his name for the photography business," she said.

I swiveled, looking for Tuck. He was no longer in sight, but the door to the kitchen was open, as if he'd walked inside and expected me to follow. I hushed my voice. "Do me a favor—right away. Tristan said he hadn't heard of mexxy until recently. Can you see if he—or any of the Lefebvres wrote an article for the *Gazetteer* on date rape drugs? I've got a bad feeling about this."

"I know what you mean—"

THWACK!

The noise reverberated out from inside the house, followed instantly by the clatter of shattering glass. Someone moaned.

Tuck!

"Call the police," I shouted into the phone. I turned on my heel, pepper spray already in my hand. Even as I sprinted into the mudroom, I could see Tuck beyond the doorway to the kitchen, stumbling backwards, slumping to the ground.

His forehead was wet with blood.

CHAPTER FORTY-ONE

Horrified, I raced into the kitchen to protect Tuck. Shoes crunching against pieces of broken bottle, I wheeled to face his attacker, pepper spray at the ready.

Frenchie Lefebvre stood there, gripping a handgun. He nodded to where Tuck slumped on the floor, then at the pepper spray. "Put it down. Unless you want me to shoot him."

I slowly crouched to put the spray on the floor. *Frenchie.* After what Kala had told me, I wasn't shocked to see him standing there. I hadn't thought about it since I'd been at the *Gazetteer* office and he'd been expounding on the newspaper's role in preserving local history, but he'd written *A Mystery in the Mountains* in the 1980s for the resort tragedy's centennial celebration. It was considered the definitive history of the resort and had been used to create the museum's new exhibit. The book Grandpa and Bucky had been working on would've proven Frenchie guilty of lazy research at a minimum, and more likely of falsifying in order to cover up his ancestor's crimes. He must've been mortified when the Bible box full of incriminating ephemera surfaced at Fisher's auction. This had never been about the Glass Widows. It was about preserving his family's reputation.

I set the pepper spray on the floor amid the shattered glass, a modern bottle by the looks of it. My gaze went to Tuck. A knot was rising on his blood-slicked forehead. More blood darkened his shoulder and hand. "You okay?" I asked.

He nodded, but his pallor and the sweat glistening on his face told a different story. He slid a hand along the lump in his left jacket pocket. His pistol. We weren't done yet.

Straightening back up, I met Frenchie's gaze. "You're not going to get away with this. People know we're here."

"But do they know why?" He smiled, a creepy, smug grin. A curl of frizzy, white hair slid out from under his Gilbert-like driver's cap. "I'll tell you what this evening's headline is going to read: *Treasure seeking Thieves Killed in Propane Heater Explosion*. Those thieves— you and your uncle—broke into an unoccupied house, lit a heater to stay warm, and kaboom!"

A heater? I glanced around. Next to Tuck a pantry door stood open. A rusted propane heater sat just inside the door.

Frenchie chuckled. "Now you've got the idea."

"No one will believe that's what really happened."

"Won't they? Tell me you've never lied about what you were up to. Does your boyfriend really trust you that much? It's no secret you're working for Graham and obsessed with the Glass Widow myth. You even went up to the ruins when you became worried someone else might beat you to the treasure."

"That's not why we went there, and you know it." I felt myself pale. *Tristan.* "Your whole family is in on this, aren't they?"

"Just me, myself, and I." He sighed. "At one point, I had high hopes for you and Tristan getting together. I even considered buying this place for you two. It would be nice to bring a new generation of Lefebvres to the old family homestead."

Tuck staggered to his feet. "Fat chance of that happening."

"Get back on the floor." Frenchie snarled. He pointed the handgun at me. "Try anything and she dies first."

Tuck swayed as he raised his hands in surrender. "Alright, don't do anything rash."

As he slumped to the floor, the sick worry in my stomach crept up into my throat. Still, Tuck had his pistol—and I had an insurance plan that he wasn't aware of. After I'd told Kala to call the police, I'd hit my phone's video app. Every word Frenchie said was being recorded, like Shane had suggested we do when we went to make our deal with Graham.

Frenchie's attention swung back to me. "I'm not happy that you made me lie to Tristan about those license plate numbers. I didn't enjoy doing that, not at all."

That took me aback. "It wasn't Megan Meyer's car?"

He laughed. "Of course not. There weren't any treasure hunters up on the mountain for you to discover—just like there was nothing wrong with our drones. The only thing I regret is not using something stronger on that mutt. That might've put an end to your snooping."

My fingers clenched into fists. "In case you're wondering, we knew it was mexxy," I snapped. Hoping he'd rise to the bait, I added, "How the hell did you get your hands on it? It's what you used on Felix Graham, wasn't it?"

He lifted his chin. "Maintaining a spotless reputation is one facet of my success. Another is assets. Mine are obvious—the stories I write can make or break people. Plus, I have connections on both sides of the law, some with access to certain laboratories." He smiled. "You should've seen Graham, stumbling around his yard like a circus clown."

"You'll never get away with this," Tuck said, voice even weaker.

"Is that so? All it takes is one touch on a remote control, and kaboom! This whole place goes up."

White-hot anger roared through me. That day, when my grandparents' plane crashed, the explosion. *Before the wheels hit the ground, not after.* "That's how you killed my grandparents. Remote control." My voice was raw, barely under control.

"You should've seen your face. You stood there on the edge of the airstrip, frozen for a full minute before you started running toward the wreckage. Of course, I couldn't stay around and watch much more. But I saw you from the other side of the airstrip. I heard you scream."

My pulse rang in my ears. Every muscle in my body longed to rush at him, to attempt to beat the trigger on the gun I knew he wasn't afraid to use. I clenched my teeth.

"Edie, be careful," Tuck mumbled.

I slid a hand over the pocket of my jeans where my phone hid, praying it was still recording. I had to take Frenchie down. But how?

His grin widened. "This time I won't be around to see your face." He eyed the pantry and propane heater. "I'll be down on the main road when I press the button."

I glared at him. "You're going to regret this."

"I can't see how I—"

A thunder of footfalls sounded against the plywood ramp.

He swiveled, looking toward the mudroom. He raised the handgun at the new target—

Too late.

Sandra entered the room already airborne. She hit Frenchie full force in the chest. He went down, screaming as she clamped her jaws around his forearm. She shook her head, thrashing the arm until the gun flew from his grip. The gun skated across the floor and into the pantry. It slid under a cabinet, clinking as it hit the wall.

I scrambled after it, sliding into the pantry on my knees. I reached into the darkness under the cabinet until I felt the shape of the handgun. By the time, I was back on my feet, gripping it tightly, Tuck had his pistol out. Sandra still had Frenchie pinned to the floor, growls emanating from her throat as she clamped his forearm.

"Get it off me!" Frenchie shrieked.

Sandra glanced my way, her expression business-like.

"It's okay. Stand down," I said firmly. I didn't have any idea what command was right, but the tone must've worked. She released his arm and backed off a few yards, hackles still raised, still on high alert, as if ready to charge again if need be.

Frenchie clutched his arm. "I'll have that dog put down for this."

I pointed the handgun at his chest. "The only thing you're going to do is stay put until the police get here."

In the distance sirens screamed, their wails exploding into the quiet of the house as they neared and finally reached the yard.

Time seemed to slow to a stop. My fingers cramped around the gun's grip. Tuck slumped forward, his sweat-dampened head bobbing as if he were slipping toward unconsciousness.

"This is Police Chief Ovitt!" The shout came from the back doorway.

"In here," I yelled. "Hurry."

There were more sirens. *Shane, please be Shane*, I prayed.

Ovitt burst into the room along with Officer Cristina Hopkins.

"Their dog attacked me," Frenchie screamed. "They broke in. I walked in on them rummaging through the house."

Sandra let out a low growl as if to disagree with him.

I raised my hands, crouched, and set the gun on the floor. "He's lying."

Tuck wavered to life. Lowering his pistol to the floor, he mumbled, "Edie's telling the truth."

Ovitt cleared his throat. "We're going to make this easy for now. You're all under arrest for trespassing."

"Chief?" I reached into my pocket with two fingers, took out the phone. "I recorded everything. Well, hopefully. Listen for yourself." I smiled at Frenchie, tilted my head to indicate the pantry and said to Ovitt, "You might want to call a bomb squad. If

Frenchie wasn't lying, there's explosives in there attached to the propane heater. The remote control's in his car."

CHAPTER FORTY-TWO

I held Tuck's hand as he lay on a gurney, ready to be loaded into the ambulance. "I'll be right behind you in the car," I said.

"Don't worry about me," he murmured. His voice went even lower. "Go see Graham."

My chest tightened. *Mom.* My deal with Graham. Obviously, the *Gazetteer* wouldn't be eager to break the news of Frenchie's arrest, but the internet and every other news outlet would be all over the news as soon as it leaked out. "You sure you'll be okay without me?"

"Few bangs, and bruises—it's nothing."

I kissed his cheek. "I'll ask Kala to meet you at the hospital."

"I'd like that. Now go get that information."

After I called Kala, I headed for Graham's shop. This time, I wasn't worried Sandra might sneak out of the car. She was asleep on the backseat, exhausted from her heroics.

I took another glance at her in the rearview. Frenchie had ranted at length to Chief Ovitt about how he wanted her put down. She was a dangerous, aggressive animal, according to him. The chief had ignored Frenchie's tirade, but he'd taken me aside and said Sandra's action would have to be looked into. Truth was, for her own good, Sandra needed to go back to her real owner. Bill was in a better position to protect her from anything that might be coming. Still, I was going to miss her, naughty antics and all.

In record time, I drove to Graham's shop. My pulse sped when I spotted Graham's Mercedes SUV parked by the front door. This was it. He'd get what I promised—and I'd get what I needed to free my mom.

After taking a second to leave a voicemail for Shane—telling him where I was, that I was okay and would call him again when I got home—I tacked on a nonchalant smile and strode inside the shop. Janet and Alison were behind the front counter, sorting through a box of antique buttons. As I approached, Alison skittered off into the storage room like a terrified mouse—which was total bullcrap. She wasn't any more of the mousy-type than I was.

Janet glanced after her. She pursed her lips, slightly peeved. "Well now, what was that all about? I was hoping that you two would have another chance to talk. Poor Alison, she doesn't have any friends around here. And that ex-boyfriend of hers is a lemon, if you ask me."

"Sometimes old relationships are best left in the past," I said, and I meant it very literally in this case.

She sighed. "At least things are going smoother for her here. Graham actually asked her to work full time."

"Speaking of which," I said. "I stopped by to see him about something."

"I believe he's in the gallery workroom."

"Perfect," I said.

As I made my way between the displays of antiques and toward the workroom, my thoughts went from Alison to Tristan. When I'd first heard about her stalking him, I'd pitied Tristan. I still did, sort of.

Also, if I were perfectly honest, I hadn't been as immune to Tristan's charms as I preferred to think. But after everything that had happened, my feelings toward him now felt similar to my feelings toward rice cakes. Not that I wanted a plague to wipe rice cakes off the earth. They were tolerable, and fine for some people. But if I never encountered one of those bland cakes again, it wouldn't bother me in the least. The same went for Tristan.

I took a steadying breath. Today might have ranked right up there with the worst days of my life, but I was on the other side of it now. Everything was going to be okay. *No*, everything was going to be stupendous, once Graham told me what he knew about my mom being set up.

My smile came easily as I reached the open workroom door. It truly was the perfect place to talk. A lot more private than his office, where Janet and her prying ears were only a handful of steps away.

"Hey, Graham," I said, walking inside.

Rag in hand, he stood at a workbench, wiping down an antler-handled riding crop. I sniffed the air. Lemon oil. Ideal for reconditioning such things.

When I pulled the door shut behind me, his thin-lipped frown flicked upwards into a smile. "Does this mean you have something for me?"

I nodded. "Frenchie Lefebvre."

He balked. "He's the thief? That seems—"

"Strange? That's what I would've thought before I knew better. But I'm a hundred percent sure. He confessed."

Graham set the rag and crop on the workbench. "When I left, he took my place on the museum's board of directors. He wrote that book about the resort... I forget the title."

"*A Mystery in the Mountains.*"

"That's it." He picked the rag back up, twisted it a couple of times, then slapped it back down. "Why would someone who claims to love his town's history steal and destroy important artifacts? And, yes, I heard what happened at the café—the Bible box, the ephemera, the Glass Widow—all of my things smashed and burnt." The muscles along his jaw tightened. "That bastard's business isn't going to survive this. I'll ruin him, and his entire family's reputation."

I quieted my voice. "Oddly enough, I suspect protecting his family's reputation was behind everything he did."

Wrinkles spanned Graham's forehead. "What are you talking about?"

"Do you remember the other day how I asked when the bloody shirt went missing from the museum?"

"I told you I wasn't aware it was gone."

"As a board member, could Frenchie have gained access to restricted areas?" I didn't wait for his answer. "If that shirt was still around, I suspect a DNA test would prove Jeb Warner wasn't a murderer and arsonist. Frenchie's ancestor, a photographer named Louis Beaumont, was guilty of those crimes—plus of falsifying crime scene photos."

"Really?" If Graham had looked puzzled before, now he looked completely mystified.

I pushed confidence into my voice. "I can't say for sure why Beaumont hated George Fielding enough to kill him, but I suspect the answer is twofold. He took George Fielding and Sophie Stebbins's betrothal photos. However, he didn't photograph their wedding. Maybe George Fielding pissed off Beaumont by firing him or insulting the betrothal photos."

"I've seen artsy-types go off the deep end over a whole lot less," Graham said. "But murder?"

"There's more to it. George Fielding had also bought up all the land on the mountainside for his resort, including a large tract that belonged to Beaumont's family. Maybe Beaumont saw the land as his birthright and the only thing left for him to inherit was a few measly acres and a farmhouse." I shifted, standing up taller. Time to quit speculating and get down to facts. "What I do know for certain is that Frenchie wrote *A Mystery in the Mountains* to make double-sure his ancestor's guilt wouldn't come to light."

"That really wasn't very bright," Graham said. A smug smile spread across his lips. He folded his arms across his chest. "You mentioned a confession. I assume that means the police are aware Frenchie stole my things?"

His smile alone told me he was up to something, and I had a good idea what. "Don't try to weasel out of our deal. I found your thief. I gave you his name before the news went public." I rested my hands on my hips. "Now tell me everything you know about my mother's forgery charge—how she was set up, where, when, and who was involved…everything including the part you played."

Sincerity replaced his smugness. "A promise is a promise, and I won't lie to you. But, like I said when we made the deal, I can't guarantee it'll be the answer you want or hope to hear."

I hardened my tone. "Tell me."

He looked me in the eyes. "I'm sorry, Edie. But I don't know anything about the setup that led to your mom's arrest—that is the full truth."

For a moment I could only stare. Until pure burning rage hit me in a wave. I slammed a hand against the workbench. "That's ridiculous!"

His voice remained calm. "My clients were happy with your mom's work. I like her. She made me money."

"Who set her up," I demanded.

He shrugged. "Like I said, I don't know. I'll give you this much —I agree, someone was out to get her. Revenge for something, but I don't know what."

Through the flames of my anger, a little voice reminded of his lack of guarantee. I'd just never fathomed that the truth could be such a vacuous nothing.

He picked up the bone-handled riding crop from the work-bench, ran his hand down its length. "If I were in your shoes, I'd look into your mother's enemies. Starting with Rosetta Ramone."

"I thought she and her husband were friends of yours?"

He scoffed. "Toady wannabes. Your mom crossed Rosetta a while back, and Rosetta has a vengeful streak a mile wide."

Now that my temper was subsiding, the ramifications of what I'd failed to learn sank in. In a few days, Tuck and I would drive to Connecticut to see my mom, and we wouldn't have hopeful news to deliver.

A knot tightened in the back of my throat, and unwanted tears burned at the corners of my eyes. "I guess that marks the end of our deal," I said. I wanted to—*no*, I had to get out before he saw me cry.

"Pleasure doing business with you," he said. But as I turned toward the door, readying to escape, he added, "I'm not sure if you're aware of it, but that new officer on the Scandal Mountain police force—Christy—Christian..."

I wheeled back to gape at him. "Christina Hopkins?" At one point, Kala'd had a passing crush on her.

"She was working at the Canadian border crossing the day your mom was arrested up there. I'd be looking into her." He slapped the riding crop lightly against his palm. "Your mom's holding something back too. I'm fairly certain of that."

"Thank you for telling me," I said. And, once again I believed he was being straight with me. Still, as I left him behind and went out into the main shop, I reminded myself to not be foolish. This time Graham had treated me fairly, but that didn't mean I could trust him in the future. He was still the same conniving, out-for-himself, womanizing eel he'd always been, and I couldn't afford to forget that.

CHAPTER FORTY-THREE

I was thankful when Sandra and I arrived home ahead of everyone else. I poured myself a citrus vodka on ice, grabbed a bag of pretzel chips and a bowl of French onion dip. Then I went to the living room and collapsed onto an overstuffed chair.

I closed my eyes, savoring the peace and quiet for a moment. On the way home, I'd called Kala to see how Tuck was doing. They were in the middle of speaking with his doctor. Good news was, they'd both be headed home soon. As I'd suspected, Tuck had sustained a mild concussion along with a few cuts that required attention. It seemed he had turned and raised his hand to protect his head when he realized someone was swinging something at him from behind. As a result, his shoulder and arm had deflected most of the bottle's impact. He needed total rest for a few days. Limited TV and reading. Limited visitors. Lots of naps. But he was going to be fine.

Leaving my drink and snack behind, I fetched spare pillows and blankets from the hall closet and made up the couch so Tuck could rest downstairs if he wanted.

No sooner had I finished than the phone rang.

Shane. Thank goodness. With him being on duty, it was likely he knew even more about the Frenchie situation than I did by now.

"I was about to call you," I said. " I just heard from Kala. Tuck's going to be home shortly."

"That's great news."

I told him about my visit with Graham and the connection Kala had found between the Lefebvres and the resort tragedy. "If it hadn't been for you, I might not have recorded what happened at the farmhouse. I hope it's enough to put Frenchie away for everything. I mean, Tuck and I were the only witnesses."

Shane said, "Don't forget the explosive device, and the remote in his car. Also, I suspect Caleb McMahon will be eager to share what he knows in exchange for a lighter sentence." Shane was silent for a beat, then continued, "I can't be directly involved with this case because of my relationship with you. That said, I heard through the grapevine the team searching the *Gazetteer* office uncovered more evidence."

"They've already searched there?" That was a surprise.

"Tristan gave them permission, but Chief Ovitt waited until a search warrant arrived to keep everything unquestionably above-board. Ovitt apparently has a judge on speed dial."

I took a sip of my drink to moisten my throat. "So, what did they find?" More explosives, I supposed. What else could it be?

"Don't be too hard on Tristan," Shane said.

I frowned at the phone. Where had that come from? "I'm counting on not having much to do with him in the future."

"From what I heard, Tristan didn't know what Frenchie had been up to, though he confessed to knowing a sordid story about a hotheaded, photographer ancestor of his altering crime scene photos and putting his own blood on a shirt to pin the resort tragedy on someone else. Apparently, Tristan's great-great-grand-mother spilled the story on her deathbed."

"That would've been Viola," I said. "She was a teenager when she married the photographer. He must've confessed to her at some point." I'd felt confident about my various assumptions, but it was nice to have them confirmed.

"Deathbed confessions have solved a lot of crimes." Shane's voice grew taut. "Tristan didn't realize his grandfather—"

I finished the hard part for him. "He didn't know Frenchie killed my grandparents." My chest squeezed. Unable to dwell on that part of the story, I circled back to an earlier point. "You said they found evidence in the *Gazetteer* office?"

"The lid of the stolen Bible box was hidden in a plastic storage container underneath a toy plane—'Flash' something or other."

My mind went back to Frenchie cradling the battery-operated plane, the Stanzel Electromatic Flash. He'd stored his favorite childhood toy with a stolen folk art painting of what he viewed as his ancestral home. Not particularly wise, but it made sense, I supposed.

Shane's voice deepened. "A K9 located several vials of mexxy in a secret compartment in his desk."

"Oh my God." I glanced to where Sandra was eyeing my pretzel chips and dip. "The last time we were in Frenchie's office, Sandra kept staring at one of the desk drawers. Frenchie took out some donuts and we all joked about her alerting on junk food."

Shane laughed. "You should ask Bill about that dog's background. The way she protected you and Tuck, alerting on drugs... Sounds like training, not coincidence."

"It's too bad none of us understood what she was saying. She probably figured out Frenchie was a skunk long before any of us humans." Now that I thought about it, she'd also alerted on Bill's briefcase, and there'd been a vial of mexxy in it too. "You don't think animal control will decide she has to be put down because of the attack?"

"Let me know if they do. I'll speak up on her behalf."

"That would be great," I said.

His tone softened. "I'll stop by later. That is, if you'd like company."

"I'd love it," I said.

* * *

An hour-and-a-half later, I'd just helped Tuck get settled on the living room couch, when the rumble of a noisy car came up the driveway. It was Pinky, and she wasn't alone. Bill was riding shotgun.

I dimmed the lights for Tuck, then dashed to the kitchen. Bill and Pinky were just walking in. "We came to see the heroes," she said, full volume.

Kala held a finger to her lip. "Sssh...Tuck's resting."

I tiptoed to the fridge and brought back beers for Bill and Kala and iced teas for me and Pinky, then we settled down around the kitchen table.

"You and Tuck are so lucky," Pinky said to me, voice hushed. She and Bill knew most everything, thanks to Kala calling them from the hospital. "Frenchie Lefebvre—not in a million years would I've guessed he was capable of those things."

"You can say that again," I said.

Kala waved her hand like a kid in school. "I just remembered. Edie, there's something I forgot to tell you."

I frowned, confused. "There's more?"

"It's something you asked me to look into. It's kind of a moot point now, but I discovered the *Gazetteer* ran a series of articles back in April about the interconnection between human trafficking and drug distribution."

I sat up straighter. "Shane was part of a team that just took down a gang involved in those things."

"I've been wondering what was keeping him so busy," Kala said. "Frenchie had an anonymous, local inside source for his series."

Bill set his beer down. "I saw the interviews he did for that on YouTube. His mystery source's voice and face were disguised.

They were only identified as someone with access to a local drug lab—" He stopped talking as Sandra wandered into the room and over to her water bowl. "Speaking of the devil. There's another reason we stopped by."

I swallowed hard. "Don't tell me animal control already called you about the attack."

He chuckled. "I wish I'd seen it." His attention went to his beer. He ran a hand down the bottle, looked back at me. "I need to apologize to you and to ask you something."

"About Sandra?" I took a not so wild guess. "She's a retired police dog. isn't she?"

"It's my fault," Pinky jumped into the conversation, "not Bill's. He wasn't around when I talked you into babysitting her. She doesn't just hate puppies. She's got a lot of weird quirks. I'm sorry I didn't warn you."

Sandra stopped slurping water from her bowl, smiled at us with all her teeth showing, then woofed at Bill as if to tell him to hurry-up and spill the beans.

He rolled his eyes. "She is a strange dog—and you're right. She's an ex-police K9." He grinned at her. "This also isn't the first time she's been a hero. She's rescued lost kids and elderly people with Alzheimer's. She trailed a bank robber over Jay Peak and kept him pinned until the police caught up. She's credited with tons of drug busts. She even retrieved a lost cat from a pond."

Kala narrowed her eyes. "If she was so great, then why was she retired? I don't believe for a second she's as old as that white muzzle makes her look."

"She's four and a half," Bill said.

Sandra strolled over and sat beside me. I gave her a scratch behind the ears. "That's not even middle age for dog."

Bill took a sip of his beer. "It was a forced retirement. Her original training included marijuana detection."

"Oh, I've heard about that," Kala said. "Drug cases are being thrown out of court when there's both legal marijuana and an illegal drug found in the same location. It brings into question which the dog initially alerted on."

I looked down at Sandra. "It's really too bad. She's the smartest dog I've ever met. And the sneakiest." I added the last part because... Well, it was true and part of what made her loveable.

"I don't think her attacking Frenchie is going to be an issue," Bill said. "She was trained to protect her handler." He wiped a hand nervously over his face. "Which gets me to my point. She and I—" He cleared his throat. "We never really clicked. She likes you. Would you consider—"

"Yes!" I shouted before he could finish. Remembering Tuck, I lowered my voice. "I'm assuming you're asking if I'll keep her?"

Pinky let out a muffled woot. "Best news ever."

Kala silently applauded.

Sandra jumped up, front paws on the edge of my chair as she licked my face. Crazy dog. I swear she was the instigator of this adoption from the start.

* * *

With Sandra's future home decided, I left the three of them in the kitchen and went to the living room with an ice water for Tuck. He was laying in the dim light, fast asleep. Bruises that hadn't been as apparent earlier now darkened both eyes. But there was no seepage coming from the bandage over the lump on his forehead, or from his other wounds, and that was a good sign.

I set the water glass on the coffee table. Before I even consciously realized what I was doing, I padded out of the room, to the downstairs library, and opened the safe. I took out Bucky's journal, returned to the living room and sank down on the overstuffed chair.

Trust your instincts, my grandpa had told me a million times. And he was right. Over the years, I'd discovered antiques and notable pieces of art by listening to my subconscious, fine-tuned from years of tagging along with my grandparents, heightened by my education and internships, and everything I'd learned on my own.

This time it was saying that somewhere deep inside I knew the answer to where Bucky had stashed the rest of the Glass Widows.

I opened the journal to the first page, then began leafing through. I stopped on *March 17. St. Patrick's Day.* According to the entry, Bucky believed the day was made for Irish whiskey not green beer. He also found a hidey-hole full of Probation-era, vanilla extract bottles while replacing floorboards in the farm-house's mudroom.

I rubbed the back of my neck. No matter how briefly I had been in the mudroom, nothing about it pinged my subconscious. But the idea of a secure hidey-hole underneath floorboards seemed likely, and prying up the floor wasn't the sort of thing Fisher's crew would've done when they searched the house.

Setting the journal on my lap, I sat back and closed my eyes.

A memory from my first visit to Hawk's Nest slipped into my mind. Doris's voice: *Took me six months to locate everything I needed for the tax people. Receipts in the living room, notebooks and papers in the kitchen, the pantry...*

The hair on the back of my neck tingled. My pulse thumped hard against my ribcage. Important notebooks and papers. Important to Bucky.

The pantry.

I sat bolt upright as the answer came to me. *A sound.* A slight reverberating noise I'd felt as much as heard. A sound similar to what I felt when I used a probe to search for bottle digging spots. Only this time, there wasn't a probe involved, just my ears and instinct taking in a familiar sound at an inconvenient moment.

A sound similar to what I'd heard when I set the crate of bottles from the auction down on the shop's front counter.

A *clink.*

CHAPTER FORTY-FOUR

The next morning, I lay on my belly in Bucky's pantry. Doris and the real Gilbert watched me from the kitchen. Shane stood next to them. He'd ridden down with me after spending the night at our house. Sandra was supposedly waiting in the car, though it wouldn't have surprised me to hear her gallop into the kitchen at any moment.

"Cross your fingers," I said as I stretched my arm out, reaching as far under the built-in cabinet as I could.

"Feel anythin'?" Doris asked.

"Not yet." As I felt along where the floor met the wall, a slow-motion replay from yesterday unreeled in the back of my mind. Sandra entering the kitchen already in midair. Her jaws clamping Frenchie's arm. The handgun flying from his grip, then sliding across the floor and under the pantry cabinet. The clink when it hit the wall—or, as I now believed, a clink sounding when the gun glanced off something else before coming to rest against the wall. A clink of metal chiming against glass.

My fingers brushed something fuzzy. A dust bunny? A dead mouse?

I ignored that thought, and I shifted so I could reach in even deeper. My fingertips touched paper wrapped around something hard. And there was a similar wrapped something right next to it.

My pulse slammed in my ears, banging like a band on the Fourth of July. My voice shook. "I—I found something."

I closed my fingers around my prize. Even through the paper, I could feel its shape—a bottle with a squatty body and a long neck. The right size. The right shape!

Tightly gripping it, I drew my arm out from under the cabinet. Doris rushed forward. "Hurry, unwrap it."

I uncoiled the paper, brittle and yellowed from age. A glint of glass appeared, glistening even in the pantry's faint light. Blueish emerald. Not amber like the lesser Scandal Mountain Springs bottles.

As the rest of the paper fell away, the embossed likeness of a plump Victorian bride became visible. Sophie Stebbins, the Glass Widow herself, the adulteress bride. And the lettering: *Maiden Springs. Healing Water. Scandal Mountain, Vermont.*

My hands trembled as I struggled to my feet. I passed the bottle to Doris.

Tears shone in her eyes as she took it. "Bucky," she murmured. "I knew you'd kept them for us. I only wish I'd been there for you at the end." She looked at me. "Thank you. I thank you. Bucky thanks you."

Shane took over the bottle hunt, his longer arms reaching under the cabinet with more ease than mine. He pulled out another Glass Widow, then a third...He felt around for more. Shook his head. "Sorry. That's it."

I rubbed the back of my neck, easing a pinch of tension. I wasn't about to second guess what my instinct still whispered. "They're all here. It's just—" I wasn't sure Doris would like my next suggestion. "I kind of expected Bucky might've kept a few accessible and the others more securely hidden. I brought a hammer and crowbar just in case..."

As I let my voice trail off, a wide smile brightened Doris's face.

"Bucky found vanilla extract bottles hidden under the mudroom floor. Are you thinkin' that gave him an idea?"

"I do," I said.

Gilbert got the tools from my car. Then, Doris and I watched as he and Shane dismantled the lower section of the cabinet. Actually, only the cabinet's lower shelves needed to go before the floorboards beneath them were accessible—and those shelves popped out like someone— Bucky—had only tacked them in place.

I pointed to where several suspiciously pale floorboards formed a rectangle the size and shape of a briefcase. "How about trying that spot first?"

"Just hurry." Doris groaned.

I held my breath as Shane used the claw of the hammer to yank out a few nails. With the boards loosened, he wedged the crowbar between them and the floor. The boards squeaked as he pried them upward.

"Wait a minute." I grabbed Shane's elbow. "We need to be super careful."

I dropped onto my knees, squeezed my fingers between the loose boards and floor, then pulled upwards. If I was right. If the rest of the Glass Widows were here...

As the entire rectangle of boards popped free, I fell backwards onto my derriere. But even from that awkward position, I could see them—or at least the top layer of them. All thirty-two remaining Glass Widows were wrapped in newspaper and safely stored away where no thief or any other sort of criminal could easily find them.

Doris pressed a hand against her chest. "Oh, my goodness."

Shane draped an arm over my shoulder. "Amazing sight, isn't it?"

I nodded, happy for Doris and proud of the part I'd played in locating the infamous cache.

Gilbert cleared his throat. "Doris, wasn't there something you wanted to tell Edie?"

Puzzled, I turned to look at her.

She smiled. "Gilbert and I were talkin' earlier. I don't know that Felix Graham guy from a hole in the wall, but I'd like to give him one of the bottles. He paid heaps of money at the auction and ended up with nothin'. Would you mind giving it to him for me?"

"I'd be happy to," I said, stunned by her generous offer. Graham certainly wasn't going to see this coming.

Her lips twitched like she was holding back a secret, then they settled into a smile. "I want you to have one too."

My mouth fell open. Now that the entire cache was found, the individual value of the Glass Widows would drop a little. Still... "That's—too generous."

She snorted. "I don't mean for you alone. You'll need to split it with that uncle of yours and that girl, Kala. I know they helped."

I smiled. "That sounds like a fair deal to me."

Secrets. When they come to light, sometimes you discover what you hoped. Other times that rough ground yields the unexpected. But in the end, isn't it what we choose to do with the secret that matters most?

—Edie Brown

Did you enjoy *Whisper of Treasure and Lies?* Subscribe to Trish Esden's newsletter to be notified when new novels are released (and for a chance to read bonus material and enter giveaways). Signup here: www.TrishEsden.com While you're there, if you like fantasy novels that are a touch dark and a bit sexy, check out the Northern Circle Coven and Dark Heart trilogies published under the name Pat Esden. Whether the novel is by Trish or Pat, rest assured you're in for a twisty tale centered on feisty women and good-hearted men who rise up with determination, heart, and passion for justice when crime—or evil—strikes their small-town communities.

ACKNOWLEDGMENTS

To the entire crew who supported me during *Whisper of Treasure and Lies'* journey from seed to publication. You are the best! Special thanks to Karen Lacey for your friendship, encouragement, and wise critiques. And to Katherine Quimby, friend and editor extraordinaire, and Lydia Johnson for your detailed and most excellent proofreading. I couldn't have brought this book to life without you. To Laurie Cooper of Pub-Craft: Marketing for Books & Brands. You are beyond generous and wise. I'm grateful to have you on my side. A huge thank you to my fellow Pub-Craft/Visible Author Method friends for your support and advice. Plus, special thanks to Melody Simmons for creating the perfect cover for this story, and to Painted Wings Publishing for their skillful formatting.

Last, but certainly not least, a huge thank-you to readers who have purchased my novels, requested them at libraries, reviewed them, and recommended them to friends and family. You brighten my days and keep my imagination lit.

ABOUT THE AUTHOR

Trish Esden loves museums, gardens, wilderness, dogs and birds, in various orders depending on the day. She lives in northern Vermont where she deals antiques with her husband, a profession she's been involved with since her teens. Don't ask what her favorite type of antique is. She loves hunting for old bottles and rusty barn junk as much as she enjoys fine art and furnishings. Trish is the author of the Scandal Mountain Antiques Mystery series, which explores the secretive and adrenaline-charged underbelly of Vermont's antique and art world. Her novel *A Wealth of Deception* was an Independent Publishers of New England silver award winner, and *The Art of the Decoy* was a Killer Nashville Silver Falchion Award finalist. As Pat Esden, she writes contemporary fantasy novels that are a touch dark and a bit sexy. Her short fiction has appeared in a number of venues including *Deadly Nightshade: Best New England Crime Stories 2022.*

Website: https://trishesden.com
Newsletter: https://bit.ly/3NiKaOd
Facebook: https://bit.ly/3gSNinI
Instagram: https://bit.ly/3TZ9yuM

If you enjoyed *Whisper of Treasures and Lies,* please consider leaving a review.

Goodreads: https://bit.ly/3SMAmgo
BookBub: https://bit.ly/3W6eFLr
Amazon: https://amzn.to/4kIi9Qr